SADIE, CALL THE POLIS

KIRKLAND CICCONE

Sadie, Call the Polis

© Kirkland Ciccone 2022

Cover illustration: Andrew Forteath
Woman reaching up by Aedrian - Unsplash.com/Aedrian
Telephone by Alexander Andrews - Unsplash.com/alex_andrews

Published by:
Fledgling Press Ltd.
1 Milton Rd West
Edinburgh
EH15 1LA

www.fledglingpress.co.uk

ISBN 9781912280568

Printed and bound by:
Print on Demand Worldwide, Peterborough

1

Useful Advice

I used to believe everything my mither told me, including her age which stayed at twenty-five for nearly ten years. She seemed to know everything, and if she didn't, she faked it better than anyone else in the world. She once told me the meaning of life, back when I trusted her every word.

−Life, she said, −is good with friends and better with money.

−But what about love? I asked.

−Love's fine if you can leave the next morning.

This was probably the wisest thing she ever told me.

That and −Always stash your cash under the floorboards.

Past Lives

According to my mither, we all brought something of our past lives into this one. Reincarnation, I suppose. She used to tell me the story of her other life, the one she lived before she became my mither. Back then, she was a happy dolphin − a daft idea really, because I saw her feeble attempts at swimming. From the steps of the pool, I'd watch while she thrashed in the foamy water, with all the grace of a sack of cats. My love of rain didn't extend to the swimming pool spray, but because I was wee enough to get into The Mariner Centre for free (and my sister still at an age where she qualified for a cheap ticket), that's just how we spent our weekends. Mither insisted we go every Sunday because it was Divorced Dads' Day. Sometimes she'd talk to someone, but it never went anywhere further than the car park. While the other kids dive-bombed into the pool, bolstered by the fearlessness of being young and dumb, I found myself at the shallow end of the water near Mither, pretending to be a mermaid, trying to turn something miserable into a good memory. Even now, I can't swim. My sister, however, took to the water like she did everything else in life – with supreme confidence. Sometimes, I reckoned Mither was right, and Lily was a beautiful dolphin in a former life. She was every bit as graceful in the water. Dressed in her one-piece green bathing suit, she turned smoothly underneath the white-speckled water, her legs kicking flecks of foam in a neat spray, knowing full well everyone nearby was watching, each one of them completely mesmerised by her unearthly elegance. *Try being her wee sister*, I'd think, looking on enviously, dreaming that I'd come back in my next life as her.

If anything, Mither must have been a cat in a past life – because most people crossed the road to avoid her. Another feline characteristic she had was her fur coat, a shiny smooth brown pelt. She wore it with everything, no matter the weather or temperature and she never sweated either. When the coat went threadbare, she seemed to find another somewhere else. Mither enjoyed the kind of glamour people rarely saw in real life, only on the front pages of expensive magazines, the type that sold clothes to rich people, stuff I'd never wear. Not only because they were too expensive, but because I couldn't get them to fit. My clothes were the sort that came with a big red Clearance sticker and an XXL tag. Lily took how I dressed personally.

–You look like a fucking tramp, she'd hiss whenever I got ready to go out and play. Sometimes I felt Lily didn't like me much. In her eyes, I was a walking, talking, drinking, eating example of our mither's bad decisions.

Lily never recovered from the fact she wasn't an only child.

−I want all the love, she explained calmly while I lay in bed listening to the rain drop. Magpie or not, it didn't matter what I was in a past life. In this life, I was an intruder who stole time, effort, love, air and money. I'd never be allowed to forget it.

DENNY, IN FALKIRK

For years, life was 87 Little Denny Road, a flat on the second top floor of a block in-between blocks. I spent most of the day and all night in my bedroom, sitting on my bed or walking on the floor, also someone else's roof. Sometimes I'd lean onto the windowsill and watch rain slide down the glass, one drop splitting into different directions. Yet, as much as I loved the rain, it also brought a lot of unwelcome problems. There was a crack in the window, a small tear that let water trickle into the house, a persistent leak that dribbled down the wall, causing long wet stains that never seemed to dry. Worse, the rainwater fed the thick fluffy black filaments of mould hidden behind my cupboard, making my clothes smell and my chest hurt.

Mither didn't have a leaky window in her bedroom. What she had was a very large, mirrored wardrobe on the far wall. Every night before she went to work, I'd hear her tell herself how amazing she looked. Lily, meanwhile, took the smallest room because it was easier to keep neat and tidy. Also, she'd spotted damp in the other room, so it was immediately passed over to me. Thank you, damp! Being at the other side of the hall also gave Lily easy access to the bathroom, a small space with just enough width for a bath and a toilet. The hall floor was uncarpeted. I heard Lily going to the bathroom late at night, her feet making tiny squeaks that yanked me out of my dreams, fun little holidays in my own head, no passport or payment necessary.

1976

Reputation was everything in Denny and it lasted as long as people were around to remember. If you asked anyone on the street, they'd tell you something about the woman who arrived by bus in 1976 during a heatwave so ferocious that even the concrete sizzled. She wasn't alone. There were two girls, including a newborn in tow. For our neighbours, just like her own daughters, Mither would become someone to revere or hate. Then again, only the most fearsome could walk through Little Denny Road with their head held high, and I moved around the street with a great view of my feet.

2

I HATE 1983

Nethermains Primary School is where I learned reading, writing, arithmetic and hiding in cupboards so no-one would find me during playtime. I'd spent too long trying to get my classmates to like me and somewhere along the line I realised it was a waste of time. They knew my name, meaning they also knew my mither. Unfortunately, they were about to know a lot more, thanks to a single question. No, not a question. The *answer*. My biggest mistake was telling the truth.

Honesty is a bad habit I've been trying to break for years.

THE QUESTION

Every Friday afternoon, fifteen minutes before the bell rang, Mrs Walker made everyone in Primary Five stand up and answer a question she'd choose from a big jar, neatly folded paper stuffed inside instead of chocolate chip cookies. The jar was old and slightly discoloured, a large Cheshire Cat with faded teeth grinned from the front. Mrs Walker would reach inside the jar and rummage around, not stopping until something felt right. Then she'd pull out the little square, unfurl it and read the question aloud. It was always fun, a nice little gift to everybody before school closed for a few days. One time, she asked us our favourite song. An easy one, because it was *Since Yesterday* by Strawberry Switchblade, who'd appeared on the *Wide Awake Club*, their harmonies stopping me between mouthfuls of Frosties. When they talked, they talked like me, their accents pure Scottish. Another time, Mrs Walker asked what we'd do if we had millions in the bank. I couldn't answer that because it felt impossible, too big a dream for my imagination. The question that ruined my life (for a few days) came soon after a second or two of suspenseful silence. Mrs Walker, a thwarted performer, knew how to work her impressionable audience and we adored her for it.

Eventually, her big moment arrived.

−What do you want to be when you grow up?

We all got up onto our feet and waited our turn to answer. Just like every other Friday afternoon, Mrs Walker started off with Heather Aitchison, because she liked to move in alphabetical order. Poor Stuart Urquhart always came last, sometimes not even getting to answer the question because we took up all the time. As Heather spoke, we waited patiently, keeping our ambitions quiet until the question came to us. I used the time to adjust my answer, depending on the other answers. Heather always set the tone.

−When I grow up, I want to be a marine biologist just like my sister.

−Your sister's a marine biologist?

−No, replied Heather, her face reddening. −That's what she wants to be.

−Okay, said Mrs Walker, who then turned her smile to Tamjeet Dallal. −What do you want to be when you grow up?

Everyone in Nethermains looked up to Tamjeet. Literally, because he was the tallest boy at school. He towered over everyone, his height making him look down at us, but never down on us. His long legs and popularity made him the first pick in every football game, even the kids from primaries six and seven chose him for their games. Being a girl, I wasn't allowed to take part. For a moment, a passing feeling, I considered saying 'football player' when Mrs Walker finally reached me. Idea noted, I waited for what Tamjeet had to say.

−When I grow up... started Tamjeet, who always seemed shy despite his height. −I want to be a breakdancer. I'm really good, Mrs Walker.

Then, as though he had to push the words out by force, he added:

−Can I show you my moves?

−Not right now, Tamjeet. We'd be sued if you broke something.

Everyone laughed and I quickly joined in, pretending I was in on the joke. Tamjeet sat down again and the question resumed its journey around the room. Sarah Everson was next. Grudgingly, she stood up and faced the room, though she couldn't look at anyone, even though her spectacles had the thickest lenses, giving her the look of a perpetually puzzled witness. She used these spectacles to magnify her feet, or a random patch of ceiling, or something outside the window, far away in the distance only she could see. I knew how much she hated speaking in front of everyone. Every Friday was torture for Sarah, who did anything she could to escape her fate. She probably wanted the bell to ring, but there was another ten minutes left and several more kids ready to answer the question. Sarah meekly accepted her destiny.

Once again, Mrs Walker asked her question.

−Sarah, she said kindly. −What do you want to be when you grow up?

−I want to be older.

Everyone burst out laughing, forcing Sarah to retreat into the comfort of her navy cardigan, because she wasn't actually trying to be funny. She just was. Robbie Ferguson, meanwhile, didn't say much when Mrs Walker reached him, just two words: *professional* and *footballer*. Then he sat down on his chair, sullen as usual. I was surprised, because Robbie spent more time lighting fires down in the shed than he did kicking a ball. Then again, *arsonist* wasn't a viable career path for anyone.

INTRODUCING GREGOR

Gregor patiently waited his turn and soon enough it came time to answer the question. He was my best friend, if only because he was the only boy at school who spent any time with me. Sometimes during a nice daydream, I'd pretend he was my brother, maybe even a long-lost twin. My sister wasn't anything like Gregor. She didn't believe in magic and thought books were for ugly people. But Gregor liked the same things I liked. We didn't wash our hair and hated being forced into nice, neat clothes, especially school uniform, always itchy and uncomfortable. Gregor agreed that polyester was one of the greatest evils in society, along with racist jokes and people with no imagination. Together, we held firm against outsiders. Like we had a choice!

–What do you want to be when you grow up?

Gregor stood up and dutifully answered the question.

–That's easy. I want to find dinosaur bones in dusty deserts.

It sounded exciting, this idea that we'd grow older and taller and probably still not be as tall as Tamjeet. But it also made me afraid of what might happen. Adults had to work jobs they hated, buy cars and pay rent to the council. How could I survive in a world that didn't bend to my spells? All the whispered words that made the magic work, the incantations that helped keep me strange in this world. Oddness was my thing. It defined and denied me.

These thoughts caught me by surprise, making me seriously think about the future for the first time in my life. One thing I knew for sure: I didn't want to work. Jobs were uncool. Truthfully, I wanted to do my own thing forever. But I couldn't say that, of course. Not in front of Mrs Walker. Looking up, taking in the room again, I saw my teacher gradually turning in my direction. How could I answer her question if I didn't have anything to say?

−Okay, she said, her eyes on the clock. −We've got another few minutes left. Let's get through as many of you as possible, including you, Stuart.

On the far side of the room, Stuart Urquhart seethed at the thought of being ignored again. Mrs Walker moved to the next name, the one that came after Gregor, that she chose every Friday at this time. It belonged to Arlene Munro, a gremlin girl with bright blonde hair that shone nearly as white as her smile. Arlene lived in the posh end of Denny, a cluster of large homes that had a dense forest out back. Gregor wouldn't go there because people used it to get drunk in secret and he had enough of that at home. But sometimes I felt like my heart was in the forest, along with the fairies and firebugs that sparked little green pinpricks of light into the darkness. Arlene probably woke up to that forest every morning. In that moment, I found myself swooning over a dream so far-flung I didn't have the words to describe it.

Something else. Something… more… than anything else I knew.

−What do you want to be when you grow up?

−*Ideally*, started off Arlene, −I want to be a lawyer like my faither.

−Of course you do, said Mrs Walker, her voice slightly strained. The only reason I caught it was because she sounded a little like my mither when she was in a bad mood, something that seemed to happen more often these days. Ever changeable, like Scottish weather in an hour, my mither could smile and snarl in succession. Sometimes, when things were really bad, she did both at once. Whenever Mrs Walker said something to Arlene, there was bite in her words. Maybe she didn't realise she was doing it, but I often got the sense she didn't like Arlene very much. No-one did, but we all pretended.

Kids are good at that sort of thing.

CHOOSE YOUR OWN CAREER

Finally, it was my turn to speak. I stood up and prepared myself for the question, even though I didn't have a satisfying answer. Frantically, without thinking it through, I tried to come up with something that wouldn't make me look bad in front of everyone, who would think the worst of me anyhow. Footballer was out because of Robbie. Numbed with indecision, I looked around at all the faces of Primary Five as they looked back at me, eyes blinking while harsh lines of sunlight cut in through the gaps in the blinds.

−Sadie, started Mrs Walker. −What do you want to be when you grow up?

Before I can stop myself, I desperately grab hold of something to say.

The first thing comes to mind. The truth.

−When I grow up, I want to be a prostitute just like my mither.

The word comes out as *proz-ti-toot*, something I'd heard someone else shout in the night, but hadn't said myself until that afternoon. The truth squeezed all other sound out of the room. Like everyone else, Mrs Walker didn't quite know what to say. All she could do was react with startled inertia, her face saying more than words in that moment. Her eyes were far wider than normal, her mouth open so wide it might touch the floor at any second. Also, I noticed her hands gripping the side of the table, as though trying to keep herself steady. That's how

14

I knew I'd made a terrible, life-shaking mistake. But it was already too late. By the time Mither arrived, the polis were waiting, hoping to ask questions of their own, like Mrs Walker each Friday before the last bell.

3

GAME SHOW

The social worker looked like someone Raymond Briggs might have sketched. She was all smiles, earthy colours, groovy spectacles, with two dots for eyes and lots of lines where there should have been hair. She arrived during a somewhat sunny afternoon to interview me about what I'd said in front of everyone in class.

Mither, still furious I'd said anything in the first place, worked overtime to make sure I looked extra presentable. Mostly, this meant having my hair washed. With a little too much enthusiasm, she forced my head into a sink full of hot water which was far less painful than my shrieking screams made it sound. Then she tipped a bottle of Vosene over me that usually sat unused in the bathroom alongside a collection of ersatz perfumes gifted at Christmas. Most of it missed my hair, instead, sliding down my nose and chin. As my head went under, the foam surged up, my hair wrapping around my face like clumps of seaweed. Mither didn't realise I was crying because my face was wet. Not that she would have cared either way. Saying the truth out loud was one thing, but saying it in front of other people was unforgivable and I had to accept that life was going to be difficult for a little while. At least until Mither calmed down a little. I just had to endure. Magic spells were duly whispered, but the words tasted of soap. By the time she was done, I sparkled, my hair artfully arranged in long wavy tresses. But I didn't feel good, because I knew this was a bad situation. Catastrophic, actually.

DOREEN

Eventually, the social worker introduced herself as

Doreen, and her lips, a thin line, curved into a smile just before she asked a question. The only time she stopped smiling was when she looked over at Mither, who met her gaze respectfully, but their conversation was hushed and urgent, conducted outside in the hall, too far for me to hear. Bugger.

Throughout my interview, Lily remained in her room, her favourite songs blasting out a racket, the sort of noise that caused the neighbours to complain to the council. Our kitchen drawer was stuffed with warnings, each signed, sealed and sent in envelopes, each one unopened and unread. If Mither ever forgot to pay the electricity bill (again), we could have used them to light a fire in the living room.

Stuck inside my head, I almost didn't see Doreen popping in from the hall.

–Hello Sadie, she said pleasantly. –I'd very much like to talk to you.

Immediately, I knew she was dangerous. I'd been warned about people like Doreen. They tied you up using your own words. This meant I had to think first and speak later, like I should have in Mrs Walker's classroom.

Her greeting seemed safe enough, so I returned it.

–Hello, I replied.

–How are you feeling?

–I'm alright.

A few seconds into the conversation and everything seemed okay. Besides, Mither had already told me what to say. We'd spent hours practicing and any question that I didn't answer to her satisfaction had resulted in tears, sadness and promises. Not mine. Mither seemed unusually worried about this meeting and her hands were never too far away from my shoulders. Because I desperately wanted to make it up to her, I made sure every question had an acceptable… no, a *believable* response.

17

Mither sold it to me as a game show, like the ones on the telly. I wasn't a big fan of quizzes, but the telly always had *Busman's Holiday* on in the background. The prize for answering the social worker's question, explained Mither, was staying with her and Lily.

I didn't want to be taken away. The thought of it made me shake.

—Do you know who I am? asked the outsider.

—Yes, I said. —You're Doreen, the social worker.

—Sort of, she laughed.

Mither had warned me she might try and make herself seem like my friend. I had to be wary. But as she spoke, I suddenly had a strong impression that she was, in fact, quite a nice woman.

—I work for the Children And Families Department of Falkirk Council. I'm here to make sure everything's fine and you're safe. You can trust me, you know that, right?

Over her shoulder and out of sight, Mither's jaw clenched tightly, the way it did whenever she wanted to headbutt someone. I'd seen that expression fairly recently, the same night she'd lunged at a takeaway delivery man after he gave her the wrong change. She'd handed over a twenty, he thought he'd taken a tenner. Who knew phoning out for a Chinese would end in an assault charge? As I answered Doreen's questions, I kept an eye on Mither, who had insisted on being in the room with me, much to the displeasure of the social worker. From the little I could see from my spot on the couch, Mither's willpower was under attack, every last nerve being tested. To her credit, she remained quiet in the background, unlike the music coming from Lily's bedroom.

—You said something to your teacher last week. Do you remember?

Did I remember? Every thought I had between waking up and falling asleep was about what I'd said in front of everyone at school. Mither talked about it constantly, obsessing over what the neighbours were saying behind her back. Lily absolutely loved it, of course. Yet another jab to join all the others she used against me. My hair, my clothes, the books I read and now the time I told everyone I wanted to be a prostitute just like my mither.

−Yes, I said with all the composure that practice allowed. −I told everyone my mither was a prostitute.

What I didn't say was that she also earned a lot of money.

BREAKING THE BAD HABIT

−Were you being honest? asked Doreen, her smile refusing to budge, not even for a frown, and I really wanted to see deeper lines on her face. Something about the kindly social worker was starting to annoy me. She was soaked in phoniness. Also, more truthfully, her presence was a reminder of my mistake.

−I said it as a joke. I didn't know this would happen.

Then, to make it sound better, I added:

−I thought everyone would laugh.

Though I wasn't looking, I could see Mither raising a thumb in approval. This made me feel like cartwheeling across the room, running up the wall, and spinning through the air. But Doreen wasn't quite done yet. She continued her interview, her hand scribbling away at a notepad while we talked. Funnily enough, I hadn't noticed the little booklet or orange BiC pen between her fingers until that moment. A thought idled its way through my head, a random visit from common sense. It made me wonder how many other names were in that notepad. How many kids like me had Doreen interviewed? Did they all say something they shouldn't have? Did they tell the truth like me? Although I didn't realise it, Doreen had been thinking along similar lines.

−Are you being honest right now?

Mither waited in the background, her breath held like a secret.

I enjoyed my power, but not too much.

−Yes.

Doreen dropped her smile, relaxed her face and ticked something off on her notepad. When her eyes came up again, so did the smile, wide and bright. Mither let out a long sigh of relief and winked at me. I took this as a good sign. The last thing I wanted was for her to do what she had done at school the other day, when she arrived like a chainsaw at a church. No-one had known quite how to deal with her, not even the police. In the end, I had to calm her down. The only way to do this was throw my arms around her waist, apologise for being honest, and beg her to stop shouting.

I waited on the seat, hoping the interview was over.

It wasn't.

DECISION TIME

Doreen decided she wanted to take a look around the flat, specifically my bedroom. Mither looked slightly startled and I knew this was because she hadn't anticipated my room being of any interest to the social worker. My room was slowly being absorbed by thick fronds of black mould, a dark stain inching out from behind the wardrobe. That wasn't something my mither considered worthy of stress, but the thought of a stranger seeing an unmade bed or crumbs on the carpet? She couldn't tolerate the thought of it!

Together, however, they made their way out of the living room, leaving me to the couch and my own company. A few minutes later and a few more hushed words, they returned once more. Doreen was now smiling at Mither.

−Okay, this seems like a huge misunderstanding, but you'll probably have to visit Nethermains and speak to the head about what happened.

I nodded but kept quiet.

Mither let Doreen out of the flat and immediately went into a West End production, shouting loud enough for the neighbours hear.

−I'm sorry my daughter tells so many fibs, she yelled, even though Doreen was barely at the top step of the staircase. −I'm so embarrassed this all happened!

As soon as Mither shut the door, her mood darkened.

−Nosy bitch, she griped.

−Did I do good? I asked, desperately hoping for her approval. Somehow, it seemed like everything would be better if Mither just forgave me. I'd hollowed out our relationship with a few honest words and now I just wanted to go back to the way it was before Mrs Walker asked her stupid question.

−Mither…?

She was in the kitchen, lighting up a cigarette. I watched her make circles of smoke, rings that drifted off into aimless, formless clouds. That's how I knew she was thinking it over, deciding whether to give me an official pardon or not.

A few words from her could make everything better.

Finally, with a flick of ash into a used cup, she passed judgement.

−Aye, she said. −You did alright.

Her decision finally made, I nearly cried with happiness. Instead, I fall backwards, hitting the wall, which is strong and dependable, unlike me.

4

AULD SYBIL

The tree outside my window was the tallest I'd ever seen. Somehow this tree had survived every storm in living memory, and it would probably survive many more to come. Around these parts, we called it Auld Sybil, because like every rural town, we had traditions that must be upheld, even at the cost of logic and meaning. For us, it was a symbol of power, magic and weirdness. Nobody outside of Denny could possibly understand the tree. We didn't understand it ourselves. Certain objects gained an abstract power when people added something of themselves to them. And so, one day a long time ago, a wee girl decided to toss a doll up into the tree. Probably some mean bully on her way back from Nethermains Primary, trying to upset a classmate by stealing their dolly, forever putting it out of reach. Whoever threw that first doll accidentally created a legend.

1985

The tree didn't just have dolls hanging from its branches. Over the years, other people have chucked shoes, bicycles and even underwear upwards, hoping the branches will catch them on their way back down. The tree catches and holds everything that comes its way. For people making their way through Little Denny Road during the rare occasions they need to be there – usually an election when the school becomes a polling centre – the sight of the tree is a shocking one. For some, it's an eyesore. For others, a piece of urban modern art.

For my friend, Gregor, the tree represented a test of courage. He'd always been fascinated with the legend around Auld Sybil, but I knew better than most that fascination was an extra thought away from obsession. One morning, as he approached my block from his, he looked up – and caught sight of a scrawny, spindly, gnarled branch. Unlike most of the other branches on the tree, this one had nothing hanging from it. The tree always let go in the end. That meant new objects could be thrown up, constantly changing the appearance of Auld Sybil, giving her something new to wear.

I noticed Gregor's eyes always flitting towards a bare branch, one that seemed to move even though there was no breeze to help it. In my imagination, full of frivolity and magic, I recast the branch as a pointed finger. It beckoned Gregor and he went to it, grateful to be wanted. Eventually, however, this became super annoying.

−It's just a tree, I said sharply, realising he was ignoring me again.

−But I've heard stuff about it…

His eyes never left Auld Sybil.

−Stuff? I asked. −What stuff?

−Someone told me she's the oldest tree in the world.

Actually, that was me, but somehow Gregor managed to overlook my contribution to the legend. I didn't want to correct him or admit that I started those rumours. Besides, most kids in Little Denny Road knew about the tree. Its power came from the same place all magic was birthed: belief, the complete absence of doubt, something each child learns and loses over time.

−It grants wishes too, continued Gregor, his eyes hungry with longing. Something was bothering him. A problem that could only be dealt with by wishing it out of existence. For a second, maybe two, the idea of not being included in his secret felt like a personal insult. As his friend, it was my right to know everything that went on in his life, including the private stuff inside his head.

23

Some of my own secrets were so private I didn't know them yet.

38 OVERTON CRESCENT

As our walk took us away from the tree, I thought about my friend, remembering how tough life could be in Little Denny Road, especially for Gregor, who suffered more than most. He was skinny to skeletal, depending on whether or not his dad remembered to put food in the cupboard. One of the reasons Gregor never missed a day at school was because at least there he'd be fed properly, whereas I'd just be fed up. The youngest of three children living at 38 Overton Crescent, Gregor looked up to his two brothers, twin bruisers who fancied themselves as hard bastards. Barry and Gary, whose names made them sound like comedy villains in a panto, were in fact completely terrifying. Worse, Gregor's faither was a notorious local alcoholic who always wrecked everyone's weekend by getting steamed up and starting fights outside in the street, always in direct view of the other blocks.

Usually this happened in the early hours of Saturday morning. These brawls became my version of an alarm clock, waking me up in time for *The Wide Awake Club*. You could set a timer for when Gregor's faither would start a fight. The only person he'd keep quiet for was my mither, who thought nothing of opening the kitchen window and yelling at him to shut the fuck up. Even in a state of complete drunkenness, Gregor's faither knew better than to push his luck. If he wasn't throwing fists and empty glass bottles, then he was singing, his voice surprisingly soulful. Unfortunately, his choice of songs were always football anthems and weird stuff about the Pope's bedsheets.

—He can't get over losing my mum, apologised Gregor

on the way to school, the same apology he made every Monday morning after his faither's latest rampage. —She did everything for us. Without her, we're not a family anymore.

For my own sins, I didn't have the heart to tell him that his faither was the same before his wife died, that his drinking made her life as miserable as he made ours. But that wasn't what he wanted (or needed) from me. We were lost in our own lies, because it made life a little more bearable.

BULLY BOYS

If Gregor's two brothers hadn't been so spiteful towards him, treating their youngest brother like sport rather than blood, then perhaps he wouldn't have been so determined to find something for the tree to hold. His brothers were far worse than Lily could ever be, the threat of physical violence always about them. They literally mugged children on their way to school, emptying their pockets for spare change, hoping to scrounge enough for a packet of 20 Club King Size. When they got bored stealing money, they'd idle away the time terrorising Gregor. We'd be out together, patrolling the streets, looking for adventure when the lads would appear and just... shout at us. There was no place they couldn't find us or trespass.

They never once tried to be friendly. Sometimes they'd call Gregor a wee poofter, other times a bent shot. It got worse when the other lads in the street were around, their presence stoking the twins into a frenzy. They favoured the bluntness of straightforward bigotry, old words passed down, transferred from mouth to ear and back again. I was never surprised to see the twins acting out in front of their friends. I'd learned long ago that a crowd for bullies is an audience for clowns.

Sometimes I thought about avenging my friend, forming a vigilante gang of our most marginalised residents. In my imagination, all the weird kids joined forces, picking up sticks to beat the twins, hitting them until all that nastiness was on the pavement along with guts and bone and brains. But for Gregor, the answer to his problems couldn't be found in the fantasy violence of my imagination. The tree was everything, or disaster.

Sometimes the Kids are not Alright

After he chose the branch (or maybe it chose him?), Gregor needed something to throw into the sky, a tribute to please the spirit in the oak that granted wishes. He couldn't throw shoes up because he didn't have a spare set. His manky old Nike trainers reeked and the left one had a mouth that sometimes stuck out its tongue, but they were his only pair, and he couldn't very well walk around in his bare feet. He also had some dolls under his bed that he played with when no-one else was around, especially his brothers. One was a scabby old Barbie with hair that had been dyed by yellow felt tip pen. The other was a silly, posable action figure. I was probably the only person in the world who knew Gregor played with dolls. He considered throwing one of them at the tree, but that plan carried too much risk. If Gregor brought one of his dolls out from the shoebox, someone might see him and make an unwanted association. He was terrified at the thought of people laughing at him, the risk their disapproval carried was enough to crush his already shrinking confidence. When I asked what he'd wished for, he didn't say.

−Friends tell each other everything, I said, my voice slightly careful.

−No, he replied, his eyes down at his feet. −This is my quest, not yours.

Eventually, Gregor found something valuable to offer the tree. He showed me one night when we were hanging around outside in the rain. Truth be told, we had nothing better to do than follow our feet, go where the paths took us both. We could walk around the world and still arrive home in time for dinner.

−This belonged to my mither, said Gregor, unfurling a crumpled piece of toilet roll, tightly wrapped around the object in his hand.

We'd been walking, wandering aimlessly around Dunipace Park, hoping to find a bench, only to spy a gang in the distance. We retreated the other way, along a path near an old bridge by a stream. There used to be a castle shaped like an *L* overlooking the field until it burned down, leaving a scar in the ground. My serotonin levels had already spiked at the thought of being the one person in the world to see what Gregor had for Auld Sybil. He still refused to tell me his secret, the reason for this misadventure. I knew better than to press the matter. Peering down, squinting to see in the moonless winter evening, I caught a glimpse of glimmering light on burnished gold.

A small gasp came from me, a childlike sound of surprise.

What Gregor had in his hands was nothing short of treasure.

−Isn't it beautiful? He whispered, as though his mither might be listening. −She wore it once a year when it was my granny's birthday.

−Wow, I said, because it was more than enough.

−It's old, continued Gregor. −I think it belonged to my mither's great granny.

−Does your faither know you've got this?

−No. I took it out of Mither's music box. He can't open it, because of the music… if he pulls that lid up, it starts singing, you know?

The sound of rowdy lads cheering and hollering was caught by the wind then brought over to us, an early warning that we should start moving again.

−Are you sure you want to give this to the tree? I asked.

−I've never been surer of anything in my life, admitted Gregor calmly.

The necklace had been important to his mither. As we walked, I realised whatever my friend wanted was something so big, so massively life-changing, that a small offering would have been considered an insult to the spirits.

I nearly asked about his wish, but suddenly we were running.

We were running because we were being chased.

THE GIFT

Two days later, on the last day of school before the Christmas holidays, I watched from my bedroom window as my friend approached Auld Sybil. Gregor needed to do this alone, or so he told me. Rested on my bed, I waved down at him, but he didn't look up. His eyes were completely fixed on the bare branch he needed to make his wish take hold. Worryingly, a slight snowfall had turned into a thick flurry. Gregor looked like the blizzard might cut him down, a tiny boy in a banana yellow tracksuit that looked a size too large. The wind worked against his aim as he swung his arm around, hurling a piece of jewelled gold at the branch. But wind always wins, and it came back down again. From behind glass, slick with warm breath, I muttered a prayer. −Please win, I said.

Gregor frantically scrabbled around, looking for his mither's prized necklace.

Recovering it, he was ready to try again. This time the wind helped, lifting and carrying the necklace into the air, catching it in a lucky gust. The shiny gold and glass suddenly suspended itself in the sky, a few inches beneath the branch, the thin chain tangling itself around the bark.

–He did it, I cried out. –Well done, wee man.

Now we only had to wait and see if Gregor's wish would come true.

5

Waiting on a wish

Nothing changed at first. Sometimes I'd waste hours casting spells, powerful incantations that I improvised with rhymes. They weren't too impressive, not on the surface, but they helped me get through each day. There was a spell of bravery to help me walk past other girls without looking down at my feet. I also had a spell that made me feel like the coolest girl in the world, even though my jacket had holes in it.

At least I still had Gregor. His magic spells were far more impressive. He could talk to animals, holding conversations with random cats and dogs. In the meantime, Gregor's wish continued to remain a stubborn unsolved mystery, known only to the animals that he chose to tell. I hadn't yet mastered the ability to talk to cats, dogs, or even the startled-looking deer that occasionally made their way down to the small field by Overton Crescent in search of food, retreating fearfully from the main road and the inevitable traffic. Gregor was there to translate and together we made our small lives into epic events.

We complimented each other because no-one else would.

Sharing slush

Denny Library was somewhere to go when I didn't want to be in my bedroom. The little branch of RS McColl's on the second floor of Denny's shopping centre had a Slush Puppie dispenser, which is where I spent most of my pocket money. If I had any change left, I'd buy the latest issue of *Bunty*, full of silly stories about white girls with yellow hair (DC Thomson's ink budget couldn't quite get a convincing shade of blonde) whose paper-white teeth could turn, depending on the shade of the paper the artwork was printed on. Afterwards, I headed into the library with my comic in one hand and Styrofoam cup in the other, trying hard to look ever-so-sophisticated in front of the watchful library assistants behind the counter, who didn't bother telling me off for bringing my drink into the building anymore.

Gregor couldn't afford to pay for his own drink, so I shared my cup with him, the two of us taking turns slurping from the same straw. Gregor took careful little sips. I didn't. Eventually, I decided to take a risk.

−Look, I said, lips dyed bright blue from the artificial flavouring in the syrup. −If you tell me what you wished for at the tree, I'll give you the rest. There's still half a cup left...

I'd hoped bribery would work where friendship hadn't, but the expression on Gregor's face made me regret asking. The ease between us, built through years of friendship, was starting to become more complicated and I didn't understand why. Reminding Gregor of his quest made him think about his wish, something he clearly didn't want to contemplate. Maybe he regretted giving up his mither's necklace? As we sat together on a threadbare chair across from a shelf of books, the two of us sharing a cup of melted slush, I sensed his wish hadn't come true. Then again, not even a tree with junk hanging from it could make good on a promise it had never offered in the first place.

LOVE AND ALL THAT ICKY STUFF

The snow started falling so hard that every step became a struggle. We walked anyway, because there was nothing else to do. We put Denny Library behind us, walking up the road with our faces down. At some point, I looked up and saw a group of people in the snow, some of whom I recognised from school. Gregor did whatever he could to avoid being seen by large groups while I tended to just ignore everything around me, including people. I'd slip into daydreams, wrapping myself tight in the fabric of fiction. Sometimes I was a witch, other times a warrior, anything but the fat girl whose clothes didn't fit and who reeked of sweat or *hard work,* as I preferred to call it. Mither despised sweat, considering it something only clatty bastards did, but the sheer amount of walking I did made keeping dry impossible. Also, I ate as much as I walked off, making my weight stay the same, regardless. Standing alongside Gregor made me look bigger. Actually, a skelf from a floorboard would look massive next to Gregor because he was so skinny. But our proportions never mattered until he made it matter.

As we passed the group of kids from our school, Gregor put his arm around my shoulder. I flinched, because it seemed to come out of nowhere. Despite how strange we looked, I began to enjoy the feeling of Gregor's arm draped around me. This power of ownership was completely new to me. But it was short-lived. Once we were safely away from the group, he took his arm off my shoulder and pretended it hadn't happened.

Over the next few weeks, Gregor would keep trying to put his arm around me or hold my hand – but only in front of other people. When we were alone, he stayed away. I quickly realised how much I liked being with Gregor, but only as friends. Sadly, my expectations were too high for him to reach, even with his long arms and legs.

When we got into a fight, our first ever, it happened at the park near the top of Braes View. The large field allowed dogs to walk their owners and kids to kick a ball without tanning any windows. I hurled accusations at my friend and he deflected them, both of us equally matched, our familiarity giving us perfect insight into the other. This meant we gave no ground, not even an inch. It was a game of chess played by Siamese twins. I sat on a swing while he opted for the roundabout.

−I'm not your girlfriend, I told him sternly. Part of me felt good about what I'd said, but another part, no matter how small, still wanted a dramatic reaction, possibly even tears. Instead, Gregor returned my words with silence. He shot past, over and over again, his face and hair a blur, returning only to be lost again in the spin. The roundabout refused to stop. I tried again.

−I don't like you that way.

−Okay, came his voice, near then far away again.

−Are we still friends?

−Maybe.

−I just don't want you to feel bad around me, I said, trying to sound grown-up, or my version of it. My teen years were on their way and I could almost feel the weight of them. I just wanted to stay here for a bit longer.

The roundabout slowed to a halt, each turn weaker than the last.

By the last stuttering spin, Gregor's expression put me in mind of a crumpled dish towel. −It's fine, he said quietly, −Honestly, I get it.

Unfortunately, I still hadn't got a reaction, or an answer to a question.

I decided to go for both.

−Did you ask the stupid tree for me to like you that way?

−No. I just want people to stop making fun of me.

My ego, still in development, was suddenly injured.

I tried to keep the situation light and fun.

−Hey, if you want people to stop making fun of you, I know what to do.

Gregor looked at me curiously.

−It's obvious, I laughed. −Just stop hanging out with me.

It was supposed to be a joke, but he took it as inspiration.

THE COST OF THE WISH

When school started up again, all thoughts of my outburst in Mrs Walker's class had been forgotten, replaced by some other minor scandal – nothing to do with my mither, for once. Instead, Gregor had made new friends. They were a gang of kids in my class, the ones I used to be friends with before I lost them to their parents' orders. Gregor was there with me, then suddenly he was gone, running around the playground with the lads, kicking a ball. Sometimes, I swear he deliberately aimed it at my head, though I couldn't be completely sure of myself, having no-one to tell me whether I was being stupid or not. I tried to get him to come back, but he was deaf to me. Eye contact was never made unless a ball was coming my way. Gregor no longer wanted to be around me. He had plenty of new friends who didn't laugh at him anymore.

The cost of the wish was our friendship.

6

If the playground was brutal, then the corridors and cupboards were slightly better, because there no-one could kick a ball at me. I spent each lunchtime haunting Nethermains Primary, forever on the lookout for something exciting to do, yet somehow always ending up in the school library. That's where I found a scrapbook about Denny, made by the librarian when she was bored. She'd put together pages of colourful photographs, scanned using the fancy new photostat machine, alongside bits of text copied out of reference books.

I sat alone, my new default status, idly flicking the pages of the scrapbook, hoping to find something interesting. On page ten, there was a photograph of the old war memorial, the one that stood near the bowling club down near the centre of town. I'd been there before, when I first arrived in Denny, yanked alongside my mither while she worked out the layout of her new home. Glued to page 12 was a photograph of an old farm. No thanks, too boring. I turned the page and found the future. *Torwood Blue Pool* it shouted. Underneath was a large photograph of a shimmering blue pool circled by old boulders. *The pool is two miles north of Denny and hidden in a dense forest*, said text underneath.

−A forest, I muttered. Enthralled, I read on. *Little is known of the pool nor its strange blue water that experts can't find an explanation for…*

Soon enough, I knew I'd found my own quest, something to fill the lonely seconds, minutes and hours between opening my eyes and closing them again at night. Torwood Blue Pool, where the water shimmered and no-one, including *experts*, could explain why. But I knew. For me, there could only be one sensible explanation.

Magic, of course.

GETTING OOT AND ABOOT

The first thing I did, the following Saturday, was stuff my backpack with supplies, all the provisions required by an adventurer on her mission to find a sacred mystical spring, long since abandoned by the wizards and witches of Falkirk. Carefully laid out on the kitchen worktop was a little bottle of water, filled straight from the tap. Next to it was a little bread brick, a piece and jam I'd scraped from the rim of an empty jar, wrapped tightly in cling film. Also, my library membership card so I could get a book with a map. That was important, because every quest needed a map to guide the adventurer safely along. I took a scarf and gloves too. The sky was a blank white, no clouds, just cold. This made me unpack my largest, warmest coat from my bedroom cupboard, shaking loose thin flakes of black mould when I shut the door. The jacket was old-fashioned, a severe black thing with triangle pegs instead of buttons. It reeked of wetness, but I decided the fresh air would blow the stink right out of the fibres.

As I made to leave, Mither stopped me, wondering where I was going.

−I am going on a quest, I said proudly.

−For fuck's sake, she muttered. −Just make sure you're back for dinner.

I lifted my right hand and gave her a thumbs up.

−Will do!

−Oh, and Sadie…

−Aye?

−Remember and keep an eye out for perverts, okay?

36

PERVERTS

Mither was obsessed with perverts and the shadowy threat they represented cast a constant darkness in my life. Perverts were everywhere. According to Mither, anyone could be a pervert. They were beyond the door, outside, lurking in plain sight, waiting to catch the unwary using kindness and cunning. The man at the shop who let me have a packet of Space Raiders even though I didn't have enough money to pay for them? A pervert, of course. Why else would he be nice for no reason? Goddamn perverts were the enemy within. Mither envisioned a world where they were all exterminated, along with drug addicts, gypsies and Skoda drivers. She was that determined.

−Please, she begged, −just be careful.

I assured her everything would be fine.

To put her mind at rest, I gave her two thumbs up.

LOOSE CHANGE

The librarian at Denny Library liked to smile even when she probably didn't feel like it, but I always appreciated her hard work. Sometimes, when I felt miserable (quite often but mostly on a Monday morning) I thought of her, the woman with the brown hair who took smiling as part of her job description. As expected, she was there when I entered through the heavy wooden doors, announcing my presence with a loud squeak of rusted hinges. When the door shut behind me, it pushed out the cold breeze, the only thing that wasn't welcome in the building. Better still, it kept the snow outside, a heavy flurry that fell on top of everything. It covered the parked cars, the people underneath their hoods, even the yellow plastic bins on lampposts were dusted in white.

−I need your help, I said to the librarian, who seemed

to be tidying up some index cards. − I'm looking for Torwood Blue Pool. I need a map to get me there.

−A map? She laughed good-naturedly. −You need a bus.

−Okay, could I have a map and a bus timetable?

A pile of bus timetables were stacked at the leaflet shelf alongside bright little posters advertising local businesses and flu jabs. The map, however, cost money.

−That'll be ninety-nine pence, said the librarian quietly, her eyes already falling back to her card index. My gloved hand rummaged around my coat pocket, trying to catch the loose change I'd brought with me, all those ones, twos and fives. Eventually, I slid every coin along the desk, each one reaching the librarian's outstretched palm. Loose change, the basics of currency, was easy to scrounge from kitchen drawers. I apologised, but she waved it away, saying goodbye to my embarrassment.

−It's fine, she smiled. −We need change for the till anyway. Really, you're doing the library a favour.

Fantasy houses

Leaving the library with my rucksack dangling across my shoulder, I walked through Stirling Street, past the chippy that was already prepping itself for business. The thick smell of hot grease and crisp potato made my stomach lurch in protest. If I had had enough change, I might have bought a few fritters, which would taste much better than the piece and jam stashed away in my rucksack. But I'd spent it all on the map that would lead me to Torwood Pool. How long that would take, I didn't know. But I had no time to spare, not even for my stomach. I kept walking, secure in my belief that soon enough, I'd get the bus and start my journey.

An hour later, I was completely lost. I blamed my map.

It was *unreadable*, each tiny line crossed other lines that led in directions I couldn't reach. After a while, horror set in, slowly eating away at my confidence, that unshakeable feeling that I'd been destined to reach the shimmering blue water. Also, my feet were starting to throb inside my welly boots. Somehow, I'd managed to make it to somewhere called Mayfield Street, a narrow road with nice large houses dotted in rows.

What made a house nice?

Stairs to an upper level, basically.

BUS SURFING

Minutes drifted by and I counted snowflakes until there were too many to catch. Eventually, something in the distance caught my attention, something bright orange on four wheels. At last, the bus had arrived! The driver, a heavyset man whose neck seemed to resent his shirt collar, immediately let me onboard, free of charge.

−Never mind the money, he said, shrugging nonchalantly. −You shouldn't be out on a day like this!

−I cannae go hame, I explained. −I'm on a quest to find a place of power.

−Fucking hell, he muttered, regretting his decision to allow me onboard.

Sitting alone on an empty bus, I ate my sandwich and laughed at my luck.

7

THE BLUE POOL

The leaves on the trees had died and dropped. Unfortunate, considering the epic story that I'd already played out in my head had me walking through a dense, luscious green undergrowth full of flowers, brambles, shrubbery and weeds. Instead, the woods looked a little frayed, skeletons of trees alone in wintertime. Worse, the sky was beginning to darken and I couldn't help worrying I'd made a mistake coming this far from Little Denny Road.

In trying to reach Torwood Blue Pool, I'd put miles between me and number 87. Some buses didn't show up during the frosty weather. Hazardous road conditions made driving a straight line into something almost byzantine. The thought of being trapped without any way back followed me through the forest. At some point, I decided to build myself a treehouse, using all the spare branches on the ground, orphans far away from their family trees.

The cold quickly started to sap my enthusiasm. Suddenly my adventure seemed like the actions of a daft wee girl who thought she could find magic in a pool of water. But I was stubborn enough to realise that no matter what happened, I was going to find that stupid pond. It was now an obsession.

Without thinking, I made a wrong turn in the right direction. Even from a distance, I caught sight of a dull blue shimmer through the branches. My legs, sore and stiff, took me to a circle of boulders. It was unremarkable, but as I got closer, the water soon made sense of my struggle. Even though there were no signposts, I knew this was Torwood Blue Pool. If anything, the water looked even brighter than it did in the scrapbook. Slowly, I approached. This was my quest, and I was about to complete it. Except... the upturned pram in the water wasn't quite what I expected to find, nor all the bottles strewn around the undergrowth. Empty wine bottles rolled across the dirt, crisp packets caught in the wind, travelling somewhere else. This wasn't how I wanted things to be. My moment, something I desperately wanted to be special, even sacred, had been ruined by alkies.

At this point, I noticed someone standing at the other side of the pool. He was dressed in a shiny yellow jacket, though it looked orange depending on the light. Even the slightest movement made it change. Juices gurgled inside my belly as nerves and hunger met head on. The man, a stranger, said nothing. He stood still, staring from the other side. The effect was unsettling.

−Hold fast, I yelled across the pool. −Are you the guardian of the water?

−Sort of, he replied. −I work for the Council.

FALKIRK DISTRICT COUNCIL

The Council were a mysterious force who controlled all of Falkirk and beyond. They were only summoned in the direst of circumstances, usually when the boiler broke in the house, or someone tried to interfere with Mither's rent rebate. The Council seemed to know everything. We feared their power, something they were happy to demonstrate when anyone on Little Denny Road got out of line. Noisy neighbours vanished overnight. Fences kicked in by kids suddenly reappeared. Smashed bus stops were replaced without fuss. They were always there, reminding us it was their world and we were just renting a small piece of it.

INTRODUCING GUS

This was a nightmare. I'd found my way to the pool only to be stuck with a council worker. Mither hated the council

41

as much as she despised perverts. The council constantly tried to steal her money, she said. Mindful of what could happen, I backed away, just to keep a safe distance.

−You work for the council, I said slowly.

−Aye. I'm the litter picker, he added.

−You're doing a really shit job, I told him, motioning at the upturned pram soaking in the water. As soon as I caught his reaction, a slightly crestfallen expression, I let my guard down slightly. Instinctively, I knew this wasn't a pervert. Carefully, I edged a little closer to the nearby pool of water.

−Why is the water so blue? I asked, hoping he knew the answer.

−I don't know, but there used to be a mine here, or a dye vat for a factory.

−Oh, I sighed. −Ah thought it might be magic that made the water blue.

He seemed surprised a girl my age still believed in magic.

−Don't be daft, he said with laughter in his voice.

I opened my mouth to say something in return, but nothing came to mind. Luckily, he said something else before I got the chance to upset him.

−It's getting late. You should head off home now.

−I can't. I'm lost.

−Well, it's lucky for you ah ken this place well.

He turned and led me up a different path, his large boots crushing petrified twigs along the way. While we walked, he told me his name was Gus and he'd worked for Falkirk Council for longer than I'd been alive. His first job out of school had been in cemeteries as a grave digger (this sounded amazing) then as a park attendant (not so amazing) and sometimes he did a shift as a litter picker. In time, we arrived on the outer edge of the forest and I stifled a bloody big yawn with my knuckles.

—Will you be alright? asked Gus, his words chittering in the cold. His answer came in the form of two headlights in the distance. The bus had come back for me. My quest was nearly over. I waved goodbye to Gus, who saluted like he was in the army. I laughed then looked away. It suddenly came to me that despite working for The Council, Gus was a decent sort of guy, not a sneaky scumbag like Mither assumed.

For the first time ever, I realised she was wrong about something.

This changed everything.

8

Mither regarded slippers as cursed objects and refused to wear them. Yet she still managed to find a pair to tan my arse the second I put the key in the lock, going until she was breathless (not long, thanks to her Benson & Hedges habit). I couldn't sit for a week, punishment for disappearing in the middle of winter. But being grounded in my bedroom wasn't such a bad thing because it gave me an excuse to catch up on the rest of my library books. Mostly, I liked the pictures because the words raced around the page too quickly for my eye to catch. Bright colours, shiny glossy pages. The magpie in me. Everything outside my bedroom and the bathroom were off-limits. Food would be passed through the temporary gap in my door. When I was really bored, I'd look outside the window at the tenement flats across the road, sometimes watching people going about their lives behind their windows. I always stared straight ahead, just so I didn't catch a glimpse of Auld Sybil.

When I looked at that tree, I thought of Gregor.

Sometimes, I wondered if he ever thought of me too.

Parole

On the last day of my jail sentence, I looked out the window... only to find the picture had changed. Something was new. A white removal van was parked in the little area next to the tree, blotting it from sight. This I took as a good omen. A group of men in bright shell suits navigated furniture towards the main entrance, noise from outside my door made me realise there were people in the stairwell struggling to get upstairs. The acoustics of the block carried their voices (and sweary frustrations) my way. Someone wasn't pulling their weight, it seemed.

Heavy objects were being bashed against the railings, accompanied by huffing and heaving. My first instinct was to have a gander through the peephole in the front door, but I didn't want to risk being caught by Mither who took major offence at any form of snooping. While watching from my window, I saw a taxi pull up. One after another my new neighbours exited the cab, each disappearing through the entrance into the block.

They were a mither, a baby, a faither, a girl, a boy, and…

My eyes were dry from staring without blinking. Rubbing them, I looked again. Yes, I was right. The girl held a dog leash with a big ginger cat on the other end of it.

−Quirky, I said aloud. The breath spent in that one word tinted the window in a small patch of fog. It faded before I got a chance to draw a flower on the glass. When I looked outside again, the new family were already gone, their noise now coming from inside the block. They didn't hide their presence, as if they could. Over the next few weeks, they'd bring with them shouting, yelling, crying, laughter and sex noises. To me, they sounded just like your typical emotionally-charged family, exactly like my own family, or the people next door. Suddenly, I was excited again, enjoying the energy of strangers, and perhaps a new friendship with them.

THE DONALDSONS

Whenever a new family moved into the block, they soon learned the golden rule: *don't fuck with my mither*. At some point on a Saturday afternoon, while Mither scrubbed the communal staircase, we came face to face with one of the new arrivals. He introduced himself as Alan Donaldson, but his pals called him King Donger. I didn't ask why.

−It's nice to meet you, Alan, said Mither coolly.

Donger smiled, making himself look like a daft wee boy, but he was a faither of his own wee boy and a wee girl too. On his top lip was a thin moustache that looked like it might jump to its death at any second. His hair was black and sideswept, proper Hitler hair. He also wore a vest that drooped loosely from his chest. Two words were inked onto his skin. FAMILY FIRST.

−We were on the housing list for months, he explained excitedly. −My girlfriend wanted a four-bedroom semi-detached. I said, don't be daft, you'll not get a semi-detached. Not yet. Just take what you're offered!

−This is a good neighbourhood, said Mither, her voice on the mild side of hostile. −It's very quiet at night. We like to keep it that way. Okay?

I nearly burst out laughing. Little Denny Road was many things, but quiet? Noise was always here, steady in the background. Shouting, crying, screaming, laughter. Noise never took a break around here, but somehow it felt like a reassuring constant in my life. However, if Donger felt offended by what Mither was telling him, he didn't show it. Instead, he nodded, as though appreciative of what his new home had to offer. −Aye, he said, −that's all you want, isn't it? That and a place for the weans to play.

He barely got a chance to finish speaking before I cut him off, stepping in to offer my services as a guide for his children. I knew Denny well, having explored it over the years, casting spells from Chacefield to Nethermains. Every shop, park, stream, underpass, field, and even the old Town House had been investigated. Who else was better qualified to show the new kids around town? Far from being suspicious, their faither seemed taken by the idea.

−Just don't wander off, said Mither sharply. She probably expected me to drag them all the way to Torwood Blue Pool, but I'd learned my lesson.

Besides, I wanted to be able to sit without yelping in pain.

I opened my mouth to say something, but Donger cut me off.

—James! Beth! Get your arses down here now!

Seconds later, a sullen little boy sloped down alongside his tiny sister.

—This is James, said Donger, slapping his son on the back, a pat of pride that looked a little too heavy for my liking. —He's about your age.

—I'm Jamie, muttered the boy. —James is an old man name.

Donger ignored him, preferring instead to introduce his daughter.

—This is ma wee princess, Beth.

She wore a bright pink t-shirt with a unicorn on it and a pair of matching jeans and trainers. Even her handbag was pink. It resembled a Fendi, but the longer I stared, the more it became apparent the branding wasn't quite right. The 'F' in the logo looked more like a 'B'. The bag was *Bendi*, not Fendi, fake but functional, never to be part of Princess Diana's impressive collection.

It was also too big for the little girl who carried it.

This begged the question… what was inside the bag?

LETTING THE CAT OUT OF THE BAG

A few minutes later, we were on our way, being waved off by King Donger.

—Enjoy yourselves, he grinned.

—So where are we going? asked Jamie, not at all enthusiastic.

—There's a stream outside, just up the street. Do you want to see it?

Beth looked down at her bag. —Can we go down to the stream? she asked softly.

My smile felt painful, but I kept quiet. I cast spells to make me feel better. Who was I to judge anyone's quirks? If this weird little kid liked talking to her fake Fendi bag, why not? Maybe it was her imaginary friend.

—He says it's okay, announced Beth excitedly.

The bag talked back, apparently. Being no stranger to weirdness, I smiled and nodded enthusiastically. All three of us crossed the road, moving in the direction of Nethermains Primary School, taking a sharp left turn towards the stream on Overturn Crescent. It was a bright day, the sun shining. A cold breeze cut through the warmth, but it came in small bursts.

Because Jamie and Beth were so quiet, I overcompensated.

—So how did you end up here in Denny?

—We got in a car and drove here, said Jamie, still making the barest effort. Beth laughed, a weird nasal yelp, the worst laughter I'd ever heard. Annoyingly, she also fidgeted a lot. Every few steps we took, Beth had to stop, just so she could readjust the weight of the bag, making sure it balanced on her thin shoulder. In time, we reached the stream. Waving my arm like an overly enthusiastic tour guide, I waited for their reaction.

Disappointingly, it was subdued.

—It's water, muttered Jamie. —Amazing.

—But there are tadpoles in it, I said, hoping that would excite him.

—He doesn't like water, explained Beth, while repositioning her bag.

—Why?

—He hates his fur getting wet.

I stared at Jamie, trying to find the fur his sister had just mentioned.

—No, not him. Mr Snuff.

As I looked at the bag, something fluffy and ginger

poked its head out from the top flap, staring at me with tiny green eyes.

Beth had a cat in her Bendi bag.

An actual literal cat.

The tabby yowled then retreated into his little bag bed.

It was times like this something in my heart stung for Gregor. What was I thinking? How could I even consider replacing him with these idiots? Our friendship was over, broken down. He wasn't some spare part I could easily replace, a friendship to be recreated with unworthy surrogates.

−Mr Snuff loves his bag, said Beth knowledgeably, not realising I'd dropped headfirst into an existential panic.

−I'm sure he does, I said while thinking of ways to get away from these weirdos. My own weirdness, something essential and defining, paled in comparison when confronted by true weirdness.

TOILET HUMOUR

−I need to go to the toilet, said Jamie out of the blue.

Thinking it over, I decided here was another chance to reassert myself in the group dynamic. Without hesitating, I took charge of the newbies.

−We'll go back. It'll only take a few minutes. I have a key.

But Jamie wasn't interested in going anywhere.

Instead, he dropped his trousers and squatted by the grass near the water. Before I could scream, he took a shit, the kind that hurt, huffing and puffing as he did his business, like he was passing broken glass. The pile left on the grass by the stream could have been from a dog, but it would have needed to be a giant. Beth and Mr Snuff said nothing. Not thinking about what he'd just done, Jamie pulled his trousers up and waited for my reaction, daring me to pass judgement. Mortified, I turned and ran back to the flat, wondering how I would explain what I'd just witnessed. The truth, still a bad habit, seemed like the best bet.

9

When Mither worked the nightshift, she kept herself hidden away in the flat. She loved that flat, jealously guarding it against outsiders who were (in order of importance) nosy neighbours, Mormons, Tories, the council and the polis. If Mither could, she'd shoot these people – but not in her flat, which had a lovely carpet she kept spotless. In fact, Mither kept nearly every inch of her 656 square foot floorspace obsessively clean, hoovering every day, polishing tables, washing windows and emptying cupboards. Dust needed permission to gather on our shelves. Lily thrived on Mither's malevolent mood swings while I lived in fear she'd discover the patch of damp on my bedroom wall, the one I'd covered with the help of my cupboard.

Even as a child, I recognised something vaguely unsettling about the way Mither cleaned our home. Sometimes I'd return home to find a stack of broken mops, handles splintered under the force of Mither's grip. She'd get so deep into her cleaning that she forgot to make dinner. Luckily, she could throw a tub into the microwave. Something in a wee white box with the Farmfoods logo on it. Farmfoods (or Pharmafoods as I called them because of the chemicals and preservatives used to keep everything fresh) were the building blocks of our daily diet. Stab the plastic film with a fork, blast it with five minutes of gamma radiation and there was a dinner ready and waiting on the table.

AYE OR NAW?

After sorting out dinner, Mither took time to get ready.

This meant putting on a beautiful dress, doing her hair and fixing her face.

—But it doesn't need fixed, I told her, not quite 'getting it'.

Mither seemed chuffed but suspicious. Eventually, she had to explain it was an important part of her work to look glamorous. She worked hard at her glitziness. Mostly, she wore black. The only bright colour she wore was the blonde in her hair. Mither hated black roots, regarding them as trashy. Her streaks were always artfully arranged, just like her daily rota.

Then, the final test. Five minutes before she left for work, Mither knocked on Lily's door. It was always the same question without fail.

—Aye or naw? she asked.

The answer never changed.

—Aye, said Lily from the crack in her bedroom door.

Satisfied, Mither walked out of the flat and into a stranger's car.

THE GET-TOGETHER

—So this is what it looks like, said Lily while peeking around my bedroom. She never came to see me and sometimes acted liked we lived on different planets. That night, while Mither was out at work, my sister decided to say hello. Immediately, I knew she was up to something. Not that I was in any position to complain. My night was sitting looking at the latest issue of *Just 17*, staring at the models, girls with bodies completely different to mine, the sort I'd secretly considered asking Auld Sybil to give me.

I almost didn't hear Lily. Soon enough, she got bored of being polite.

—Helllooo, she sang. —Are you a sandwich short of a soup or something?

—Huh, I replied, not knowing how else to welcome my sister into my domain.

—What are you reading? she asked, not caring in the slightest.

I waved the magazine at her face.

—That's… interesting.

—Okay, I sighed. —What do you want?

She answered with a surprised expression, the sort she probably practiced in the bathroom mirror. After a few seconds, she quit pretending to care and told me why she was lowering herself to breathing the same oxygen as me.

—I need your help, she said.

Swinging my legs around, I circled round on the quilt, bunching it up, clustering the fabric into a twisted pile. Readjusting myself, I was soon sitting up straight. Not that I was particularly obsessed with my posture, but I wanted to see my sister properly, savour this moment — because it might never happen again.

—You need my help? I asked. —You want me to do something for you?

—My friend is coming over, she explained, her eyes rolling slightly. —Only for a wee while, but he's going to be here while you're here.

—Oh, I replied, my disappointment too great to hide.

—I don't want you saying anything to Mither.

—What do I get in return?

That question had either arrived from a place of bravery or good old-fashioned overconfidence. I'd find out soon enough.

Lily thought it over for a few seconds before offering me a deal.

—You get to walk around without a black eye.

I had to accept her gracious terms, albeit reluctantly.

Before I could say anything else, the buzzer sounded in the background, an air-splitting, unyielding screech that

53

made me want to dive under the nearest pillow. Lily ran to the intercom. Quickly, she lifted the receiver and pressed the entry button. Voices from the ground floor came up, followed by laughter and the tuneless clanking of glass bottles. Wine for a get-together, I guessed. Whoever they were – and they were more than just one friend – they made a lot of noise. Then again, a tip-toeing tortoise would have caused a racket in our block. Footsteps and slammed doors sounded explosive if followed by a long period of silence.

–They're here, said Lily, acting like I didn't have ears.

SHERBET DIP

While I sat in my room, Lily unlocked the front door. The voices belonged to party people and they sounded delighted to be in the flat. Intrigued, I poked my head around the corner to see who owned the voices. A small group, two lads and another girl, none of them matching the image I had in my imagination. One of the lads was tall and pale, a lamppost dressed in a black bomber jacket. His friend was shorter in height and he looked like he was being eaten alive by his Adidas tracksuit top. Finally, there was the girl, who smiled as she passed by. Smaller than my sister but she stepped past with a strut that told me everything I needed to know. Her walk said she was cool as fuck and someone had to tell her.

My mouth opened to say something, but the living room door slammed in my face before I could get the words out. Clearly, I wasn't invited to the get-together. The door didn't budge no matter how much weight I put on it. Lily had somehow jammed it shut. I *screamed*. What my reaction lacked in sophistication, it more than made up for itself in impact. My sister, worried that one of the neighbours would call the polis and report a murder, relented and let me into the living room. Her three guests were sitting on different parts of the same couch, a blue plastic bag with bottle heads poking out the top sat in the middle of the group.

The girl who wasn't my sister introduced herself as Kelly.

−I'm Sadie, I said.

Her teeth were lined with tiny stainless-steel studs.

−They're my braces, she explained. −My teeth are a wee bit squint.

Before I could ask how I'd go about getting braces just like hers, one of the other boys, the tallest of the two, shifted his weight on the couch so my sister could sit between his legs. Somehow it looked really uncomfortable for him. The other boy, who seemed interested in Kelly (he clearly wasn't good enough for her), lifted a bottle of Buckfast out of the bag, unscrewing the cap with one quick flick. He offered Kelly a drink and she took it very gently. The bottle was rapidly snatched away so Lily's boyfriend could empty it down his neck.

−Bastard, she called out, her hand wiping her chin dry.

Lily's boyfriend found it so funny he almost burst into tears. If there was a joke being played, I didn't understand. Almost immediately, I realised something wasn't right. It was their eyes. They all had the same eyes in different faces. Dark, wide and unblinking. Not Lily though. She was her usual self, not necessarily an improvement. But as I studied her face, still surprised by how little she looked like me, she took to her feet and headed into the kitchen, pulling her lanky and wanky boyfriend off the couch. Together, they shut the door and left me alone with Kelly and the other one, who couldn't stop cackling. I waited quietly, but my curiosity (nosiness, let's be honest) was never going to settle, so I just ran over and opened the door, poking my head in to see what was happening. My sister and her boyfriend were hunched over the counter, the worktop where Mither would sometimes sit when she wanted to look out the window at a fight. There was usually one every few nights, sometimes in this block itself. Both Lily and her boyfriend weren't looking out the window though. They were sniffing along the worktop surface. Fascinated, I watched quietly. Kelly tried to yank me away, but I wanted to see what happened behind the closed door.

−Get her out, cried my sister, conscious of being spied on.

−What are you doing? I asked.

−We're eating sherbet, said her tall, nameless lank of a boyfriend.

−Up your nose?

−It's nice and sweet. Would you like some?

Even Lily found this too much to bear and let him know by slapping the back of his shoulder. If he felt it, he didn't react. There was still a line of gritty powder left on the worktop. −Go on, he said. −Just try it.

Cautiously, I approached the powdery line, intrigued to see what was so special about it. Lily said nothing. She seemed interested to see what would happen next. Craning my head up slightly, I tried to smell the powder, but the thickness of it scraped the back of my throat. The grittiness immediately made me hack up thick wet coughs. This led to a sneezing fit, scattering the rest of the powder across the worktop, leaving a greasy line-shaped stain.

−Fuck, said Kelly, darting over to try and capture some of the bitter mist I'd sent drifting upwards into the air. My face was red with heat. Quickly, I got to the sink and filled a mug with water, cooling my throat as I gulped it down in one long swig. The little get-together completely ruined, Lily made sure everyone was gone before she sat me down for a sisterly discussion.

−Remember what I said earlier?

−About what?

−About what would happen if you told Mither about my wee get-together?

−Yes. Why…?

Before I could finish my sentence, just shy of three words, my sister drew her fist back and slammed it against my face. My nose split open, staining my top lip, chin, and – *oh my god* – Mither's nice carpet.

Lily was looking down on me as I looked up.

−That's a reminder. Okay?

I wouldn't forget, especially when I looked in the mirror the next morning. My face was puffy and red, a tell-tale blackness forming under the surface of my left eye. When Mither asked what happened, I told her I'd walked into the door while sleepwalking on my way to the bathroom.

Funnily enough, the same thing happened to Lily, later that same night. When I asked what happened, Mither took it upon herself to answer the question.

−Sleepwalking, she said firmly. −There's a lot of it going around lately.

We said nothing more and the matter was quietly dropped.

10

The strange family in the flat above us declared war on the block without warning us. At first, they seemed jovial, even helpful. But King Donger started treating me less like a child and more like a childminder. He would literally knock on the door and ask if I wanted to take Jamie and Beth somewhere far away for the day, so he and his girlfriend could 'spend time' together. Not even his offers of free Irn-Bru and a packet of KP Nuts could tempt me, especially after the incident at the river. His girlfriend was just as bad. A space cadet without a spaceship. She chapped the door one day to ask if we had a spare tenner for her leccy meter.

—I'll pay you back when ma rent rebate comes in, she said.

I assumed a rent rebate was like winning the lottery. Mither, similarly unimpressed, soon became wise to their ways. However, as much as I disliked my new neighbours, there were benefits to having Jamie at Nethermains Primary. He'd easily taken my position as the least-liked kid at school. His sister wasn't as harshly ignored, if only because she had a certain silly charm – and a ginger cat in a bag that delighted the other kids in the playground. But soon enough, the whole family became a continuous pain for everyone on Little Denny Road.

Mither led the charge against them, of course. Taking on my mither was like leaping into a fiery pit with cardboard wings strapped to your elbows. But as much as I wanted the Donaldsons gone and the block back to the way it used to be, a part of me also didn't want them to suffer too much – just enough.

The only cure for Sundays was television. At some point in the afternoon, Mither decided we needed a pint of milk for her endless mugs of Nescafé. She was barely away when she stormed back into the flat, the door slamming so hard behind her that it nearly bounced right off its hinges. I'd been flicking through the four channels hoping for something interesting, even a game show, when there she was behind me. Slowly, I looked up to see her red face, wide eyes and lips pinched in a thin line. I recognised this expression.

Someone was in deep shit.

Literally, as it happened.

−Someone took a shite downstairs, she shrieked. −In my block!

−What?

−There's a shite downstairs at the door, and it isn't dog shite.

I'd already seen the large brown blob but had avoided looking right at it. She was right, of course. It wasn't an animal. It was far too chunky. Mither was taking it personally, as though the shit was somehow aimed at her character. But that didn't explain the jumbo jobbies being laid across the street. Residents had no idea who was behind the outbreak, but they'd already dubbed him The Secret Shitter, deciding it had to be a 'he' because no girl could possibly squeeze out anything *that* substantial. Mither, however, knew more than she realised. −Wait, she said, suddenly connecting this with that. −The dirty wee bastard upstairs took a shite at the stream, didn't he?

Ah. She remembered. I was worried she might.

TAKING ON NUMBER NINETY-THREE

I saw the poster on my way to school, a little A4 sheet

of paper, a patch of white on a white wall. It had been placed beside an exit button that had to be pressed for the hydraulic clamp of the front door to unlock. Everyone would have seen it by now.

BEWARE, said the poster. DIRTY SMELLY BASTARDS LIVE IN THIS BLOCK AT NUMBER 93!

Even before I reached the final paragraph, it was obvious who had written it. I recognised Mither in the words because she wrote the exact same way she spoke. Even the man on the moon could see her personality in the paper.

−The faither is a smack lord, I read aloud, my voice bouncing off the walls.

A smack lord. I thought. What the hell is a smack lord?

Nevertheless, I kept on reading. Each accusation became more lurid further down the sheet.

−The Donaldsons lock their kids out of their flat so they can do drugs. THIS IS WRONG. The kids are forced to shite outside because their toilets are blocked with drugs. If you want the Donaldsons out of Little Denny Road, sign the petition. Together we can make a difference!

There were five signatures already.

Carefully, I took a closer look at who'd put their name on the petition. I didn't recognise any of them, but I sure recognised the handwriting.

Mither had signed the petition on behalf of people she'd invented.

Sighing, I punched the green button, unlocked the door and headed out.

Five steps outside and I nearly put my foot on another shit, and promptly marched back inside to add another fake name to Mither's petition.

Old wounds reopened

Gregor was in the playground when I passed the gate

on my way to the main doors, but he looked away, his arm around Arlene, an arm that drew her nearer to him as I walked past. Arlene smirked, her favourite facial expression. Even a smirk on Arlene looked like a *Just 17* front page; a glossy photo on a wall of an agency that booked children for modelling or acting jobs, and my goodness, could Arlene do both easily. Even though I fought the pressure to compare myself, it was impossible to win. She had blonde hair, blue eyes and expensive designer labels on her clothes, all funded by her faither, a lawyer who drove a car that looked like the Batmobile. Gregor had replaced me, just like I tried to replace him – but unlike me, he was successful in his attempt.

To cope with my new reality, I spin everything into a manageable new version, giving myself permission to be happy for the friend who put a knife in my heart. Really, I should take it as a compliment that he replaced me with the likes of Arlene. She's so perfect that feeling happy for them is the only victory I have, but it's one too many for Arlene. She can't help lashing out and spends most of the time during lessons kicking the back of my chair whenever Mrs Walker isn't looking. Not happy with my lack of reaction (the result of a Spell of Nonchalance I cast under my breath), she starts to kick my legs. It's so bad I nearly scream out in pain, but somehow, I endure. This has always been my greatest talent. Eventually, Arlene tires of tormenting me and stops. Her short attention span takes her off in new directions – one girl to hate is never enough. I'm the latest in a very long line, a lineage stretching back to nursery.

ANOTHER NAME ON THE LIST

During lunch, I return home to find Jamie outside the block, sitting on the ground, as though waiting for something to happen. My first thought is to ignore him, but he's sitting at the door, his back pressed against it. In order to get inside for lunch, I need to shift him away from the entrance. My only other option would be to go around to the other side of the block and head through the back door, but that would mean turning around and walking away. Having been bullied enough, I decide this is my stand to take. But the decision is made for me. Jamie gets up and moves aside. His sister, her bag and her cat are all nowhere to be seen. It's just me and him.

—Your maw's a cunt, he tells me as I press the button marked 87.

—Fuck off, I snap back.

—She's telling lies about my family!

—You're the liar.

Not a great riposte, but all I had to offer. The door finally unlocks, but before I can get inside, Jamie runs past, and he's gone. Unsure of what to do, I finally made a decision I wouldn't regret.

I lifted the BiC pen and signed the petition on the wall. My real name this time.

Just like Arlene, I needed someone to hate.

11

1987

Mither always returned early, with the birds, their staccato chirping a regular wakeup call. After their song came footsteps, sharp heels on concrete stairs. Then the key in the latch, clicking and turning, the best sound. That meant she made it back home. At last, I could go back to sleep. On the rare occasions Mither arrived home late, I struggled on the pillow, my head bursting with possibilities of what might have happened, none of it good. Things changed dramatically one morning as I lay there, listening, as four wheels tried to reach an agreement with the gravel. This time something was different. It took me a second to work out Mither wasn't alone. My ears were attuned to her footsteps. This time there was a voice and it belonged to a stranger. A man. When he spoke (and I couldn't quite make out the words), his voice sounded gruff and leathery. My belly shivered, giving me the sort of queasiness that happened before a lengthy stint on the toilet pan. Keys went into the lock, though it no longer brought me any comfort. Then the front door opened and two sets of voices came in alongside two sets of feet. He was in the flat now, laughing like the kids at Nethermains. Mither shushed him and his voice went lower, but not much. Lily, meanwhile, slept through it all.

I shut my eyes and tried to dream away my worries.

RAINTOWN

A few hours later I had to get up and face the new intruder in my home. He wasn't alone. Ricky Ross and Lorraine McIntosh were with him, their voices spilling out of the speakers in the living room. Mither had never previously expressed any liking for Deacon Blue. Now they were never off the turntable. Accepting my fate, I pulled myself out of bed and made my way through the hall to the living room. Dressed in my favourite scabby pink housecoat, I waited for the inevitable introduction. Mither was sitting on the chair by the table, a glowing dot between her fingers. Not that she noticed me. She was too busy belting out her version of *Dignity*, the one that sounded nothing like the actual song. Her friend, the gravelly-voiced stranger, was on the other chair, his legs positioned across and under her legs, an intimate tangle of limbs. He wasn't much to look at in comparison to my mither. His light hair was long, almost reaching his shoulders, but not long enough to make a full ponytail.

His smile was crooked, but something about his overlapping teeth made him seem insecure. He never ever failed to put his hand in front of his mouth whenever he laughed – and he laughed a lot, the loud laugh of a man who wanted everyone to look at him, even though he wasn't much to look at.

−Hello, wee yin, he said in a voice so rough it sounded like he'd gargled battery acid. I didn't respond because I was waiting to be acknowledged by someone who mattered.

−Sadie, cried out Mither, abandoning her karaoke.

−What are you standing out there for? Come in and meet your Uncle Tam. He's been waiting all morning to see you and Lily.

−He's not my uncle, I snapped, my worst fears confirmed.

−Don't be so fucking rude, she snapped. −Show some respect.

Oh God. Not this *again*.

−Hello, Uncle Tam, I said between clenched teeth.

There were no good men for Mither to depend on, no-one like Gus from The Council. She saw the worst of them, the scumbags and cheats, drivers hidden by tinted windows, who didn't want anyone to see them out with other women. Their money was rent and food and clothes. Anything I owned (not much) came from these men and their bank accounts. They were always with us, these men who needed my mither in the only way certain men want women. Over and over again, I suspected Mither saw a gap in her life for someone respectable, a good man to form the family unit she seemingly wanted. But because she never met any decent men, opportunities for her dreams to come true were exceptionally limited. That didn't stop her from trying, though.

Every now and then, Mither would bring home a man and test drive his potential, hoping he'd fit into her life. She wanted the faither figure she felt Lily and I needed, though she'd never told me who my real faither actually was, something that kept us at odds. These replacements became our Uncles. In Mither's mind this camouflaged their outsider status. There had been a lot of Uncles in my life over the years. Uncle Jack was tall, skinny and spotty – but he also had the best record collection, most of which got stomped on when Mither decided he wasn't suitable for the role she had in mind. Then there was Uncle Malky. He was an ex-Mr Scotland. He still had some of his old muscle and showed it off by wearing t-shirts so teeny they looked like bikini tops. His other vice had been his favourite aftershave, Denim. He used to empty whole bottles across his face and neck, making my eyes and nostrils drip. For some reason, Mither had found Uncle Malky physically irresistible until the night he put her through a small glass table she'd bought in the Woolco sale. They'd been arguing over her career, the source of every tension in our lives. As soon as I saw the blood, I tried to call the polis, but never got the chance.

Eventually, Uncle Malky was gone and we were alone again.

Now I had another Uncle in my life.

But for how long?

LILY MEETS HER NEW UNCLE

Lily was still in bed, completely wiped out from the previous night's party, She'd spent the evening drinking, snorting, laughing and crying. Now, she was sleeping. That morning, minutes after being introduced to my new uncle, I crept into Lily's room and made my way to her bed, where she lay with a quilt over her face, snoring muffled by polyester and stuffing. For a second I waited, hoping my footsteps on her floorboards would wake her up, but she was out cold. I needed to make more noise.

−Lily, I whispered. −Wake up.

She muttered some half-defined words, possibly a threat too.

Nonetheless, I had to keep trying.

−LILY! I screamed. −WAKE THE FUCK UP!

She groaned, then pulled her quilt tighter across her face. It was a horrible bedspread, a quilt of creamy beige with a crochet design across it, the sort of thing you'd find covering a miniature bed in a Victorian doll's house instead of an actual bed. Lily had been allowed to design her own room, approaching the task with all the seriousness of a professional interior designer. My bedroom was decked out in Clearance everything, including the light fittings.

−Lily, I sang, each letter hitting a different note.

Sluggishly, Lily opened her eyes.

−Don't hit me, I pleaded. −I need to talk.

She didn't speak, but I knew she was listening.

−Mither's brought someone back.

−Oh God, groaned Lily, her hangover suddenly cured.

−His name is Uncle Tam, I added, knowing it wouldn't go down well.

−For fuck's sake. Not another one.

−Aye. I think he's a hippy.

She seemed to be thinking something over.

Finally, she sighed. Then sniffed. She sniffed a lot these days.

−I'd better go out meet him.

Together we went into the kitchen where Mither and Uncle Tam were sitting. The needle had been put to the start of the vinyl again and *Raintown* was spinning for the second time that morning. Lily waited for someone to acknowledge her, but Mither's full focus was on her man. It was one of those rare instances of Lily knowing how I felt, being the one ignored all the time.

−Who's your new gentleman caller, Mither?

−Lily! said Mither brightly. −Tam, this is my eldest. Her name's Lily.

Then:

−She's going to be a famous model.

−I'm already halfway there, sniffed Lily, her hand wiping her nose.

−She looks exactly like her maw, said Uncle Tam, his arm going around Mither's shoulder. He pulled her closer, nearly bringing her right off her chair, but somehow, they met in the middle. Mither blushed and smiled, her eyes not once leaving her man's face. They were in love for now. Lily wouldn't say anything else, of course. She knew how risky it was to piss off our mither.

That left me to be the whiny, complaining daughter. I hated it.

−Welcome to the family, said Lily calmly.

—Aye, I said. —Welcome.

Mither glared at me, as if to say *why can't you be more like your sister?*

If only.

12

What's cooking?

In a bid to impress his new girlfriend, Uncle Tam threw himself into being a faither figure. He decided that I was *bigger than Godzilla* (his exact words) and blamed all the microwave meals I ate.

–You might as well eat hot shite, he said unhelpfully.

Mither agreed with him even though she was in charge of filling the freezer in the first place. Hypocrite! Luckily for me, Uncle Tam once took a cookery course at Stow College. This came in useful when he got a job, years later, at Fratelli's in Glesga. A whole three weeks he lasted, before he decided to pursue his dream as a nightclub DJ. But that was his past and we were his present. From now on, everything was to be made from scratch using only the freshest of ingredients.

The pasta came in a box, the sauce in a jar and the potatoes in frozen pellets – but everything else was made by Tam, who oversaw every dinner, both good and bad. Mostly bad. Worse, we were forced to eat together, including Lily, who preferred being out at Wimpy's with her friends, not suffering a family meal every single night. We bonded in mutual suffering, brought closer by the stranger in our lives.

To his credit, Uncle Tam made an effort to create a stable environment for his new daughters. We were embraced by Tam like his biological children, all of whom didn't speak to him anymore because they thought he was a wanker. Mither told us this but said very little more on the matter. She was just grateful to have found someone who didn't feel threatened by her career. In fact, Uncle Tam drove Mither to work every night, staying out with her until the early hours. He'd do anything for 'wifey' – which was just as well, because she had something specific in mind, a favour repaid in love and late-night lust. They were at it constantly. I was grossed out. Once they stopped, they talked. Mostly about the Donaldsons in the flat upstairs. They were starting to royally piss Mither off.

–Manky bastards, she complained one night. She hadn't got over the fact her petition had failed and the Donaldsons were still living in the block.

–What about them? asked Uncle Tam eagerly.

Another noise came through, muffled but immediately recognisable. It was the sound of nicotine being siphoned through the end of a cigarette, inhaled then exhaled by the same set of lungs.

I knew that sound well. It followed me around the flat.

–Could you sort them out for me? asked Mither calmly.

I already knew what she had in mind.

Skoda of evil

At some point the Skoda had mysteriously appeared in our communal car park. It was a large, squat, ill-proportioned mint green box on wheels, the bonnet sticking out too far, its once bright paintwork jaundiced with neglect. Each wheel looked like it belonged to a different car, giving the car an odd lopsided appearance. Mither saw it when she came back home in the early hours, her horrified expression visible even from my bedroom window. Mither despised Skoda cars in general. It was an inexplicable hatred she couldn't hide or fake away. That morning, when she discovered the Skoda parked outside the main entrance to the block, she freaked out. As I watched from above, face hidden by the net curtain, I noticed blinds in other windows parting slightly, giving the neighbours a good view of the action. They were waiting for a show, of course. They'd get one for free.

–What in the *fuck* is that fucking abomination doing here?

Evidently, the car belonged to the Donaldsons. Uncle Tam tried to calm Mither down, though he may as well have handed a lollipop to the Loch Ness Monster for all the good it would do.

–It's just a car, he said, trying to keep her mood steady, because it was early and he didn't want everyone to see or hear them. Too late. –The Skoda Garde is quite a reliable car, actually.

Ah, I thought. His first mistake. I'd learned a long time ago that disagreeing with my mither was more dangerous than throwing a petrol bomb into a hurricane. The results were never going to end well for anyone. I cringed.

–I want it out of here, said Mither quietly, her voice tight. The car was too untidy, an eyesore that she couldn't erase with a bottle of Domestos. Somehow, I knew there was more to it. She was throwing excuses, reasons, explanations out so at least one might stick.

Uncle Tam didn't respond.

–Get rid of it, commanded Mither.

–Okay.

I snickered, finding humour in my latest uncle's subservience. But like my mither and her man out on the street, I was too loud. Uncle Tam glanced up, almost catching me by the curtain. Pulling away abruptly, I lost my balance and fell down onto my bed, missing the wooden headboard by inches. As I lay on the mattress, thankful that I managed to avoid putting a dent in my skull, there was a sudden movement from nearby. Footsteps above me. Someone upstairs had literally just stepped away from their window. As they moved around their room, the floorboards creaked under their weight, confirming a suspicion I had about the flat upstairs. They didn't have carpets down on the floor. Every single footstep made the ceiling squeak.

Whoever it was (and it could only be one of the Donaldsons), they'd probably overheard Mither and Uncle Tam. Everybody in the street had been listening. My mither, bless her, didn't know how to whisper, but if I complained, she blamed it on her mysterious bad hearing, an ailment that only seemed to benefit her more than anything. Even the softest word had to be shouted, including their secret plans to get rid of an eyesore on four wheels. If I hadn't been so tired, I would probably have laughed. Instead, I shut my eyes and snored for a few hours.

Eggy bread against French toast

The flat was unusually calm that morning. Mither was in bed, meaning Uncle Tam was in charge of the kitchen, holding court at the table while Lily paced about in the background, waiting for the microwave to heat up a bowl of oatmeal for breakfast. Last week it had been the soup diet, now it was oats, oats and oats. As far as I could see, it looked like a bowl of cement. Worse, porridge always backed me up worse than the M8 at its peak. I'd be stuck eating nothing but apples (or 'roughage' as Mither called it) until I finally managed to empty myself. Every morning, I had some toast with margarine or a bowl of Sugar Puffs (if we had any left). Lily liked the odd bowl of Sugar Puffs too, but only at night when no-one was watching. She went through periods of eating in private, out of sight but never out of earshot. The flat just wasn't big enough for that level of isolation. For now, she was eating with us, if only because Uncle Tam had a weird obsession with keeping us all together during breakfast and dinner.

–Eggy bread? asked Tam as I slumped onto a chair, the table keeping a satisfying distance between us – but not far enough for my liking.

–It's called French Toast, I said, –and no, I just want toast with margarine.

–Nah, it's called eggy bread. I should know. I'm a trained chef, remember?

I nearly laughed in his face but kept it inside, my body shaking slightly. At the same moment, Lily decided to enter the debate with her own opinion.

–Someone I know calls it Turkish Toast, actually

–They're wrong, said Uncle Tam, quickly correcting her.

He did this more often than I liked.

–Turkish Toast, I mouthed, my brow furrowed in confusion.

While I contemplated what to call bread soaked and cooked in egg, Uncle Tam was already up off the chair and at the frying pan, his entire body fizzing with weirdly nervous energy. –Listen, it's no trouble. I can make some eggy bread for you if that's what you want?

–Just toast please. Toasted. By a toaster.

But he already had the bottle of cooking oil out from the lower cupboard, emptying a thick stream of it into the pan before I could protest. Healthy eating, indeed. The ring on the hob was heating up. I sighed. This was my life now. Even the simplest of situations had to be complicated by adults constantly trying to prove themselves in some way. Uncle Tam couldn't just stick a bit of bread in the toaster and heat it to a nice crisp. He had to cook! This would have been lovely except for the way it made me feel. Somehow, I couldn't quite shake the impression that there was some bad acting going on, and I was stuck in the audience against my will. Mither had inserted this wanker into my life and I was stuck playing the role of

73

happy daughter. If I knew who my real faither was, none of this would have mattered. Sometimes, I thought about him. Thinking about him was better than asking about him. Oh, I'd tried that more than once, and every time the conversation ended in tears.

Not mine.

–The toast is burning, said Lily absently, her eyes on Uncle Tam.

I sniffed the air at my side of the kitchen.

She was right. Something was burning, but…

It wasn't the toast.

My first reaction was to get up off my chair and follow the smell.

–Sit down, said Uncle Tam, his voice suddenly hardening.

–But something's on fire, I cried out.

–Eat your fucking breakfast.

Two pieces of bread soaked in egg plopped onto my plate.

The smell of fire was now unbearable. I felt a dry boke in my throat.

–I'll close the window, said Tam, who was looking out of the kitchen door, right into the living room where the window overlooked the car park. Without waiting for permission, I tore off into the living room. Before Tam could stop me (and he tried), I was at the window looking out. Thick black plumes of smog curled up into the greasy sky, twisted all the way up from something far below on the kerb. My brain translated everything in short bursts. A fire. A blazing box where a mint green Skoda Garde once sat.

Directly above our heads, feet banged wildly on the floorboards. The Donaldsons sounded like they were running around, completely in a panic, moving without doing anything. Faintly, I heard the sound of crying. It might have been Donger, but it sounded like a little girl in distress. Lily looked at me but said nothing. Our thoughts were probably very similar, if not the same.

–Bloody hell, I muttered as the framework around the car started to collapse into a heap of smouldering iron rods and liquefied plastic. The hysterical sounds of weeping were quickly drowned out by sirens in the near distance. Residents of nearby blocks were watching from a safe distance, their windows firmly shut to stop the smell of burning. Suddenly I took a strange notion that the fumes might be poisonous. Immediately, I backed off from the window while Lily and Uncle Tam looked down at the improvised bonfire.

The smell of petrol seemed to push itself into the air in the living room. Where was it coming from? I followed my nose to Tam's t-shirt, the one he currently had on. It was a faded old Joy Division t-shirt he wore more than anything else from his duffel bag. It reeked of something flammable, a chemical backsplash in its fibres and threads. The smell was in the house.

The door from the hallway opened and Mither sauntered in, still half asleep.

–What's happening? she asked between a long, slow stretch of her arms.

–There's a bonfire outside and it isn't even November, said Lily smoothly. –Someone's car, by the look of it.

–An insurance job, said Mither groggily. She wasn't a morning person. Actually, she wasn't an afternoon or evening person either. At night, she came to life, but this early, while in her old fluffy bathrobe, she wasn't herself. She normally never let anyone see her without a face of neatly applied makeup and nice clothes. That's how I knew she was in love. And the burning car outside? It was a gift from Uncle Tam, his version of flowers or chocolates.

Then, without giving us time to react, the car's fuel tank ruptured.

The skyline flashed briefly, but the glow lingered in my eyes for days.

13

Mr Chadha's garden

The most beautiful garden in Little Denny Road was owned and loved by Mr Chadha, who kept to himself, though his singing voice (just as lush as the garden) always announced his presence. He was a fan of opera singers, specifically Pavarotti, which immediately marked him out on a street where songs about murdering the Pope were blasted from windows at weekends. Living on the third floor of a housing block, we didn't own a garden, so I had to be content to look out the window at Mr Chadha's garden whenever I wanted to see something beautiful.

On the occasional warm days (the sort Lunn Poly sent sun worshippers to Spain for), Mither would sunbathe for hours. Really, she didn't need any excuse. Even the barest break in the clouds was enough to make her strip off into her favourite two-piece for an all-over tan. She would head downstairs to the shabby patch of grass at the far side of the block and lie there with a scabby old towel under her back, the same tatty green thing she wrapped around her shoulders when it came time to fix her roots. *Better that than my good towels*, she snapped that one rare time Lily complained to her about how it looked to neighbours. I found it difficult to care, completely overwhelmed at the demands placed on me by my daydreams. I dreamed of the day I could live in a house with two doors, one of them leading to a garden.

There was, however, another reason for my interest in Mr Chadha and his garden. Something I'd overheard the shopkeeper's wife telling a customer at the Little Denny Road Mart down the road, a bare snatch of conversation I'd earwigged whilst looking for a box of Tampax, the same box Mither insisted on buying every month. If I got

77

them quickly enough, I was allowed to spend the change on a ten pence mixture.

–It's true, said the woman at the till while adding up the final total –Mr Chadha built a wee town in his garden. He says it's for the fairies.

They laughed, clearly finding it all very silly. Me? I was so taken by their discussion that my fingers suddenly lost strength. The purple cardboard box I'd lifted from the shelf in front of me dropped out of my hand, landing at my feet. It bounced once, then came to a final rest, waiting to be picked up again.

My thoughts were too busy to be diverted elsewhere.

A little town for fairies in Mr Chadha's garden?

Suddenly nothing else mattered but seeing the fairy garden.

In a daze, I walked out of the shop and back up the road.

Mither freaked out when I walked through the door without her Tampax.

–I need them, she shrieked, her head poking out from the space between the bathroom door and frame. –Don't you come back without a box!

–I'm not getting them, muttered Uncle Tam in the background, his voice sounding more worried than anything else. –Fuck that, he added.

I wasn't bothered either way. Going back to Little Denny Mart meant passing Mr Chadha's garden and that gave me an opportunity to look over the fence.

BEHIND THE GARDEN GATE

The sky was blue and bright, but the air felt wet and soggy, the worst sort of weather. My chest got tight when the air went this wet. Taken by the urge, I turned my step into a skip and moved down the street quickly, getting closer to

Mr Chadha's house with each leap. He lived alone, by all accounts. I hadn't ever seen him with anyone, but it never occurred to me that there was anything wrong with being alone. Mither really didn't like him, not just because he lived by himself, but because he put up posters in his window for the SNP and Mither felt this was a personal attack against her values, whatever they were.

As I stood alone at his garden gate, I started to think about Mr Chadha. There wasn't much, to be honest. He wore nice clothes, always tweed, with a white shirt and green tie. I'd seen him waiting at the bus stop to go into Falkirk. What he did after he got off the bus, no-one knew. Colleen, one of the residents of a nearby block, had once seen him at The Yorke Café, a famous award-winning chippie near Falkirk bus station. She'd told Mither he was alone in there as well, seated at a table reading the latest Evening Times. This old man, who'd spent decades living on my street, slowly started to take on near mythical status in my mind. I raised my knuckles to Mr Chadha's garden gate, ready to knock – only to stop with my knuckles inches away from the wood.

Someone was belting out a beautiful tune, singing a song with notes that soared all the way to Heaven. I stood still, absolutely captivated, trying hard not to draw in air in case my lungs made a noise and ruined the song. None of the words made sense – but I knew it was opera, music for rich people. Only when I felt dizzy (from unwittingly holding my breath far too long) did I realise the singing had suddenly stopped. That's when I mustered the bravery to knock on the gate, hoping he would answer. The wood was a nicer colour than the other nearby fences, treated with a golden gloss coating. The other garden fences were speckled with green stains, tell-tale signs of encroaching moss. It made me think of the wall in my bedroom, crawling with blackness.

Lost in my head again, I almost didn't see the gate swing open.

Mr Chadha stood in front of me, looking down, his eyes watery and wide.

–Why are you knocking on my gate?

Unprepared for such directness, I didn't know what to say. Not at first.

Then, I found the words.

–This is going to sound so weird but…

–You want to see the fairy garden, don't you?

–Yes, I cried out. –If that's okay?

He stepped aside, giving me permission to see his garden.

FAIRY HUNTING

The view from inside was even more amazing than looking at it from above. The fence was covered in vines, beautiful green bindings that must have taken years to grow. The ground was grass, thick and tall, but paving stones were neatly placed around the lawn. In order to get from the gate to the back door of the house, careful steps were needed, because it would feel deeply wrong to step on the grass. Turning my head to the right, I saw a cluster of colourful houses in the corner next to a little pond.

–How did you know about my garden? Mr Chadha asked gently.

–I saw it from my bedroom window.

A lie, but he didn't need to know people were making fun of him.

–Can I have a closer look?

–Of course. Just watch the pond. I've got a lot of frog spawn in it.

I was completely dazzled by the little town. It looked even better that I could ever have imagined. There were

80

funny little houses with silly roofs, each of them hand painted in bright playground colours. But there was a sort of harmony in the paintwork; the walls of one house were purple, the roof cherry red. Another had yellow walls and a grass green roof. Together they made a row of houses on a little rainbow road. The cherry blossom tree that sheltered the houses was the only part of the garden that looked sad – literally, it was hunched over, the branches ready to drop the ornaments that hung from them. Before I could stop myself, I asked Mr Chadha a question.

–Why did you do all this?

He seemed to consider what I'd just asked, giving it a little thought.

A minute later, he explained everything.

–I made it for my daughter.

Jealousy made my heart heavy, but I fought it off, hating the idea of being so petty. It occurred to me that Mr Chadha's daughter was very lucky. To have a father who would do this for her? I wanted that too.

Once again, I thought of a mystery man I'd probably never meet.

–What does your daughter think of it?

–She was daft on fairies, unicorns and magic.

–I used to love all that stuff too, but it seems silly now. I don't know why.

Mr Chadha knew exactly why and explained, treating me like an equal.

–Everything changes, people most of all.

–No way, I said boldly. –I want to stay this age forever.

–My daughter never got to be your age, said Mr Chadha quietly, his eyes on the cherry blossom tree and the little town hiding underneath its hunched branches. Without going into details, Mr Chadha told me everything I needed to know about his daughter. I said nothing because words were pointless and only feelings mattered in that moment. Strangely, I felt closer to this old man than my own family, the two of us bonded by something quiet and exceptional.

A few minutes later, I left the garden and stepped from green back into grey.

14

Uncle Tam drove us to Spain, the journey lasting over three hours in his car. As expected, my legs kept cramping in the back seat, making me want to stretch until my feet dangled between Mither and Tam's shoulders. Lily, an unwilling traveller, seethed at my side. This would prove the least of my problems. Spain wasn't what I thought it would be. Not only was it a damp miserable mess, but it was also filled with caravans. I grinned, excited to finally get a chance to stay in a nice box without mould growing up the walls. Mither, however, wore an expression of utter dismay as Tam finally stopped his car in the car park, neatly settling it alongside all the other cars, each one owned by families who had driven all the way to Spain from various parts of Scotland in order to enjoy a holiday.

I was first out the Volvo, my legs painful from being cooped up in the back seat. Mither was next. She swung herself around and primly stepped out of the car (in what I referred to as 'the Lady Di style'), only to be caught by a brutal gust of cold wintry air. Standing in the parking area outside the caravan park, dressed in her favourite fur coat and leather skirt/black knee-high boots combo, Mither suddenly looked like she might burst into tears. This would have been a disaster for her carefully applied eyeliner. It was July, yet it felt like December, only without the promise of presents and multi-coloured lights to make everything look beautiful. Uncle Tam got out next, leaving Lily the last to exit the car. She took her time, making us suffer in the bad weather.

–I thought Spain was meant to be warm, I whined, my teeth chattering.

–Don't worry, came Uncle Tam's terse response. –It'll get warm again!

–Aye, added Mither. –When we switch the gas fire on it will.

–A gas fire, gasped Lily, her fingers instinctively touching her freshly crimped hair, already frizzing up in the damp weather, making her look like a female Fido Dido. –But I've got half a can of VO5 keeping this in place.

We started shouting at each other in the middle of the car park, all of us getting everything out into the open. Everything from the lack of warmth to the negative effects of hairspray on the ozone layer (Uncle Tam's contribution to the argument), we didn't stop until the rain started. Surprisingly, bickering always brought us closer together, making us feel like a proper family.

CATCHING THE WAVES

Our caravan was at the far end of the park and nothing worked because the gas tank outside hadn't been connected properly. Uncle Tam quickly sorted it out and finally, at long last, we were able to warm ourselves up with hot air. We had a little television in the corner, a couch that turned into a set of beds, and a nice kitchen that impressed even Mither, who was notoriously difficult to please. Grateful to be away from Little Denny Road, the Donaldsons, Auld Sybil, Nethermains Primary School, and everything else that held bad memories for me, I quickly learned to appreciate our little box on wheels.

But even in a caravan, all the way in Spain, some things never changed. I found myself looking out of the window, staring past distorted patterns caused by the streaks of running rain on the glass. Something in me was agitated. In all honesty, I wanted to get out and see everything, look

84

everywhere. Mither would be less enthusiastic for me to wander around Spain unaccompanied, but there was no way Lily would be an escort. Besides, I felt old enough to be alone in a strange place. This was my holiday as well. I deserved some fun.

Uncle Tam was keen for me to look around. He'd spent weeks talking Spain up, telling me all about the amusement arcades, pinball machines, candy floss stalls and skiing resorts.

First though, the television needed sorted. The picture kept breaking up.

−Sadie, said Uncle Tam, his full concentration fixed on trying to get the aerial in the right place. −Hold this here, will you? No, there. Wait. Stand here.

A few seconds later, STV came through. If the presenter's expression was stark, his headline was starker. I caught a little of it before the crackling started up again.

−One hundred and ninety two people are still missing after an explosion on an oil rig, said a voice before it dissolved into noisy waves.

−I wanted to see that, shouted Mither. −Stand still for fuck sake!

By the time I got the picture back, the news had gone, replaced by Ulrika Johnson and John Fashanu together in front of a gigantic stylised 'G'. At last, Uncle Tam settled down, his attention fully directed at the television screen. Gladiators was his favourite thing to watch and he *had* to see it, even all the way in Spain. It wasn't my favourite show on television, but the novelty of watching something familiar in a new setting was too strong to ignore. I moved to sit down, only for the picture on the box to fuzz up and the sound to crackle violently. Everyone in the caravan went frantic and I froze on the spot.

−Don't move, shouted Uncle Tam threateningly. − Keep that position.

And so I was left holding a piece of wire on a bit of black plastic for nearly an hour (including the commercial breaks) just so my family could watch a group of steroid-loving behemoths bash members of the British public with giant cotton buds. It quickly occurred to me that I'd probably need another holiday just in order to recover from this holiday.

SPANISH SNOW

The next morning came with a blizzard that trapped us all inside the caravan until the late afternoon. The camper suddenly felt too small for four people, the lack of space affording no privacy whatsoever. Even a trip to the toilet had to be timed so I could go in peace, because I couldn't do anything knowing someone was at the other side of the door, listening to every squeeze and push. I'd always been funny that way. The same couldn't be said for the rest of my family, who would hold lengthy conversations with the door open, one of them sitting on the toilet seat, the other chatting about BBC Breakfast's Frank Bough, who had been caught at a brothel a few weeks earlier.

–I heard he was a good tipper, said Mither approvingly when Uncle Tam brought it up.

Worse, rotten smells fermented in the toilet (really just a cupboard with a seat and cistern) and seemed to drift around the caravan, suspended in the air above our heads, waiting until I got close – then it would envelope me. I needed to put some space between me and the rest of my family – and fast. The blizzard was starting to calm itself and brightness seemed to peek through the cloud. At last! Without asking permission, I swung my denim jacket around my shoulders, covering my new sailor's white and blue striped polo shirt, an early birthday present from Mither and Uncle Tam. Denim jackets were very trendy.

Next, I had a quiet look around the cramped caravan for Lily's Walkman, something she jealously guarded from me. It didn't take long to find it hidden beneath a pile of Uncle Tam's underwear. Quickly, I set about ejecting Lily's beloved Tracy Chapman tape, replacing it with New Kids On The Block. Tape rewound to the start, headphones pressed against my ears, it was time for me to get out and see what Spain had to offer a twelve-year-old girl from Falkirk.

Not much, it turned out.

I followed a path that took me away from the rows of caravans, walking until the view changed. Sadly, I still walked with my head down, so I found myself looking at my feet as they stepped across the ground, watching as it changed from rough gravel to smooth concrete. Eventually, I found myself standing on pale stone circles, each one offset by a slate-grey concrete border. Slowly, I looked up to see my surroundings had totally changed. There was a huge building in front of me, a brick with windows in it. The other building in the distance looked sort of like a chalet, suddenly making sense of the chairlifts that seemed to move diagonally against each other, up and down the snowy hill. Craning my neck upwards, I glimpsed a large billboard sign that announced a cinema, a restaurant, an ice rink, go-karting, and games.

Welcome to Aviemore, it said.

AVIEMORE, 1988

Everybody burst out laughing when I got back to the caravan, cackling so loud that someone else in the park yelled at them to shut the fuck up. This didn't set Mither off, thankfully, and she remained in high spirits for the rest of the night, doubtlessly helped by the half-empty bottle of Tia Maria on the worktop. Even better, while I'd been out, she'd taken the opportunity to go shopping at a local supermarket for stuff to fill the little refrigerator at the far side of the kitchen.

—We're eating traditional Spanish cuisine tonight, she said snidely, handing me a curry flavour Pot Noodle and a plastic fork. For a second, I had a vivid fantasy of giving her a nose piercing with the fork, but common sense won out in the end. Later, the noise of rainfall outside caught my attention, one of my favourite sounds in the world.

—Hey, said Uncle Tam. —Do you think the rain in Spain falls mainly down the drain?

Everyone howled with laughter again, all of them delighted to be in on the joke. Before I could tell them to fuck off, something else caught my eye.

Mither didn't see it, couldn't possibly have realised, but I'd turned just in time to catch Uncle Tam place his left hand on Lily's arse, patting it softly. If I'd expected Lily to react indignantly, I would be disappointed. Her reaction was no reaction, except the quiet smile on her face and a look in her eyes. It immediately became clear to me that not only were they seeing each other behind Mither's back, but it had been happening for a while.

15

We got a shell suit zipper jacket as a gift for surviving seven whole years of Nethermains Primary School. It had a logo on the back, a circle filled with the names of every single one of us in the year group, a reminder that we once had a time and place in common. Arlene's name was at the top, of course, so it wasn't alphabetical. And her faither was a lawyer, after all. He'd probably donated the money to pay for the gift. And my name? Near the bottom, where people felt it belonged. My new shell suit top was white, red and blue, the colours of a can of Pepsi or Rangers Football Club. Mrs Walker presented our jackets at a ceremony in the gym hall. The jacket said more than our names. It announced high school was happening in a matter of months, the next phase of our lives. I didn't know how to feel. School made me miserable. Why would anything be better in another school up the road?

As I left Nethermains Primary for the last time, grateful to be gone at last, I found myself thinking about what Mr Chadha had said last year. He told me everything changed. It was true. My life had suddenly fluctuated in random new directions, including the worst change of all: two lumps on my chest, growing every day, something everyone in my house immediately noticed.

My hormones were pulling me into an unwanted adulthood.

–I'll need to take you out for a bra, said Mither, excited at the prospect. She knew things, secrets that had to be passed down from mither to daughter. It gave her an opportunity to act out the role of mither in front of people.

–No, I wailed. –Don't do this to me!

–It's fine. I took Lily shopping for her first bra. It's natural.

–Ugh! came my response. It wasn't anger for the sake of it. Every time something happened that I disagreed with, my feelings were immediately disregarded with two small words: *it's natural.* When Uncle Tam bent over and farted? Or Lily clipped her toenails on the couch while we watched the telly? Mither walking around without clothes? These things were very *natural.*

I couldn't win. Winning for me was unnatural.

SHOPPING WITH STYLE

Mither brought me and her Style card to Stirling Street where we spent an hour in a shop I called Closing Down Sale because it always seemed on the verge of shutting. Once inside, my nose surrendered to the stink of rubber shoes. The shop sold them by the dozen, piling them up alongside racks of schoolwear, pieces of uniform bought separately so they could be worn together. There were also bras and a fitting room that was a small cupboard with a raggedy curtain on a rail, the sound of which made my back teeth hurt when someone pulled the rings across the bar. The sales assistant made her way across the shop to greet me and Mither. She wore a blue overall and a yellow t-shirt.

Her smile was part of the uniform too.

–Good afternoon, she said warmly, her voice putting me in mind of Super Gran off the telly. –Do you need any assistance?

Eager to escort me through a rite of passage, Mither nodded eagerly and replied, –Oh yes. It's my daughter. SHE'S HERE FOR HER FIRST EVER BRA.

The entire shop stopped and everyone looked right at me, making me want to melt into the carpet. This was

90

torture. How many more ways of inflicting humiliation on their children would parents think up?

Gudrun Ure–AKA Super Gran–AKA the sales lady eagerly joined in.

–You've come to the right place. We just received a new delivery today. Also, we've got a sale on school bags going on, as well as these lovely new bomber jackets. They're very popular. All the kids are wearing them.

–No thanks, I said.

–That jacket has a stain on it, said Mither, using her tried and trusted scam of finding mysterious marks on clothes she didn't want to pay full price for. Sadly, she underestimated the superpowers of the sales assistant, who instead whipped out a long, yellow measuring tape. Without stopping, she wrapped it around my chest, her eyes looking for the right numbers.

–Get off me, I hissed, squirming against the pressure.

She retaliated by pulling the tape even tighter, nearly cutting me in two.

–Okay, came her cool assessment. –We need a small size.

–Silly cow, I muttered. This was not the way I wanted to spend my afternoon, but the world was whirling out of reach and everything was changing. My life, my body, my opinions. Nothing made sense anymore. Even in the shop mirror, flanked by my mither and the saleswoman, I could see how much I'd changed over the last year. My face was longer, less round. I was taller, the way I used to look whenever I dressed up in Mither's heels, back when I was a little girl, only now they would probably fit my feet better.

–Okay, said a voice from the left. –Let's see if this one fits.

The bra was basic and white, the sort a girl wore for her first time. Reluctantly, I took it and moved across the shop

91

to the fitting room. Though I didn't have a door to slam shut, at least I could yank the curtain over as viciously as possible. Take that, curtain! Unfortunately when I did this, it came right off the railing, the pole following it to the floor.

Sheepishly, I apologised. My little moment of rebelliousness had backfired spectacularly and now I'd wrecked part of the shop. The saleswoman's perfectly placed smile faltered slightly, but she recovered and assured me everything was fine.

—That happens all the time, she said unconvincingly.

With that potential catastrophe averted, I sidestepped into the next booth and closed the curtain as carefully as possible. Except there was someone already in that booth, a young woman trying on a skirt. Before she could protest, I ducked out and found myself in the last changing room. Despite this, I still wasn't completely alone. Just like the small toilet in the caravan up in Aviemore, I could hear people standing around at the other side of the curtain, making an awkward situation even more agonising.

Then, in another moment of madness, I decided to do something to make everyone (especially myself) laugh. Struggling to fit the weird thing with straps and clasps over my chest, I put my new bra on over my jumper and walked out into the shop as though it were the most normal thing in the world.

—Is this how you wear it? I asked innocently.

Mither's face when she caught sight of me made everything worthwhile.

—Take that off!

I tried, but somehow it got tangled on my arms. Eventually, after twisting and thrashing around like Houdini in a tank of water without a key on his tongue, I felt the bra go very loose, then watched it swing down until it dangled from my left shoulder. That's when I knew I'd snapped the strap.

Before Mither could say anything, the saleswoman got in first.

—You break it, you buy it.

—But I didn't break it, I said hotly. —I snapped it.

Mither quietly, coldly, paid the bill and escorted me ear-first out of the shop.

—I'm going to boot your arse when I get you up the road, she snarled.

In all the commotion, she forgot the reason we'd gone to the shop in the first place. That suited me just fine. Eventually, I'd go back and get the bra I'd tried desperately to avoid because, as my chest continued to grow, my confidence continued to shrink. However, by that point I had other problems to deal with, other things in mind. Trouble, mostly. That and a new school.

16

TAKING THE ROUGH WITH THE SMOOCH

Denny High wasn't anything too exciting, just another place that kept me out the house during the day, safely away from Uncle Tam and Lily. They were probably grateful as well, because with Mither sleeping off the nightshift, it meant they could be alone together. The very thought of it made my skin shrivel, but I kept my mouth shut regardless. Despite this, I couldn't help looking at them, wondering what Lily saw in Uncle Tam. Was it the same inscrutable qualities my mither found in him?

One evening, I looked hard at the man who'd taken over my home, breaking him down into a list with ruthless accuracy. His personality was irritating and smug. He was short, pot-bellied and his teeth looked like tombstones on even ground. So what was so appealing about him to my family? The answer was too awful to contemplate. This was a man who told AIDS jokes, pissed all over the toilet seat without wiping it and blamed me whenever he burped or farted. Whatever his appeal, I didn't care. So long as he kept away from me, I'd keep quiet about the affair.

But… as much as I wanted to deny it… something in me wanted Mither to find out the truth. Worse, I really wanted to be the one to tell her what was really going on. Somehow, that didn't make me feel good about myself.

FANTASIES

In my imagination, the little scenarios I dreamt up during moments of boredom, Mither threw Lily out of the house and promoted me to the position of #1 daughter, where I belonged. Better still, in these daydreams, Uncle Tam ended up leaving too. Mither, finally seeing the light, quit the nightshift and got a job in the Co-op, working behind the checkout, bleep, bleep, bleeping groceries through the little scanner. It was a good dream, but it could only exist as a fantasy, another life in a different world I could reach in instalments. Mither tried hard to hide her other life from me, but as much as I wanted her to give it all up for a normal life like everyone else here in Little Denny Road, there was something I had to acknowledge, a truth that even my fantasies couldn't avoid. Mither did what she did, not just for money, but for me and Lily, to give us both a good life. Everything we owned, from the clothes I wore to the food I ate, was due to Mither's work.

I knew that. Everyone knew that.

It was the reason people avoided me.

A new school, however, also meant a new beginning.

DENNY HIGH SCHOOL, 1989

Everybody in the playground at Denny High was dressed in fluorescent colours because that's what we wore in 1989, my year of shell suits and shell shock. Our bright, colourful clothes made us stand out against the grey drabness of Denny's concrete landscape, always unyielding in its remorselessness. Worse, the sky was the exact same colour as the concrete. Every day was grey here and though we were meant to wear our functional school uniform, most of us favoured shell suits because we all wanted to belong to each other. Uniforms were uncool except in Summer Bay, a million miles away (or STV at ten past five).

Everyone sized each other up from afar, because cellulose triacetate lined with polyester is as thin as paper but as durable as steel wool, and just as flammable. Thankfully, none of us smoked. Not yet. But everyone knew to be careful around flames, especially Arlene, who carried a can of L'Oréal Studio Line hairspray in her bag. She was so paranoid about her enormous peroxide hair (copied from Madonna) that she'd developed a system to avoid passing the smokers, girls and boys from Nethermains we used to know before they left. They had been hardened by life at the high school, but I feared nothing. What could possibly shock me? Instead, I headed into the building with a sense of calmness, a new maturity that had been developed through years of drama. Nothing could touch me, especially words, daft names shouted over corridors or across the packed playground.

I walked forward, my eyes facing the same way.

AN EMPTY CHAIR

My new friend (though she didn't know that at the time) had black hair that matched the thick black smears around her eyes. Normally we wouldn't have met each other, but a new term at high school meant throwing people together, some of whom didn't know about my mither. Our first meeting happened during an English lesson, the only empty chair being the one next to her, a chair meant for me, whether I realised it or not.

−Hello, I said politely, while taking my seat.

She blinked twice, then looked away.

−I'm Sadie, I added. −Sadie Relish.

−Oh God, she blurted. −Your mither's the crazy hooker, isn't she?

I went to stand, try for somewhere else in the room.

−I'm sorry, she said, −I shouldn't have said that.

A few seconds later, she tried again.

−I'm Valerie, she said, though she didn't smile. Valerie never ever smiled. She was a goth and looked like she was dressed for a funeral instead of school. Whatever funeral it was, I wanted to go with her. I wanted to throw wreaths onto dirty holes in the ground and look miserable in the sunshine.

Slowly, carefully, I made a statement I prayed wouldn't be laughed off.

−I think we're going to be friends, I said quietly.

She agreed, and together we found safety in numbers.

17

We considered ourselves too cool to associate with the
boozebags outside Little Denny Mart who spent their
weekends begging people to get them a bottle of Buckie.
This meant we had to look for other places to get drunk
on a Friday night. No matter what happened through the
week, every teen in Scotland knew Friday was about
getting drunk and hanging around the streets, no matter
the weather. Usually, it was cold. And wet. But none of us
cared. We traded one day for another, choosing Friday and
losing Saturday, which was spent nursing the unavoidable
hangover. Luckily, I'd learned from Mither all the tricks
necessary to survive a lost weekend. She put her faith in a
miracle cure called Bon Accord. Sweet and fizzy, it came
in a bottle like the cheapo wine Valerie shared with me.
Mither insisted on drinking some Bon Accord after her
boozing.

−It lines the stomach, she claimed.

Her miracle cure may or may not have been connected
to the fact Uncle Tam delivered it door to door. And
although the limeade flavour looked like disinfectant, it
tasted of joy and diabetes. Friday officially kicked off
with a glass of Bon Accord, continued with half a bottle of
Buckfast, and ended in kerbs being sprayed by the insides
of our bellies. At some point, I started to enjoy my Friday
nights a little too much.

GOTH AT THE BUS STOP

Our favourite place to hang out was a small bus stop in
Braes View, the one just up the road from my flat, near
Denny High. It gave us a place to sit and drink, shelter

ourselves from the rain. Even under the protection of the glass, little drops still made it through tinier cracks, but this was preferable to being soaked. Buses would arrive to pick up small groups of pensioners, women who would only leave their houses on a Friday night to visit the bingo down the road. They were all fabulous and I couldn't stop staring at their hair, different shades of blue, as punk as grannies could get, though they'd probably disagree. Seeing them made me want to dye my hair a bright new colour too.

It was on Fridays at that bus stop that I started learned more about my new friend, who became livelier with each bottle of wine. Her favourite subject was Margaret Thatcher, her ultimate enemy. According to Valerie, Maggie was Satan's secret servant, a helper from hell, sent here to make everyone miserable. The mere sight of Maggie made Valerie feel utterly homicidal. Unfortunately, my meek support (or lack of enthusiasm) suggested I didn't care, that I didn't consider politics to be important. That itself was unacceptable for Valerie. Sober, I could get through to her. Steaming drunk, nae chance. Worse than that… she was hogging the bottle of Buckfast.

I reached out to take it from her, but Valerie suddenly had a theory.

−You aren't a fan of her, are you?

− No, I could never support someone with that hairdo.

−Boat sinking bitch, muttered Valerie, while tipping back her bottle.

The moment was over and we sat in silence, the traffic our soundtrack.

−I'm smashed, said Valerie, snickering.

−Oh, totally.

−My parents are going to kill me.

Her parents were the least of her problems.

−Never mind *them*. I'm going to kill you.

—Why?

—Because you've finished the wine.

—Oh, she hiccupped.

We waited in the shelter and let each bus pass us by. We had nowhere to go, no place to be except underneath a rusted tin roof with each other, reinforced glass keeping the wind away from our faces. After a while, the lack of wine started to make the bus stop feel far too small. In the end, it became about the next bottle. Sadly, there was a new problem we had to fix.

—We've no money left for wine.

—Damn, said Valerie. —We need more money. How about I ask one of these old crones for cash. They'll win it back at the bingo anyway.

—Don't you dare, I snapped. I was always the serious one in the friendship, the girl who had to shoot down Valerie's most outlandish ideas. A far cry from the little girl who believed in magic spells and ancient guardians protecting mystical puddles.

—Sadie, said Valerie abruptly.

—What?

She laughed and motioned down at her legs.

—I've just pished myself.

A puddle had gathered around Valerie's Docs, a wet patch on the concrete connected to a trail that dripped down her left leg. Moving aside in a drunken waltz, I tried to avoid the stream as it inched towards my feet, treating it like a pool of corrosive acid. Valerie was sobering up fast, wondering how this had happened. Somehow, in the midst of her crisis and my daft dancing (just to avoid contact with her piss) we both burst out laughing. The pensioners tutted their disapproval, but that only gave us permission to laugh louder. It felt good to laugh, even better when someone else was there laughing with you.

18

Waking up to find Uncle Tam standing over my bed was the moment I decided to run away from home. At first I thought it was a ghost vision, an unwanted echo from a nightmare, something that would flicker and fade away. Then I smelt his breath in the dark. It reeked of overcooked eggs and rotten teeth. Worse, he was just there, standing still, simply… staring, watching for something. What that was, I couldn't be sure. I literally opened my eyes and saw him in the darkness, his outline backlit by the lamp outside.

My first reaction was to scream. The shock of the unexpected, of course.

He looked at me, blinked twice, two slow flutters of his heavy eyelids, and then tilted his head to the side, as though not understanding why I'd reacted so badly. Before I could scream again, his hand shot out and covered my face. No more noise came out except a muffled scream. My heart thumped so loud he probably felt it through his palm. His hand smelled bad, like chip pan oil.

−You think I don't know what you're about? he said, eyes wide in the dark.

I didn't reply. I couldn't. My lips were squashed under his skin.

−Fucking hoor, he spat. −You better shut your fucking mouth or else.

His hand wrapped itself tighter around my face, the pressure almost capable of bursting my skull open. Now I couldn't breathe. I *had* to move, to get some air through my nose and mouth. Without meaning to, my body reacted and I thrashed under the covers, trying to free myself from him.

−If you tell your mither about me and Lily, you're dead. Right?

Footsteps from the far end of the hallway moved closer and Uncle Tam quickly released me. The door opened and Mither poked her head into the room, her eyes creased with sleep.

−What's going on?

Before I could point my finger, Uncle Tam immediately got in first.

−She had a bad dream, he explained.

Mither rubbed her eyes then turned away, completely uninterested. From her perspective, it was a credible set of events. The truth was probably too horrible to even consider, so I was alone again with her boyfriend. I lay there, too frightened to speak, my throat dried out. No matter how scared I was (and I was fucking shitting myself), there was no way I'd cry in front of him. He'd probably enjoy that and I wasn't going to give him anything except hatred and disdain. When everything was quiet again, except my breathing, the noise loud enough to fill the room, that's when Uncle Tam retired to bed.

On his way out, he smirked in the dark.

−Goodnight, he said slowly, −Sleep tight.

I waited for him to finally leave before I reached down underneath my bed and patted the floor until I found what I needed: a half-empty (definitely not half-full) bottle of Smirnoff. Slowly, underneath the quilt, I unscrewed the cap and swigged on my version of water. It went down smoothly, burning a trail down my gullet, but it felt so good, like my life didn't make sense before I found Friday nights and the spirits that lifted my spirits.

GETTING OUT OF DENNY

Two things happened the following morning, one after

the other. I packed my clothes into a rucksack and made sure to include Mither's bottle of Malibu, a Ghost of Christmas Past that had been left under the kitchen sink, lonely and waiting. To be fair, Mither's tastes were far too evolved for *Caribbean rum with a coconut flavour*, so it had gathered dust until I liberated it from oblivion, as I prepared to liberate myself in the same way.

Actually, I wasn't the only one. After nearly three years of shitting on pavements and carrying cats around in bags, the Donaldsons were on the way out too. Their departure turned out to be far quieter than their arrival, the entire family having kept themselves away from everyone else on the street for months, the incident with the Skoda having knocked the stuffing out of them. For me this was brilliant, because while they were being watched by all the eyes behind the blinds, it meant no-one was watching me. With this in mind, I dressed in dark colours, wore shapeless baggy clothes, including a tracksuit top that I wore around the flat, something loose-fitting to hide inside. Leaving the block using the back door, I headed up towards the Braes View bus stop, the same one I'd spent too many Friday nights in, watching buses go by. This time, however, I was going to stop one of them and leave Denny forever – well, that was the plan.

The bus to Glesga didn't turn up when it should have.

–Fuck's sake, I muttered, resigned to my fate.

At some point, possibly nearly an hour later, I considered sticking out my thumb to try and entice a driver to help me on my way. But I'd seen too many episodes of *Crimewatch* to know that hitchhiking inevitably led to death. Nick Ross, in his drab suit, standing in a gloomy BBC studio was not going to tell *my* story. That privilege belonged to me. In the end, I decided to wait it out, hope against all odds that the next driver wouldn't just bypass Denny on his route again. I thought back to the time I went searching for Torwood Blue Pool, how I'd met a nice man who helped me get the bus. This time I was on my own. But that was fine. I could do this, or so I kept telling myself.

Nearly four hours later and legs numb with the pain of standing, I finally got on the bus. The driver, a woman with white-blonde hair and laughter lines around her eyes, smiled as I pushed my way up to her little compartment.

–Where to?

Where indeed? I only had one real option. I didn't know anything about my faither. His face, his name, where he lived. Nothing. In the end there were only my grandparents, who I hadn't seen in years. Mither loathed my grandfaither, despising him more than both the council and undercover polis.

That made my choice easier.

–Cumbernauld, I said. –Near Glesga.

–I know where it is, said the driver, her smile making me feel safe.

GREEK COLUMNS

Mither always tried to make out she came from nothing, but I knew she came from Prospect Road, a street in Dullatur, forever the posh end of Cumbernauld. It was full of houses so large that families living underneath the same roof could often become strangers to each other. She was my age when she lived there, but not for long. Something pushed her out of the nest, something that made her fly all the way to Little Denny Road. Remarkably, years later, I was making the same journey – but in reverse. I'd only met my grandparents a few times that I could remember, but it was more than I'd ever had with my nameless, faceless faither. Something I never ever forgot were the Greek columns that held up their hoose: two large Doric (or Ionic?) pillars at either side of the front door, both large and polished black. Each house, elegantly arranged in sequence, was a mansion compared to my poky flat in Denny. Somehow they'd been touched by ancient Greece, stone columns holding hard against time, taste and dreary Scottish weather.

Walking Doon the Street

I walked up from Cumbernauld Village and moved slowly in the general direction of Dullatur, passing by hills and houses on my way. It was a bright day, the clouds thick, fat and lazy. They moved slowly, a slide that seemed like it might take forever. Underneath those clouds (currently a dull grey), people played golf, their gruff voices sounding unhappy even when they were cheering another hole in one.

As I gradually came towards Prospect Road, I couldn't help but smile at how good it felt to finally be away from my mither's grubby boyfriend. 'Uncle' Tam was a bad memory without reach or influence anymore. Also, I liked the idea of being special for once. The thought of being doted on by my long-forgotten grandparents was an exciting prospect. Now that I'd put distance between me and Little Denny Road, home felt farther away than Spain (or Aviemore) and I was starting to relish my new sense of freedom. With all of that in mind, I stopped several times along the way to take a quick swig of Malibu, loving the taste of melted Bounty chocolate.

By the time I saw Greek columns, I was absolutely blitzed out of my tits. Staggering down a bend, which seemed steeper to me than it should have been, I felt my weight pulling me towards a simple wire fence with wooden blocks propping it up. The air reeked of cow shite and cut grass. Suddenly I took the boke, letting everything come out of my gullet, up, up, up over my throat, across my tongue and then out onto the path by my feet – a scungy pool of Malibu, bile and blobs of undigested Weetabix. Mercifully, I felt a little better. As I staggered down the road towards a vague memory of a shiny black door and the faint hope that I'd be welcomed like a hero, long gone but now returned, I fell down. The bottle of Malibu broke in my rucksack, dousing my clothes, thick dark smells and flavours soaking through the nylon lining.

–Fuck! I yelled, picking myself up off the ground, the way I always did whenever I fell hard. My clothes were ruined, my knees scraped raw.

Eventually, I got to the shiny black door I'd recalled in daydreams. Taking a breath, filling myself up with air, I knocked a tune with my knuckles, thoughtful enough to do it more than three times – the last thing I wanted was my grandparents to think the polis were waiting for them.

The door opened slowly and half a face peered out from the fissure.

Almost immediately a voice came from the hallway, loud and happy, whooping with excitement. It was a voice I hadn't heard in years.

–Archibald, cried my grandmither. –You'll never believe who's at the door!

Before I could say anything, I was pulled into the hallway and wrapped in thin arms. Then, after a few seconds of being held close, my grandmither looked right at me, taking in my face, inch by inch and plook by plook.

–Look at you, Sadie. You've grown so much.

–You're... smaller, I said quietly, somewhat shocked at how much time had passed between us, something I had known but didn't feel until that very second.

My grandfaither didn't say much, but his eyes never left me. Not once.

Though the outside of their home was the same as I remembered, the inside had changed completely. Not the layout, the actual skeleton of the house itself. As I remembered, there was a library full of cheap cowboy books just beyond the front door, the living room was still where it should be, the kitchen still easily accessed through the far end of the hallway, the conservatory at the far side of the house still led down into the garden. None of that was different. But the colours and the furniture had changed over the years, the decorations, the vases and framed photos. One of them was me as a little girl, chubby with a gap in my grin. Lily was there, of course, her face prominently displayed above mine, a pout where a smile could have been.

Mither was on the wall too, but her photograph showed her as a little girl. She seemed incomplete somehow, like she hadn't quite decided who she wanted to be. Her hair was a different colour, for a start, and her expression was deeply sullen. For some reason, I never enjoyed seeing the past printed and pinned to a wall. Immediately, I sensed Mither wasn't a happy child.

In that second, we suddenly had something in common with each other.

—I can't remember the last time I saw you, said Grandmither, fussing over me with her hands that kept rubbing my face, pulling at my cheeks, making me squirm in her grip. My skin was sensitive in every way that mattered to a teenage girl: a sensitive topic and sensitive to the touch. I'd taken to smearing cream across my face to try and soothe all the tiny eruptions dotted over my cheeks, nose and chin. For whatever reason, it never really worked.

–It must be five years since you were last here, said Grandmither.

–Nearer ten, I replied quietly, unexpectedly feeling overwhelmed by everything. I was beginning to regret my idea to run away from home.

–Ten years? No, it can't be. Where *has* the time gone?

We loitered in the hallway because I didn't want to just barge in. I needed permission, something to make me feel like this was all mine too. Grandfaither still hadn't said anything, his silence a physical barrier that kept me in the corner. Finally, after Grandmither glanced at him with a look FULL OF MEANING, he said something vaguely encouraging.

–Do you want a drink?

It wasn't much, but it was something.

–Aye, I said. –I'd like a Hooch or some Bacardi, if you have any.

Their expressions told me I'd said the wrong thing. Worse, I suddenly realised how bad I smelled. They must have caught a whiff of it too, because it was suffocating. I'd arrived at my long-lost grandparents' house reeking of bile and booze.

–I'm joking, I said quickly, hoping to salvage the situation before I was told to turn around and go back to Little Denny Road. –Just water, please.

–Bottled or from the tap?

I stared at my grandfaither like the mothership had just deposited him in front of me. Bottled water? Water… in… a… bottle? That people *paid* for?

The very idea of it seemed ludicrous to me.

–The tap, please.

–Look at us, said Grandmither. –We're being so rude. Come on, let's get you into the living room. We've got so much to talk about… like… well…

–Everything, I replied with a smile.

−Here's your water, said Grandfaither gruffly.

I slugged down half of the pint tumbler he offered before stopping mid-gulp.

It needed something extra.

Flavour, mostly.

Alcohol, preferably.

19

We spent the rest of the night in the garden, a space that felt as big as a farmer's field, especially for someone used to living in the confines of a three-bedroom council flat. As I sat on a swing planted down on the overgrown lawn, rocking in the breeze, my thoughts shifted to Little Denny Road. Mither would probably know I wasn't coming home, but there was no way she'd come for me. That would mean facing her folks, standing in front of them for the first time in over a decade. Somehow, I knew that wouldn't happen. Too much had gone on. What? I didn't know, but that was something I needed to discover for myself.

I touched the ground with my toes, feet sinking into grass, and pushed myself back on the swing, lifting my legs and letting myself fly, if only for a second. But soon enough I had to stop. My stomach didn't feel right and the motion of the swing was beginning to make me want to throw up again.

−So… started Grandmither. −Does your mither ever mention me?

−Or me? added Grandfaither, who was sitting with a copy of the Daily Mail.

My first instinct was to lie and pretend they were all she ever talked about, but the bad habit won out. It always did. Once again, I told the truth.

−No, I said. −She doesn't even have any photographs in the house.

−Photographs? Of us?

−None of herself either, I said, suddenly realising this for the first time. My grandparents looked at each other but said nothing. Their eyes communicated their feelings, none of it decipherable. Eventually, I asked the obvious question, because no-one else was around to do it.

—What happened?

Grandmither opened her mouth to answer, but the voice that came out belonged to her husband. This happened quite a lot and it was beginning to irritate me. Any opinion Grandmither tried to express was often rerouted through Grandfaither, until he agreed with what she had to say.

—Your mither wouldn't live by the rules of this house, said Grandfaither, his arms crossed tightly around his chest, elbows propped up by his gut. The flesh heaved up over the rim of his black trousers, plain and simple, the sort men wore to a job interview or a funeral. I had a violent fantasy of taking a long pin and sticking it into his belly, bursting him – or at least letting out some trapped wind, all of that accumulated hot air.

—So you stopped speaking because she broke some rules? I asked, deeply disheartened by the explanation. From what I'd seen and heard over the years, it seemed like something truly unforgivable had occurred here, a battle that broke familial bonds beyond repair, an apocalyptic fight over *something*. I'd watched my mither cut old photos of her parents in half and cram them down the toilet, only for the council plumber to be called out to unblock the drain, bringing up memories she literally couldn't flush away.

—Your mither got caught up in the wrong crowd, explained Grandmither gently. —She was shoplifting, fighting, seeing boys, staying out too late, and…

—Drinking, said Grandfaither icily.

—And we really couldn't have that, said Grandmither, giving me stereo.

I waited for something else to be said, but they just smiled.

Their hint was received and accepted.

111

I finally had a bedroom without even the slightest trace of black mould on the walls. That was far more exciting for me than it should have been. The room had one window, a small circle on the roof. The walls, meanwhile, slanted up, giving me the sense of being inside a turret. Finally, I was living in a fairy tale, complete with a castle to call my own. Here, I was the princess, a girl whose whims were completely catered to without a sister to steal even a second of attention. But as I stood alone in the new room, something felt… amiss. I quickly corrected myself. Not amiss – *wrong*. But that was always the way for me, wasn't it? I wanted something, worked hard for it, then managed to achieve my aims… only to feel hollow and unfulfilled.

I never ever learned. But the journey itself was important, or so I assumed.

After cleaning myself up and changing into a pair of plain green silk pyjamas, an old Christmas gift from Mither, I found myself on top of my new bed, thinking about the future, dreaming myself a new world.

I fell asleep for an hour and woke up two days later.

The lightbulb, however, was so bright it burned my eyeballs.

–Ugh, I said aloud. –Turn the light out!

–The light isn't on, said a voice gently from the corner of the room. Opening my eyes, I realised Grandmither was standing in the doorway, a pile of washing in her arms. Smiling without feeling it, I repositioned myself on the mattress, using the slanted wall to push myself upwards.

–It's a lovely afternoon, she added, –the sun is out.

–Turn it off.

–You can't switch off the sun, laughed Grandmither, quite bemused.

Then, after a laugh at my expense, she said,

—Besides, your grandfaither wants you up and out of bed.

My thoughts, chaotic and unrefined, suddenly found a thread to follow. My instinct was to pull the quilt over my head and stay safe in the dark, but I felt Grandmither's presence there by the door, a reminder that I couldn't just do whatever I wanted. There were rules, of course. But I felt deathly. The vein on my forehead pulsed noisily, the worst sound in the world. Floaters drifted slowly across my eyes, the way they always did after a night with a bottle of Malibu. Also, I was starving. Hunger made my stomach gurgle, my bones shake. My thoughts soon skipped towards food, breakfast in particular.

—Come on, said Grandmither gently. —Get yourself washed and dressed. I'll see you downstairs.

Her voice was so slight, almost a sigh, that I felt something approaching pity in that moment. This wasn't the woman I remembered. The forceful, loud woman who shouted at Grandfaither about getting a job. She seemed diminished somehow. What had happened, I wasn't sure. An illness she was still recovering from? A breakdown? Maybe it was her age? Maybe I'd never know.

Eventually, I had to put thoughts of my grandmither aside and open my eyes. Ailing, but alive, I rolled out of bed and forced myself onto my feet.

That's when I heard something that sounded vaguely like a bottle of wine being uncorked… or a small gun being fired. Either I really wanted a drink or someone nearby was shooting a gun up at the sky.

Wee Herbie

Grandfaither had a psychopathic hatred of seagulls that made him act like a fool. Every single morning, he'd stand outside in the garden with a gun, his eyes never once leaving the sky. I watched from the patio, held by the same sort of fascination one might experience whilst watching the Big Wheel toppling over at the fairground. His gun wasn't anything with real power in its barrel, just a rusty old air rifle that popped whenever it was fired. Grandfaither fired it a lot, yet the seagulls always escaped, mocking him with shrieks and squawks. Either he was a bad shot or they were far too smart for him, and the more I got to know my grandfaither, the more I started to respect birds. As I watched from a safe distance, up the stairs that led into the house, it soon occurred to me that a pea shooter would probably do the job better than the antique Grandfaither carried at his hip.

–How's the poached egg?

I wasn't sure whether or not I had enjoyed it. I'd never eaten a poached egg. My eggs were always fried or mashed up into a cup with a chunk of melting butter dropped in for extra flavour. Grandmither wanted to impress me, keep me in her house with good food and kind words, but she didn't need to worry. Nothing could make me go back to Little Denny Road. I'd never fart in the same room as Uncle Tam, let alone breathe the same air as him.

The sound of a gun popping startled me again.

–What's his problem with the seagulls anyway?

–Oh, it was a long time ago.

Did I really want to hear a story right now? My head was ready to burst like a ball with a blade in it. A few seconds passed. Another shot was fired. In the end, I just accepted my fate and asked to hear the story. Grandmither didn't need to be asked twice and I got the impression she was enjoying having someone else in the house, another pair of ears for her to confide in.

–We had a dog for seven weeks, a lovely wee puppy. Your mither loved him!

—I've always wanted a dog, I confessed. To be honest, I couldn't see Mither caring for an animal. She wasn't very good at caring for me, for a start. Grandmither, meanwhile, was still talking. It was starting to get too much. There was an intensity in her words, the way she got words out before someone could tell her to stop. Grandfaither, probably.

—We loved that puppy. His name was Wee Herbie. He was a mutt, but lovely to look at. Your grandfaither won him at the snooker club during a night out.

—How exciting, I said, hoping to bring her story to an end.

—The wee yin was out in the garden one day when a seagull came down.

I nodded even though I was nodding off.

—And he swallowed the pup…

That woke me up. I actually thought I'd misheard.

—What?

—In two bites. It just came down and then took off again. Oh, your mither was devastated. Grandfaither went out and threw his shoes up in the air, trying to knock the bird out of the sky.

—A seagull ate Mither's dog and… Grandfaither threw… huh?

I couldn't even bring myself to finish the sentence. I wouldn't need to. The door at the far side of the conservatory swung open, slamming the wall with force enough to shake the panes of glass in the surrounding fixtures. It was Grandfaither, of course, his gun held tightly in both hands, eyes stern.

—Some day I'll get the one that got away, he told me calmly.

He had to be talking about the seagull, right?

115

20

Grandmither wanted to make my sixteenth birthday special and though they got the year wrong, I wasn't about to correct them. Maybe she knew something I didn't? Despite Granny's enthusiasm, I appreciated someone looking at me as though I were worthy enough of celebrating. But as I looked in the mirror, I didn't feel worthy of *anything*. To the bare eye, my naked body needed to be clothed at all times, even in the bathtub. My legs were thick, the knees nobbly. Then there was my belly, which looked unhappy at being part of me. It drooped, folds of flab hanging there, pulling me down. My skin, previously smooth and pale, was covered in angry red dots, the whole lot ready to pop. My greasy brown hair was flatter than a floor. But the worst thing about being me were the cramps. They were worse than my family, my life, my spots, my hair and my Herman Munster legs.

The cramps came slow and hard, their power intense like their pain.

—Cramps, said Lily years ago, —are a bit like being fisted by Freddy Krueger.

ENJOY YOURSELF

My grandparents' house (still not mine) was in that strange phase of feeling both familiar and vaguely foreign. My memories of the house from a lone visit twelve years ago had to be superimposed on the current layout. Worse, I didn't know where to find anything other than food, drink, cutlery and plates. The iron, it turned out, was in a cupboard near the fridge, while the ironing board was at the other side of the house, in a cupboard along with an unused Ariston tumble dryer. At some point, I'd need to explore the house until I got confident with it. There were parts of it sealed away from me, including a garage that I never cared to go near. Besides, there was always more to do. It was a beautiful bright day outside, meaning I could dress lightly. Now that I'd escaped Little Denny Road, I could give myself a whole new look and personality, become someone else, someone... not Sadie Relish.

First, I sprayed pink streaks through my hair like the girls from Summer Bay, who always looked trendy and sun-kissed. Next, I glossed my lips with a thin layer of apple green, the first time I'd ever used the stuff. Mither would have gone mental at the thought of me with makeup, even a hint of fake tan on my skin. But she was far away and I was better than free. I was brand new.

−Enjoy yourselves, said Grandfaither gruffly, a manky bit of paper pushed into my hand as I headed out the door. When I opened my hand, I saw Robert the Bruce's wrinkled face peering up from the crumpled purple banknote.

−Thanks, I told him, but found myself being hugged a little too long.

DINO'S, IN GLESGA

Grandmither wanted to take me into Dino's for a birthday lunch. I'd never heard of it.

−A Glesga institution, she declared, suddenly alight with oomph and umph. −I used to go there with your grandfaither all the time.

−How did you meet? I asked. Not that I was particularly interested, but I wanted to kill a little time on the bus, currently stuck on the middle of a road in Moodiesburn, waiting for a green light to flicker. When I asked why we couldn't have taken a car instead, Grandmither promptly told me there was no car to take.

−What's in your garage? I asked. There was no response. Instead Grandmither started talking about the day she met Archibald.

−I saw him playing the flute one day and I thought he was the most beautiful specimen of a man I'd ever seen. His beard was so neat. I swooned.

−Playing the flute? I asked politely. −You met at band practice?

−No, she laughed. −At the Orange Walk.

The smile calcified on my face, but I kept quiet. Grandmither, however, did no such thing. Worse, she was loud so everyone on the bus heard us. Ignoring my alarmed expression (the same one Bambi had on his face when he watched his mither get shot by hunters), she continued telling her story, framing it in a soft golden glow. Truly, the best days of her life! I continued to stare at the back of the seat in front, tracing the red pattern on the fabric with my eyes.

−Well, even though I knew it was love at first sight, not everyone was convinced. My parents hated your grandfaither. They tried to split us up. He was this and he was that. But I knew he was the one for me.

−A forbidden love affair?

I couldn't even pretend to sound enthusiastic, though she didn't notice.

−Aye. But we managed to get around them.

−How?

Grandmither leaned closer, her eyes white and watery.

−Your grandfaither used to walk me home from school.

That didn't sound so bad, I thought. Sometimes I wondered what it would be like if one of the lads at school walked me home. Not that I would have ever said that aloud to anyone. Not that I had anyone my age to talk to,

118

not since I abandoned Valerie in Denny. She was probably still at the bus stop, waiting.

−How exciting, I said quietly, thinking of last week and the life I'd left behind. Grandmither took it as a validation of her story and continued.

−Aye. He used to wait for me at the school gates too. We kept our love secret.

−That's lovely, I said, trying to be polite. I felt like I had to keep asking questions, make myself important to my grandparents so they kept me in their house (not yet my home). Sadly, Grandmither still hadn't finished.

−He wasn't allowed into the school grounds, obviously. He was too old.

She burst out laughing again, nudging me with her elbow. The other passengers on the bus tutted their irritation just as loudly but said nothing.

−Obviously? I asked, stretching the word out. −What age was he?

−Twenty. But I was mature for fourteen. Our folks didn't understand that.

−Jesus Christ, I muttered, wondering if I could just open the emergency door and roll across the road to freedom. For a second, even less than that, I considered grabbing the handle and twisting it just to get away from my grandmither and her gross story. But I decided against it. After all, I wanted to celebrate a birthday with my arms, face and hefty legs intact. Instead, I took the grubby twenty quid note out of my pocket, Grandfaither's surprise contribution to my big day. I looked at it, thinking about what to do next.

Before I could change my mind, I tore the note in half, making a ragged line down the middle. Immediately, I knew I'd done the right thing. Then, with Grandmither looking the other way, I dropped the two pieces of paper, now useless, onto the floor of the bus, hiding the evidence with my feet.

—Is something wrong? asked Grandmither from her side of the seat.

—Just stretching my legs, I said, a sugary smile sweetening the lie.

Seconds after the bus pulled up into the stance, I was off and outside.

GOOD FRIENDS

Glesga has always been a good friend for anyone lucky enough to know it. As I left Buchanan Bus Station with my grandmither, who tired very quickly, I found myself watching complete strangers as they moved around the city. The pavements were a constant battle for space, with everyone trying to walk in a straight line, only to correct course or risk being elbowed over the kerb. People pressed and pushed against each other, a battlefield from opposite sides with commuters from Buchanan Bus Station and Queen Street Train Station moving against visitors from Central Station as they moved uphill, everybody meeting and mixing in the middle.

For Grandmither, the city was another opportunity to tell stories about her past. Each street had something to do with the past, every building full of people living, working and sometimes dying. I listened politely while my grandmither talked, because she was paying for dinner. She told stories about the Empire Theatre, where she saw Frank Sinatra back in the fifties. She cackled at the night Des O'Connor pretended to faint so he could get off the stage because the audience thought he was shit. And just like her breath, our journey was made in short bursts. Eventually, we made it past The Apollo, a dirty-looking blot on the horizon, down into Sauchiehall Street, finally reaching Dino's for dinner.

Stepping into Dino's was like walking all the way into Italy without a passport. Though the interior design verged on the tacky, for someone who'd spent her entire life in Little Denny Road, it was the height of sophistication. Not that I would have minded going to Wimpy's for a burger, but this...

–Yes please, I said quietly.

TABLE FOR TWO

A short man with no hair and a neatly trimmed moustache took us through the small hallway into a room full of nicely-dressed people seated at tables. Heads immediately turned, validating my choice to dye my hair. At least that's what I thought until I saw the expressions on all their faces. That's when I realised that having bright hair was worse than wearing bright clothes, that people in Glesga had little patience for anyone who thought they were a cut above, especially when they spoke in my accent which was pure *teuchter*. Making small talk with my grandmither, I suddenly realised how different I sounded to everyone else. My accent was a lovely sing song, but the tune didn't seem to be appreciated by anyone in the room. The attention caused by my hair and voice was transformed in my imagination into some sort of endorsement. Eventually, after being shown to my table, I took a seat and a look at the menu. Unfortunately, I couldn't understand a bloody word of it. Everything was in Italian. Looking up at Grandmither, I asked,

–If I tell you what I want, can you order it for me?

–Of course, love.

–I want ravioli, chips and a glass of red wi...

Instead of raising a glass, Grandmither raised an eyebrow.

–Water, I said, hoping to sneak a glass of Smirnoff without her noticing.

The waiter stood in the background smiling benignly, his routine perfected, decent tips assured. Every now and then he added a little small talk to the table, something Grandmither turned into a long discussion about Italy. Before I realised it, their conversation had switched to Italian. Grandmither was literally speaking another language. This immediately made her a million times more interesting to me. Once she was done and the food ordered, I asked how she knew Italian. She drew herself up to her full height on the chair, not very high at all. Regardless, she seemed happy I was interested.

—My mither, your great grandmither, was Italian. I grew up in Italy.

—Really?

—Yes. We came here in the fifties. Your great grandfaither wanted to sell ice-cream, but the sleekit Nardinis and Capaldis got there first.

—I love ice-cream, I told her, suddenly validated in a way I hadn't been. In my head, I said the words: *I have Italian blood. I am part Italian.*

This changed everything. I'd discovered my unique selling point.

Later, after our meals had been plated and served, the waiter passed by.

—Is everything okay? he asked.

—Si, I replied grandly, answering with the only bit of Italian I knew.

The waiter's only response was to look at me like I was a complete bampot.

PAYING FOR DINNER

Later, when the bill came to the table, I waited for Grandmither to get out her purse and wave her Visa card at the waiter. Instead, she sat completely still, staring right at me as though waiting for something to happen. So we both sat still until one of us said something. It had to be me, of course.

−Is something wrong? I asked.

−You've got the money, she replied.

−What?

−Your grandfaither gave you money to pay for the meal, didn't he?

She stopped, assuming I'd forgotten about the gift he'd given me in the garden.

−That... was for our dinner?

−Yes. What did you think it was for?

−My birthday, I screeched, my voice breaking the sound barrier.

−Oh God, said Grandmither, her eyes wide in barely concealed horror.

−Don't you have any money on you?

−Not enough!

−I've lost it, I said, frantically improvising a lie that sounded like one. −It must have fell out of my pocket while I was sitting on the bus.

We looked at the table and the empty plates and glasses we'd gathered during the three courses of our celebratory dinner. We both had time to think and face a certain immutable fact: we were totally, completely fucked.

Eventually, Grandmither looked up, shrugged and made a suggestion.

−We could always offer to wash the dishes.

21

If the eighties looked bright then the nineties *felt* bright. Not for me though. I'd been living with my grandparents for two months, from 1989 to 1990. I'd spent most of that time upstairs, drinking in secret, out of pure boredom, pishing the bed and sneaking the bedsheets into the washing machine, wondering when Mither would make her move to bring me back to Little Denny Road. She was far away, yet her presence was always there, a ghost of a living person. Grandfaither, in particular, wanted to know everything, much more than I was willing tell him. He wanted to know where she worked. What her friends were like. Was Lily anything like her mither? But the strangest question came without warning one quiet afternoon, while the sun shone through the windows, filling every inch of the house, everywhere but the garage, which remained out of bounds.

−Who is she seeing? he asked.

−Huh? I said, not prepared for the question. He tutted, something he did often to show displeasure. Worse, he asked the question very slowly, as though helping me out in some way.

−Who is your mither seeing?

−No-one, I replied, feeling weary with the whole subject.

We were in front of the television, a gigantic box with wooden panelling that didn't match the actual table they'd set it on. Somehow, this seemed important to me. I was slowly feeling my way towards all the likes and dislikes that would carry over into adulthood. This feeling became more persistent when I got up to change the channel, the clashing wood grain never failing to make me wince.

Grandfaither was dressed in black shorts, colourless socks that used to be bright white and a pair of black shoes from Clarks. His bare chest was always on show, but it looked blotchy, the skin withered like a rotten apple. Earlier that day, Grandmither had let slip she thought he looked like Buddha, but I told her that Buddha always has a smile on his face.

Not like Grandfaither at all, really.

−She *must* be seeing someone, said Grandfaither, trying to get me to talk. His tone was soft, as though that might make me more amiable to his interrogation. Sadly for him, I wasn't as compliant as I had been when I first arrived. In fact, I'd started blanking him, feeling closer to my mither than I'd ever felt in my life. Sometimes, I understood why she fell out with her parents.

−I like him a lot, said Grandmither, trying to break the building tension.

She was talking about Michael Barrymore on *Strike It Lucky*, who always seemed a little too pushy in his attempts at making the audience laugh. But the pensioners seemed to adore him, delighting in his cheeky chappie schtick.

−What's he like? continued Grandfaither, clearly not giving Michael Barrymore even the slightest bit of attention. −Does he earn good money?

Finally, I'd had enough. Before I could stop myself, I snapped back.

−For God's sake, it's none of your business!

Grandfaither looked at me, but said nothing.

I could feel his eyes on me as I turned to face the television set.

From behind me, he spoke.

−If I ask you a question, I expect an answer.

I gave him an answer.

It wasn't the one he wanted, but it was something nonetheless.

–Fuck off, I muttered.

He was up off the couch and halfway across the room before I could react.

–DON'T YOU FUCKING SPEAK TO ME LIKE THAT YA WEE CUNT, he screamed, his breath nearly blowing my hair right off my head.

–You're as bad as your mither. She was a cunt the second she came out the delivery room.

–Bawbag! I shouted, squaring up to him. He was larger than me, despite being decades older, but after waking up to find Tam in my bedroom, here was a chance to correct my lack of action. Before I knew it, I was being slapped about by a pensioner.

–Fuck you! I screamed.

I hit him between the legs where it hurt, then hit him some more just to make sure. Grandmither tried to put herself between us, accidentally re-enacting old events with a different girl. The fight suddenly changed direction and my grandparents started slapping each other, both yelling names. He made fun of her breasts and she made fun of his breath. I took off into the hallway and picked up the phone. There was only one number I knew by heart, two if I counted the polis. I didn't, because calling them was strictly forbidden. That left one number. The only number I could call. Without hesitation, I pressed a sequence into the keypad. Looking over my shoulder, I saw they were still battering each other. Somehow, in the upheaval, they'd forgotten all about me. Months of poison had been building up, festering beneath the surface, hidden because they wanted to show me a false version of themselves. The ringing in my left ear told me somewhere else, in a street roughly twenty miles away, the phone was ringing.

Like most atheists, I only prayed to God whenever I wanted something.

−Pick it up, I whispered. −Please, please, please pick it up.

−Hello, said Mither, the sound of her voice the gift I never knew I needed.

−Hey… I started, before stopping.

It turned out I didn't need to say anything else.

−Sadie, she cried out. −Where are you?

In the background, a few metres away in the living room, Grandfaither roared something about *hoors*, followed by the racket of a television set being toppled off a display shelf. It hit the floor with a bang, causing the lights to flicker around the house. I hoped their next television would come with a sympathetic wooden grain, but of course I kept that thought to myself.

−You're there, said Mither on the other side. −With *them*.

−I didn't have anywhere else to go, I told her, hoping she'd come for me.

−We can deal with that later.

−I need your help, I said quietly.

But the phone went dead, leaving me helpless in a house with crazy people.

Help wanted

Hours passed, with me upstairs in the bedroom with a barricade between me and the door. Hastily improvised, I'd shoved the bed between me and my grandparents, who were still fighting. In my head, I knew Mither was probably taking the bus to get here, but a part of me wondered if she'd just decided to leave me here to suffer.

When she finally arrived at the front door, she announced her presence – not with a knock or a ring of the bell, but with a ferocious kicking that nearly burst the hinges. Standing up, pulling the bed frame away, I rushed downstairs and let her into the house, watching as she entered without even the barest glance in my direction. I didn't even get a chance to say a word before she was in the living room. That's when it occurred to me that in calling my mither, summoning her into battle, I might have made the situation worse.

Head held high, I entered the living room and surveyed the aftermath. Grandmither was on the couch, staring over at the space where the television used to be. Her eyes were watery and wide. She'd been crying. Grandfaither, bright red and slick with sweat, stood staring at his daughter, who was equally steadfast. I felt like this was history in the making and I'd made it happen.

–Get your bags packed, said Mither. –You're coming back home with me.

–Like fuck she is, snarled Grandfaither. –She stays here with us.

–Aye, you'd like that, wouldn't you? Another wee girl in the house.

–Don't start this again, said Grandmither, suddenly on her husband's side.

The betrayal was too much and I couldn't keep my cool any longer.

–He treats you like shit, I yelled. –What the fuck happened to you?

–She'll say nothing, said Mither coldly. –That's what she's good at.

Then something remarkable happened. Mither looked at her faither, trapping him in her eyes – and then she walked away. Gently, her hand on my shoulder, we stepped outside, past the Greek columns, walking up the street in the direction of a bus stop that would take us away from Dullatur.

–What about my clothes? I asked.

—I'll get you new clothes, said Mither, lighting up a cigarette. The breeze and pollen pushed the smoke into thin strands, curling it up into nothing. I waited, wondering what to do, until it came to me there was only one thing I could do in this situation. On tip-toe, I hugged my mither. She hugged back with one arm, the other still being used to hold her half-sucked cigarette.

Then I remembered why I came here in the first place.

—I can't go back while Tam's there, I said.

—He's not there, she replied.

—How? When?

—Pretty much the day you left.

I was furious.

—Why didn't you tell me?

—You didn't stick around long enough. When I found him in your room? Oh, I knew. I told him to get his stuff and fuck off.

—And... Lily?

I wasn't sure how much she knew about the situation, so it felt wise to approach it cautiously, as I did most things where my mither was concerned. Her cigarette smoked into a stub, Mither flicked it at the house she grew up in, like she hoped it would catch fire. For a heartbeat or two, I thought she'd tell me I was a liar, that her man would never do anything to her daughter.

Watching in real time, I saw her struggle to process some obscure trauma.

Instinctively, I knew it was an old memory, the sort she wanted to avoid.

—She told me everything, she said, smiling, lines around her lips.

—Everything? I asked.

—Yes, and I believe her.

Then she looked away from me towards the house we'd just abandoned.

129

–I BELIEVE MY DAUGHTER, she screamed at the Greek columns.

She stormed away from the house and I moved quickly to follow, but as I walked, something caught my attention. The garage next door to the house was open for the first time since I'd been there, wide and exposed. I finally got to see what was hidden inside, locked away from me.

Unsurprisingly, a car was parked, old and rusted, but undeniably there.

It was a Skoda.

My discovery

The journey out of Cumbernauld didn't take long once the bus picked us up. Halfway between towns, she suddenly burst into tears. That afternoon, she was wearing mascara, thick clumps of it. Her tears made trails and the streaks kept filling and falling down her face.

I didn't know what to say, but as usual I tried my best.
–What's wrong?
–I've been a shite mither, she sobbed, not caring that her eyeliner was dripping down onto her blouse, a shiny metallic number from Jane Norman. I knew this because the label was sticking out. If she cared that people were staring, she didn't say anything. Then again, my mither didn't care what anyone thought. I cared too much. For her, we might as well have been all alone on the bus while I was always conscious of other people. It gave our conversation a stilted, one-sided tempo.
–I'm so sorry, she wept, continuing to be oblivious to everything else. –I don't want to be like this. I hate it. I hate *me*. But I can only be me. Do you get what I mean?

Honestly, I didn't. Maybe one day I'd welcome what she was trying to tell me, once I'd experienced more years of life. Or not. Only time could say.

—So you don't hate me? I asked, hoping to finally know the truth.

—Hate you? Fuck off. Having you was one of the few good things I've done.

My jaw plummeted, giving anyone looking a good view of my tonsils, because it seemed almost impossible my mither would feel these things, let alone say them aloud. It started to feel like I'd misjudged her completely.

She kept talking, giving me (and the rest of the bus) more to gawk at.

—I love you, but sometimes you remind me…

She stopped. I waited. What else could I do?

Eventually, she took a shaky breath and started again.

—I look at you and see your faither.

—Don't you mean my grandfaither?

She said nothing.

She knew exactly what she meant.

22

Exorcism

Mither had an exceptional talent for making her enemies disappear. Hadn't she already chased an entire family out of the block? I didn't think of the Donaldsons or their noisy, messy children much these days. But when they came to mind, I liked to think they were happier in a different town, probably harassing their neighbours with random piles of shite. With that in mind, ridding the world of my latest 'uncle' would have been simple enough for someone of Mither's temperament. Better still, there was literally no trace of Tam left in the flat. Whatever had happened was fast and final, an exorcism of an ex. For years his smell, a sort of hot, mammalian armpit stink had thickened the air. Even in my bedroom. Not anymore. As soon as Mither opened the door, I knew he'd been scrubbed out of the very particles in the air. He was gone in every way that mattered. If only she could do the same to her faither, my faither too. He was still out there, still dangerous. A pervert, a molester, a scumbag.

I often thought about calling the polis, but never quite made it.

Scoured clean

My time away was too short to miss home, but long enough to forget it. 87 Little Denny Road seemed so small compared to my grandparents' hoose. Surprisingly, a tangy lemony scent had replaced the foetid stink of damp in my bedroom. Someone had scrubbed the walls with Zoflora. Immediately, I rushed over to the wardrobe and peeked behind it, knowing the patch of mould was gone. A discoloured patch showed where the stain had once spread. Mither, meanwhile, was already in the kitchen, probably lighting up a cigarette and making a cuppa. She liked her tea to look like fake tan and taste like Tetley. The low rumbling noise of water boiling in the kettle confirmed my theory. It felt like an old friend.

Suddenly this life was mine again and I didn't mind it at all. Everything I needed could be found in Little Denny Road. My clothes. My records. My comics. My CDs. Oh, and possibly a spare bottle of Hooch I'd stashed underneath the bed. Squatting onto the ragged carpet, I pushed my arm deep into the crevice between the chest of drawers and the headboard. Grasping, I felt around. Fearful Mither had found my booze stash, I conjured up several excuses, none of which seemed remotely believable. There I was, on the floor grasping, when two feet appeared. Nice shoes, I thought.

Looking up, I saw Lily standing over me.

−Looking for this?

Something swished through the air and bounced onto the mattress.

Sitting up, I realised she looked slightly different. Her hair was shorter, for a start. She wore a large parka jacket, a huge fur hood hanging over her neck. On her feet were large black boots, the kind she used to make fun of me for wearing. Her trousers were army khakis. Infuriatingly, she looked great.

Months had passed but I was glad to see her again.

−You better not be trying to blackmail me, I said.

Lily smirked, before her expression softened.

−Do you think I'm a grass or something?

She spat out the word 'grass' like she might fluid from a burst gum boil. Without saying a word, Lily closed the bedroom door. Meanwhile, I tensed myself for a punch or a headbutt. Instead, she burst into tears.

−This was my fault, she said, eyes thick with black

clumps. Clearly, she'd decided to stay away from the waterproof mascara. I corrected myself immediately. She wasn't acting. Somehow, I knew she was sincerely upset.

−I'm glad to be back, I told her, not knowing what else to say.

Already, she was cleaning her face, wiping away evidence of tears.

Before she could leave, I called out her name.

−Wait, I said.

−Your Hooch is done, she told me, a slight smirk on her face, familiar and welcome.

−No, I wanted to ask... well...

−Why him? With Mither, it was bad enough. But you? What did you see in him?

Lily didn't need to explain, but she seemed to waver at the door, considering whether to tell me, and how honest her response should be. Soon enough, she decided to do one but go halfway with the other.

−He was nice to me, she said.

I didn't know what to say, so I defaulted to the obvious.

−That's it?

−Yes.

There was more, of course. Much more. I'd learn that later.

BACK TO THE BUS STOP

Nothing had changed when I found Valerie, including her brand of wine. Not that I expected much to have happened while I was away, but I'd hoped for a bigger reaction from my friend. Though I wouldn't admit it, I wanted her to scream happily, throw her arms around me, beg to know where I'd been and make me vow never to leave her again. Instead, she casually necked the green bottle as I walked up the road, bringing the two of us together under the bus stop, away from the rain. As I walked, I was careful to stay on the narrow path while cars zipped by. I felt a trickle of sweat running down my back. The combination of summer humidity and the rain meant I wasn't going anywhere without somehow being soaked.

In all honesty, it made me feel disgusting.

No-one else was at the bus stop in Braes View.

Casually, I took a space on the seat next to Valerie.

−How was your holiday? she asked coolly.

−Holiday? I ran away.

−Oh. I thought you were gone a long time.

I looked at her, not knowing if she was being serious or not.

She took another swig from the bottle. Valerie, I decided, was the worst sort of friend, the kind who refused to share her booze.

At last, she asked about me.

−Did you get up to anything exciting?

−I was living in a huge house in Cumbernauld, I explained, going through the story I'd already planned in my head. −I'm going to inherit it when my granny and grandfaither die. You can come round if you want, for a party.

We sat there quietly, not quite knowing what to say to each other.

Meekly, I attempted to restart the conversation.

−Listening to anything cool?

−Two words, she said. −Happy Mondays.

−What are they like?

−They're the best fucking band in the world.

That's when I realised she was no longer a goth. It took a minute or two, but the black hair had vanished, her natural murky blonde now back in force. Her eye makeup had switched from black to bright purple. Even

135

her clothes had changed. Loose, light and *baggy*, just like her new favourite music.

−So… erm… how's things?

Valerie didn't respond. This was going to be harder than I had thought. Against my better judgement, I kept pushing, trying hard to resuscitate my friendship.

−Anything cool happening at school?

−Nothing, she said. −I've just been hanging out with other people.

I couldn't bring myself to say anything. How could I? What right did I have?

−I was fine when you were gone, continued Valerie, her tone almost defensive. −Honestly, I've got other friends. Nothing changed. I knew you'd be back at some point. I'm surprised you didn't run off sooner, to be honest.

−Really?

−Everyone knows what you put up with, said Valerie mysteriously.

A bus pulled up while we were talking, but it didn't stay long. I always felt awkward talking when buses were nearby, like the driver could hear everything I was saying. Obviously, they couldn't, but sometimes the paranoid part of my psyche overrode the sensible side. Eventually the bus drove off, heading to Bo'ness. Finally, I had the space necessary to explain myself to my only friend in the world. But just like my sister, I had to go halfway with the truth. Valerie could never know about my real faither.

Instead, I told her about the other dramas in my life. The reason I ran away.

−My Uncle Tam… well, he isn't really my uncle…

−I honestly had no idea, said Valerie sarcastically. I took it graciously.

−He was going with my sister behind my mither's back.

136

The bottle of Buckfast nearly slipped from Valerie's fingers.

–No way, she said quietly, –Your sister's a goddess.

Valerie stopped herself before she could say anything else. Her response had been that of a girl who'd said far more than she'd intended.

–Mither kicked that arsehole out, I said, grinning, really feeling that smile for the first time in months. –He's gone forever.

–Good. He didn't… you know…

–No, I said firmly, thinking of Greek columns and Skoda cars. –He didn't.

Despite my insistence, I felt I'd had a lucky escape.

–Well, I'm glad you're back. Have a drink on me.

Eagerly I reached over and took the bottle out of Valerie's hand, only to find it was completely empty. She burst out laughing and eventually, I did too.

–Cow, I said, only half meaning it.

–There he is, shouted Valerie, looking in the opposite direction.

For a moment, I assumed she meant Uncle Tam, but someone else was walking up the street, coming through Braes View towards the bus stop. I watched as they came down the stacks of stairs, each step crumbling into pavement powder. Whoever it was, they were using the underpass. Somehow, I had little regard for people who used underpasses, though I wasn't sure why I felt that way. It was a lot safer than crossing the road, of course.

–Who is it? I asked.

–I *told* you. I've got other friends. While you were running off, we were hanging out. He's in some of my classes at school. You'll *love* him, doll.

Watching carefully, I followed his progress through the underpass until he emerged from the other side. My eyes lost him briefly when he vanished out of sight again, though it was a brief disappearance. He reappeared at the bottom of some stone steps, climbing them slowly until – at last – he was at the bus stop. Our eyes met and all the memories came back. I remembered a tree, a wish and best friends who used to go on quests together.

–Hello, Gregor, I said shyly.

–Hey, he said back, his face hidden under hair that was pure Shaun Ryder.

Suddenly, I believed in magic again.

23

Suddenly there were three in the shelter, all of us watching buses passing by on their way to different places and better towns – or so I used to think. I'd already been far away from Denny and found nothing was that different. Besides, I had Gregor in my life again and whatever magic we'd shared as children was still there, more powerful than ever. Sometimes I caught him looking at me and we'd smile, for no reason other than we were both happy to be near each other. I'd start a sentence and he'd finish it. Our closeness created an entire new lexicon, a language both of us were slowly learning as we went along, a new dialect that Valerie struggled to understand.

Gregor had changed over the years, becoming a different person, but not so different he was lost to me. Puberty had deepened his voice and lengthened his bones. When we talked, I had to look up at his face and he had to look down. His favourite song was *The Only One I Know* by The Charlatans, and he listened obsessively. Sometimes, when we were sitting quietly, our conversation slowed down, he'd hum the song under his breath. He wore large headphones, huge enough to give him a handle on his head, making him resemble a human-sized handbag. Meanwhile, my favourite song had become *Lazyitis* by Happy Mondays, the song that made most sense to me, at least at the time. I was still a little smaller than everyone, chubbier, but I hid it underneath baggy clothes. Valerie, meanwhile, yearned for something noisier, brighter, sweatier and squelchier. Her ambition in life was to take ecstasy and usher in a third summer of love, even though the second summer of love lasted nearly two years.

Basically, Valerie wanted bass in her face in a darkened place.

Together, we made sense. I thought this could be my life forever.

THE NUMBER ONE NIGHTCLUB IN DENNY

Sylvester's, also known as Molesters, was the largest nightclub in Denny. It wasn't that large though. Located centrally in the town centre, it was a cupboard with a small bar, spotlights dotted in darkness, a few mouldy seats, and a sticky floor that never failed to pull a stray Reebok off somebody's foot, making their walk of shame into a stumble. There was a painting of a cat outside the club. It vaguely resembled a Hanna Barbera character, but with a bow tie different enough to prevent a lawsuit. Whoever drew the cat made him look terribly depressed, like he'd been pinned to the plyboard and all he wanted was to leap out and dance like that stupid cat in the Paula Abdul video. At some point during one of our many late-night bus stop booze sessions, Valerie suddenly became obsessed with the idea of getting into the club. She thought her third summer of love could be found behind the bouncer, a large man with a bald head and a ratty ponytail, like him from Status Quo. Late one Friday night, we found ourselves outside Sylvester's, watching from a safe distance. There was a small queue lined up by the drawing of the cat, boys and girls ready for a night of noise.

THE LOST FIELD OF LOVE

–Do you know the worst part about going to Sylvester's?

We didn't but implicitly understood Valerie had something to say.

–The only reason people are here is because they couldn't find the field.

140

–What field? I asked, trying to understand.

–The field where the rave is happening.

–What rave? asked Gregor.

–Exactly.

By the time I turned to get Gregor's reaction, he'd already turned away. There was something on his face close to amusement, at least vaguely gleeful.

–Alright, said Valerie after a few seconds of silence. –Here's the plan. We join the queue, stay calm and I'll show off my fake ID. Let me do all the talking and we'll be fine. If anyone asks, you're eighteen years old. If they think you look too young, just tell them you were born with Foetal Alcohol Syndrome and you're completely offended by the very notion that anyone would *suggest* you look younger than eighteen. Okay? Comprende? Do you get ma jist?

Gregor's monobrow moved up over his forehead, but he said nothing.

Like me, he wasn't totally convinced this was going to work.

A few minutes later, we quietly joined the queue.

Every now and then, we shuffled slightly closer to the door, stopping to wait while people up ahead were checked over. As I waited, it suddenly came to me that we might not get into the club. Not because we were obviously too young, but because the venue was already packed full of people. I wouldn't have minded being turned away, if only because I didn't fancy a night of standing around awkwardly in a stuffy, cramped room listening to shit music. Really, I could recreate the same conditions in my own bedroom by switching off the light and turning the radio dial to Tiger Tim's show on Clyde 1 FM.

–We're nearly there, muttered Valerie, her voice low and excited. I hoped after all this work to get inside, all the planning, the fake IDs, the clothes she thought would make her look older... I wanted it to be worthwhile. More than that, I didn't want Valerie to be disappointed. Gregor wasn't too keen on hitting Sylvester's either, but he was likely worried about bumping into one of his brothers. They were always around, constantly trying to make him feel small.

We moved up again. Soon we'd make it past the bouncer.

−This is going to change my life, I can feel it.

−Life is mad, I said.

−It really is, added Gregor.

This was our new catchphrase because we started and finished it together. Valerie, meanwhile, was getting a little too excited and couldn't hide it. She started hopping on the spot, bouncing up and down, her head appearing over the crowd, then dipping, then appearing again. It was a bit much. Somehow, she put me in mind of a puppy leaping for treats.

−Do you really need an eccy? I asked scathingly.

−I'm going to have an amazing night, she said indignantly. −I just know it.

Gregor was quiet, probably nervous he might be caught by one of his dreadful brothers. Sensing his uneasiness, I took him by the hand and squeezed softly. He looked down and smiled, eyes bright behind his tousled fringe. His headphones were on, music playing, soothing his anxiety. I mouthed the words ARE YOU OKAY? His response was to nod once very slightly. We all moved up again and *at last* we were at the main door.

In the time between the queue moving and stopping, I realised three things. They just happened in my head, three thoughts in succession, each one as quick as the next. In turn, I realised:

I still had his hand in mine.

I didn't want to let go of it.

142

And most importantly…

I'd fallen in love for the first time.

SUMMER OF LOVE

The bouncer let us through without bothering to check Valerie's fake ID that she'd spent time, effort and money (not her own) acquiring. Slightly irritated that her hard work was for nothing, she stopped bouncing around enthusiastically, preferring to stomp her way into Sylvester's, her only form of protest. Gregor and I followed closely behind her, not wanting to lose our friend in the crowded room. On our way inside, we passed the familiar cartoon cat on the wall, the club mascot, his painted expression still frozen in a strange place of happy sadness. I would have waved at him, but Gregor still had his hand around mine and it seemed silly to break his grip to greet a large drawing on a wall. As we headed deeper into the room (at this point I decided that calling it a *nightclub* felt like an infringement of the Trading Standards Act), I literally felt music hit me, the bass loud enough to rattle my ribcage. The sound system was small but the noise it made was anything but.

−*Moments In Soul* by J.T. And The Big Family, said Gregor, as he lowered his headphones, letting them droop around his neck. It took me a second to realise he was referring to the song making the speakers wobble.

We stood there in the middle of the dance floor, looking and feeling out of place, not knowing what to do. Valerie, however, was already busy trying to find the local dealer. Luckily for her, most of the other clubbers dabbled in a bit of weekend drug dealing. While Valerie did the rounds, I headed for the bar, where I waited for ten minutes. The stink of BO and Brut made my nostril hair recoil in fear. Soon enough I stopped caring and so did my nostrils.

At last, the barman got round to serving me.

−What do you want, love?

−Do you sell Merrydown in here?

The barman snickered slightly, as though he knew I shouldn't be there. Instead of throwing me out, he answered, −We sell Tennent's Lager.

−Okay, a can of your finest Tennent's Lager, I said, giving him my biggest smile. Though I didn't realise it, my smile made me look like a letterbox.

He paused, as though reconsidering his earlier stance.

I deepened my voice, made it sound slow, like the way Mither spoke.

−Please, I added.

−Okay, he said. −Here you go. That'll be one pound thirteen pence.

Standing by the bar with Gregor, who had his headphones back over his ears again, I pulled the ring and let the can hiss at me. Without giving my taste buds a chance to negotiate a peace treaty, I slugged back a long gulp of beer. It tasted like someone had siphoned all the bum sweat from every clubber in the room and tipped it into a can at room temperature. Despite the taste, Tennent's Lager was as Scottish as haggis, tartan and casual sexism: on the side of the can was a woman in a white negligee. Her name, according to the florid writing, was Fiona. Not that it mattered. I'd soon forget that *and everything else* by the time I got to the last drop and the next drink.

At some point during the night, Valerie battled her way through the crowd to show me a pill on the palm of her left hand; her eyes were as wide as her smile.

−I've already taken one, she grinned.

I raised an empty can to her success at finally getting someone to give her what she wanted. Before I could do anything, she threw her arms around me, then hugged Gregor. The lager made me act without thinking. Reaching

144

over, I yanked Gregor away from Valerie, pulling her off balance. Unfortunately, I was also struggling to stay on my feet. Together, we fell over, landing on the floor and each other.

–Fucking hell, said Gregor dismissively. –You're both in a state.

I motioned at his headphones until he lowered them.

Step On by Happy Mondays had just started playing in the background.

Gregor heard the opening bars and just… smiled.

This, I decided, was our song and nothing else could ever sound better.

GIVEN THE BOOT

The bouncer's hand was large enough to fit around my neck, giving him something to hold while he dragged me out of the club. Outside, in the breath-curling cold night, he threw me away from the main entrance. Momentum quickly took me down, pulling my knees along the pavement, causing me to yell out in startled pain. Valerie soon followed and she found herself on the ground next to my feet. Her promised land taken away; she couldn't help but laugh anyway. Gregor came out on foot, the bouncer firmly (but not so politely) warning him to tell us how disastrous it might have been for Sylvester's if the police discovered they'd let us inside the club.

–Our licence could be taken away, he snapped. –Where would everyone go if that happened?

–Somewhere good, replied Gregor calmly.

–Wee prick! yelled the bouncer, his hand motioning us to leave immediately. That didn't happen, but only because I couldn't be bothered getting up onto my feet. Eventually, I did and all three of us stood together in Stirling Street, watching people coming and going from

Sylvester's, a literal hole in the wall. We looked at each other, waiting for someone to speak, but none of us knew what to say, or we felt we'd said enough that night. It was late and we were tired, drunk and cold.

But that night I couldn't sleep. Mither was away out on the nightshift, so she didn't see me staggering around the house, tipsy but mostly in control. Lily, meanwhile, didn't care. She spent the night talking on the phone, chatting to someone about someone else. I was alone with my thoughts. Soon enough, I found myself ransacking the kitchen drawers in search of a bingo pen. Mither had a few stashed around the house and though she didn't often go to the bingo hall in Denny toon, when she did, she always returned with coasters and large dabber pens.

It didn't take me long to find a handful of colours.

Then I headed out just in time to hear the birds sing.

Making the Unhappy Cat Happy Again

My unsteady feet took me back down the road to Sylvester's in just over twenty minutes. The entire street echoed with emptiness, though in the distance I could hear people screaming at each other, probably down in Shanghai, the area of Denny that had the worst reputation, alongside Little Denny Road. Standing near the main entrance of Sylvester's, safely locked up for another night, I contemplated what was about to happen. In my head, it made sense, but would it really change anything? Did it even need to?

Before I could stop it from happening, I scribbled a smile over the drawing on the wall. Suddenly, the cartoon cat had a big happy face, the one he'd deserved from the start. In my boozy state, I'd decided cartoons deserved to be happy as well. Feeling accomplished with my work, I headed home, only stopping once to spew my guts up on the pavement.

24

When Mither asked what I wanted for my birthday, I couldn't answer. I'd already been to Dino's with my granny, our version of a sweet sixteenth before the actual day. But trying to talk Mither out of something once she'd made her mind up was about as sensible as trying to get superglue back in the tube after you'd squeezed it out. She was determined to show me a good time. Deep down, I think she saw my birthday as a chance to redeem herself after the Uncle Tam incident. Also, I had a feeling she regretted telling me about my real faither, the consequences of which neither of us had confronted. The best way to cope was to close my eyes to scary monsters, just pretend nothing had changed. Mither was good at pretending too.

−I'm quitting the nightshift, she announced one morning at the kitchen table. −It's the right time. Who knows? I might retrain to become a social worker.

Laughter nearly shook the screws out of my seat. In the end, I decided to just enjoy what came my way, allow people to make a fuss over me for surviving sixteen years of Little Denny Road. My birthday, I told myself, was an opportunity to show everyone how far I'd come as a person. Oh, and an opportunity to get drunk on Merrydown. With luck, everything would go well.

Sadly, I've never been particularly lucky.

THE KITCHEN TABLE CLUB

Lily was with us at the kitchen table, puffing ferociously on a cigarette, no longer hiding her new habit. Not that Mither cared. She now had someone to give her a cigarette when she ran out. Between them, they formed a credit/debit system where one always owed the other. That way, they never ran low on nicotine or conversation. They smoked, talked and smoked again.

—Okay, said Lily excitedly, —let's get dressed up and go out for dinner.

—Maybe a few drinks, I added hopefully.

—A few dozen drinks in your case, muttered Lily.

I was by the sink looking for a glass. There were no bottles of Bon Accord in the cupboard, so I had to run the tap. Worse, a brawl was happening inside my brain and each punch made my skull shake. *Never again*, I thought. *That's it, I'm laying off the booze*. It was a promise I made every Monday; the same one I broke on a Friday. The rest of the day would be spent trying to hydrate away my hangover.

—Okay, said Mither. —That's it settled.

—You're going out? I asked, not quite hearing the whole conversation.

—No, *we're* going out.

I stared dimly at Lily, hoping she'd help me out.

—For your birthday, explained Mither, as though I were daft.

—Oh. Where are we going?

—We're heading to Dino's in Glesga.

Oh. Shit. How would I put this into words?

—Well… I started, —I've already been.

Mither raised a neat eyebrow while the rest of her face remained absolutely impassive. It was a talent she'd developed over the years. That expression was a warning for the unwary. I had to be very careful now.

—How were you there?

She already knew or at least she'd guessed but needed me to explain.

None of us had talked about my time living with her

parents. After she'd broken down on the bus (this made a change from the bus itself breaking down), it was never mentioned again. Lily, curious to the point of sheer nosiness, hadn't said anything either. Not once. It was almost as though it hadn't happened. I stood by the sink, knowing what might happen if I told the truth, ultimately realising it wasn't a choice for me.

—Grandmither took me there for my sixteenth birthday.

Mither lit up another cigarette, saying nothing until she was ready.

The next thirty seconds felt like five slow minutes.

—But today's your sixteenth birthday, said Mither, drawing in some smoke.

—I know, but she wanted to take me out anyway. As a treat, you know?

Lily kept quiet. She knew this could go badly wrong and wanted to stay out of the blast zone. Besides, she was trying to stay in Mither's good graces.

—When did that evil auld cow take you to Dino's?

Mither was referring to her own mither, of course.

I thought back, carefully rewinding the dates until I remembered.

—Mid-December, I said.

—The fourteenth?

It seemed important that I got this right, so I thought it over carefully.

—Yes. The fourteenth of December. It was a Thursday afternoon.

Mither made a strange noise, clicking her tongue against the top of her mouth. Then she shook her head in a way I took to be dismissive.

—The fourteenth of December is *my* birthday, she said softly.

It took a second to process what she'd just told me, my

150

brain not quite fitting the bits together quickly enough.
She was right. I should have known.

−Dirty creepy bastards, was all Mither wanted to say
on the matter.

EATING POPCORN

Thankfully, we didn't go out that night. I decided to stay
in and watch my favourite film, *The Breakfast Club*, an
eighties classic. Mither and Lily sat beside me on the
same couch, watching the movie, not quite enjoying it the
way I did. One bucket of popcorn for three hands, though
I ate sparingly. I loved John Hughes's oeuvre, taking his
words and work deep into my heart. Later that night, both
Mither and Lily did the obligatory lights out, lit candles
birthday cake moment.

−Happy Birthday, sang Mither like she was auditioning
for *Stars in their Eyes*, giving it real *Tonight, Matthew,
I'm going to be Sheena Easton.*

When she came into the living room with a wonky
slab of marzipan on a plate, I pretended to be surprised.
As much as I wanted to eat, I couldn't because my belly
felt like it might fall out through my arse. The rest of
the night went by quietly, just popcorn being crunched.
Mither didn't say much. She was lost inside her head, a
far noisier place than the inside of mine, hangover and all.

25

Valerie quickly started to resent my crush on Gregor. Though she never said it aloud, I knew she preferred it when we were alone. Gregor, whether in person or just by name, was now an inconvenience.

−Why don't you just tell him how you feel? she suggested wearily. This happened while we were in the bogs between lessons, the two of us applying concealer and dabs of Clearasil to our skin. My first instinct was to deny it, just lie. But I didn't, of course. It would cheapen my feelings, somehow.

−He doesn't see me that way, I said, sounding just a little bit pathetic.

−How do you know? Just tell him. What's the worst that could happen?

−That's a multiple choice, I said. −He could say no, never, or fuck off.

−Or all three, cackled Valerie, much to my annoyance. Then, after fixing her fringe (always ready to leap off her forehead), she glanced at me.

−But even if he isn't into you, at least you'd know. Isn't that a good thing?

I thought about it but caught sight of a stray zit underneath my nostril, so small it might have gone unnoticed. Pressing the Clearasil nozzle to the tip of my finger, I massaged the tiny dot of cream into the little blemish. In the background, other girls arrived, backpacks slung over their shoulders.

Quietly, we conferred so no-one would hear what was being said.

−If you were me, I said, −would you tell the person you like how you feel?

Valerie's reflection to my left suddenly looked very sombre. When she realised I was looking at her, she immediately readjusted her expression.

This happened so quickly, I started to think I'd imagined it.

–No, she said. –I prefer to like people from a distance.

–How far?

–Ten miles at least, she laughed.

The cap was screwed back onto the tube of Clearasil and thrown back into Valerie's backpack, a huge sack that looked like something a mountain climber would put on his back for the journey to Everest. Everything could be found in that bag. Spot cream. Concealer. Even a bottle of Buckfast. Valerie had it all.

–So you really like Gregor a lot?

–Yes, I really, really, really like him a lot.

–Tell him, she repeated. –Just get it over with.

Thinking it over, I finally jumped on a decision.

–Alright, I'll ask him over tonight and tell him.

Valerie grinned and suddenly anything felt possible.

In hindsight, I might have been a little naïve.

DATE NIGHT

Gregor was on the floor, back propped up against the end of my bed frame, television and VCR directly in front of him. I was on the mattress, slumped over some pillows, sipping on a glass of vodka with a pinch of Pepsi. We'd been watching *Female Trouble* and *Pink Flamingos* all night long and Mither had kept a respectful distance, giving me the space I needed to make everything as comfortable as possible. While Divine chewed on dog shit, I decided to find the third film of the night, something a bit more romantic.

−What did you get? asked Gregor, who couldn't believe what he'd just watched.

−A future classic, I replied, hoping my excellent taste in cult cinema would prove me right. Gregor couldn't wait and threw some guesses my way.

−*Judgement Day*?

−No.

−*Steel Magnolias*?

−Erm… no.

−I give up. What?

Reaching over the bed, I lifted the cassette box and waved it at my friend.

−*Grease*, he said, his eyebrow raised high enough to touch his hairline.

−No, even better… *Grease 2*!

He didn't react. I took this to be a good sign.

−Oh, it's amazing. The songs! The acting! The fucking stupidity of it all.

−Ooooh, he said, suddenly interested. −I'm in the mood for stupid.

I rolled off the bed and landed roughly on the carpet, keeping myself out of harm by making sure I didn't go too hard. Once on the floor, I rolled across the room, reaching the television and VCR, something Gregor found hilarious.

−You're a rocket, he kept yelling, −an absolute rocket!

After feeding the tape to the video player, the mechanism snatching it in, I moved back to sit by Gregor. We were literally shoulder to shoulder. The film lasted into the night, the streetlamps flicking to life in the background, adding to the milky gamma ray glow of the television screen. Later, deep into the film, shortly after the cast performed *A Girl For All Seasons* (my favourite), something happened, something important.

The only thing that mattered, actually.

I realised Gregor wasn't enjoying himself.

—Is everything okay? I asked quietly.

He didn't say anything. That's how I knew he was upset.

—I'm sorry, he said, finally looking me in the eye. —I can't be who you want.

—What?

—Valerie told me everything.

Stung at the thought my friends had been talking about me behind my back, I put myself on pause for a moment, desperately trying to gain time to work out an escape scenario from an embarrassing situation. But something else came over me. A calmness. Maybe this wasn't a bad thing, I thought.

—I really like you, I said, cursing myself for not being a liar. —Is that so bad?

—No. I like you too.

—You do? I asked, not quite sure if I heard properly.

—Not like that, said Gregor a little too quickly.

We sat there quietly, our touching shoulders suddenly itchy and painful.

Then Gregor said something that would change our lives forever.

—I need to tell you a secret.

Panic made my thoughts fly hard like kamikaze pigeons.

—You do?

—Aye. I trust you more than anyone in the world, Sadie.

—What is it? I asked, hoping he wouldn't ask if I had a secret. The thought of explaining the truth about my birth, the identity of my real faither…

No. Never. I wouldn't. Instead, I focussed on Gregor's secret.

It occurred to me that my friend was going to tell me what only Auld Sybil knew. Years after he confronted the tree with a wish, I'd finally discover the truth. But something had spooked Gregor and I knew from his expression he was already starting to regret saying anything. Quickly, I mollified him.

–Honestly, I won't tell anyone.

At last, Gregor spoke aloud something he'd kept hidden for over ten years.

–I'm not a boy. I'm a girl.

Seconds passed while my brain processed the words.

Then I did something I'd never forget or forgive.

I burst out laughing.

Right in his face. I shrieked until tears fell down my cheeks.

Gregor's eyes widened. His face fell – and so did our friendship.

Hurting the ones we love

Without a sound, not even a creaking floorboard, Gregor stood up and walked away, only this time he kept walking until he was out the flat, down the stairs, and away from the block. I begged him, no… I begged *her*… to wait.

–I didn't mean it! I screamed.

One last time, I tried to say something, anything that would make Gregor stop in her stride and come back to me, where she belonged.

–I love you, I cried out. But not even that worked. Suddenly there was a noise that I couldn't place. It was everywhere. A screaming wail or a howl that came out and carried itself off into the wind. Once I realised it was me, I stopped. There was no point in giving the neighbours another show, after all. As I turned, I caught a glimpse of the tree that knew Gregor's secret. He had trusted me and I had laughed, unlike the tree, whose silence was neither judgement nor endorsement. Anxious, depressed and half-cut with the Smirnoff, I returned to my bedroom and threw my videos across the room, watching them hit the wall, shattering into spirals of black tape. I'd need to replace them, of course, but I'd worry about that later.

Nothing mattered now except that I was a deeply shitty person. My soul was dirty, corrupt and vile. Nastiness was in my personality, my very essence.

Suddenly Mither was there, totally unfazed by what she'd just witnessed.

−What happened? Did he try anything? Did he touch you?

−Fuck off! I screamed, all my frustration and rage finding a new target. −Of course he didn't touch me. Who do you think he is? Your faither?

If I'd slapped my mither across the face, it would have hurt far less than my words. She didn't know how to react, simply standing there, eyes looking straight ahead, fighting to keep herself from saying something we'd both regret. I saw it on her face, the struggle, and for a second I honestly thought she'd leave the room without saying a word.

A vain hope, it turned out.

−He's your faither too, she said quietly.

Then she left me to sob while the credits rolled. Eventually, the tape stopped, fading the picture out of view, replacing it with noisy static. I didn't care. I was content to sit in the dark, staring at the telly, chasing ghosts on the screen, half-images that might have been projections from the back of my brain or mere eye floaters. For the next few hours, I tried to lose myself in the blizzard. Eventually, after what felt like no time at all, I realised it was time to get ready for school.

26

Valerie was waiting the next morning at the bus stop, waving merrily in the distance as I stormed up the path, my hands clenched tight into fists while my rucksack swung off my back, bobbing with each forward step.

−How did it…?

Go? she was about to ask.

She knew as soon as her eyes took in my face that it hadn't gone well at all. I stood there, glaring at her without saying a word. Time had turned my anger cold now that there was someone to blame for my catastrophic date night.

−What the fuck did you say to Gregor?

Valerie blinked a few times. She was trying to work out what to say, knowing the wrong answer would tip our friendship into an abyss. What she couldn't work out was whether telling Gregor was good or bad.

Eventually, she came out with it.

−I gave him a heads up… but I just wanted to help you out.

−Did he tell you his secret? I asked.

−No, she said quietly, −But I know there's something going on with him.

−You suggested I tell him everything.

−Yes, said Valerie nervously.

−No, that's not right. You didn't suggest. You *pushed*.

−What? No, Sadie. I was trying to be supportive.

Confused and agitated, I was still struggling to understand how last night had happened and I needed someone else to blame. But it wasn't easy to blame anyone, so I went for the nearest bystander. I couldn't blame Gregor, of course. I lacked the language, education, even the words to describe the life Gregor was due. She was a girl born into a body that didn't fit. A girl who asked a so-called magic tree to transform her outside to fit what she felt on the inside.

−I laughed in her face.

That was all I could say about what happened.

−Her?

Apparently, I'd already said enough. But my silence made Valerie uneasy enough to keep talking, if only to keep the conversation from turning awkward.

−Look… Sadie, this isn't a bad thing. You've still got me.

−What?

−I like Gregor too. No, not like that. Don't worry. I like him as a friend.

Valerie looked away before finding her resolve again.

−I don't want to lose you, she said, her voice wobbling.

−Stay away from me, I snarled, finger aimed at her face. −I mean it.

−Don't be daft, she cried out. −You're acting like I set you up somehow!

−Maybe you did.

Again, I'd gone too far. My karma mileage was getting higher and higher.

−If that's what you think, then we were never friends to begin with.

−No big loss, I said bluntly.

Valerie didn't respond, except to try pull her shoulders up, glaring at the sky in frustration. For a wee bit of a second, I thought she was going to say something, but she reconsidered. Turning around, I walked towards Bulloch Crescent, eventually taking the path to Denny High School but really wanting to go in the opposite direction. I couldn't help thinking about what the next few months would be like now I had no friends except for me, a friend in myself.

Hopefully, that would be enough.

Forget the old me

Finding a new me, someone I could like again, was as easy as a change of clothes and a batch of CDs from the Falkirk branch of HMV. With this in mind, I took a bus into town when I should have been at school, preferring the breezy feeling of walking around the shops to the cramped, overly energetic corridors of Denny High. Even though I didn't have a job, I'd saved up enough money, keeping the small change any time I did something for Mither or Lily. In fact, I deliberately made myself indispensable to them.

Whenever they needed a packet of 20 Benson and Hedges, I offered to go on the condition I could keep what was left. With the amount they smoked, I was out at the ice-cream van nearly every night. The loose change I saved went from a handful to an old cake tin full in less than a month. Eventually, when I had enough, I emptied the tin into an old purse that belonged to Mither, abandoned in one of the kitchen drawers. It was bright pink, instantly appealing to my magpie eye, and it closed tightly thanks to a large bronze clasp. Even though I hadn't saved as much as I'd have liked, I could still buy clothes from the Clearance racks if I was canny enough. There was always a sale somewhere, you only had to look for red signs with large white letters.

Clearance is my favourite designer label

This time around I tried on the clothes without any fuss, going out of my way to find bright colours and trendy silhouettes. Actually, I wasn't too worried whether or not they fit. Mither had a sewing machine, a huge antique she

160

dragged out of the hall cupboard on occasion, using it to put double stitches into old blouses she refused to bin. Sometimes, I overheard her muttering about how that sewing machine was the only good thing she got from my grandmither. Now I understood exactly what she meant.

There was a woman in the shop who kept looking at each item of clothing I picked up, moving with me as I worked my way around the racks. Eventually, I glared at her, hoping she'd say something so I could tell her to fuck off. That was something the new me would do, but I didn't need to, because the woman (whoever she was) remained stubbornly quiet.

Glancing down, I noticed a large walkie talkie on her belt.

Ah, she was a security guard.

Offended at the mere thought of being taken as a klepto (even though I was when I needed to be), I made a scene of pulling out my large pink purse, waving it around as some sort of proof I intended to pay for my items. This seemed to satisfy her and she moved away, further up the racks, until she was on the opposite side of the room. With her back turned, I quickly pocketed a pair of sunglasses and a packet of temporary tattoos. Satisfied no-one had caught me, I headed over towards the girl behind the counter, offering the clothes I'd chosen to pay for hanger-first. She smiled, told me my new jeans looked beautiful (they were just denim jeans like any other pair), before swooning over my new blouse, which had a distressed, torn-up, heroin chic vibe to it. I had to agree it was fabulous. Finally, she finished removing the tags and ringing through the items.

–That'll be twelve pounds and forty five pence.

–Thank you, I replied evenly.

I opened the red purse, ready to dig out some cash, when something slid out and dropped to the floor. Taken aback because I thought I'd checked the purse beforehand, I looked down at my feet, where the object had landed.

It was square, wrapped in silvery foil and had the word DUREX on it.

I let out a sound that was somewhere between a scream and a laugh.

−I think that belongs to you, said the girl behind the counter.

−No, I cried out. −This isn't even my purse.

−Of course it isn't.

−But it really isn't, I screeched.

She nodded sympathetically, but I knew she didn't believe me. Before I could do anything else, my legs took me out of the shop, all the way down to the ABC Cinema, where I passed dozens of mini billboards, each one showing posters of Whitney Houston and Kevin Costner. Only then did I catch my breath, before losing it again when I realised that in my haste to leave… I'd forgotten to take my clothes, already folded in a poly bag.

I returned to the shop apologetically, trying hard to appear cool.

The condom was still there on the floor, unopened and untouched.

−Have you forgotten something? asked the girl at the checkout, all white teeth and black roots. Beyond mortified, I lifted the Durex and slipped it back into Mither's old purse. Taking the bag with my clothes in it, I left the shop again, not stopping until I outran my embarrassment.

27

Though the new me was old news before the day was done, my nice new clothes still did their job. It was when Arlene asked me to her party that I knew my fancy threads were having a positive effect on my reputation. Arlene's father, still a lawyer, was going away for a weekend with his latest wife. This meant the house *and his bar* were open. Arlene caught me in the library, trying to cram a little bit of study time in before an exam. I heard her steps before I realised she was at my table. Arlene couldn't just walk quietly into a room, she was far too ostentatious for that, especially after her stint as the lead actress in the school show, a role that earned her great acclaim with her father, stepmother and friends.

−Hi Sadie, she said, pulling a chair out.

I looked up from my books, the pages I needed vandalised with underlining and highlighter pen. Arlene might have seemed untouchable to most, but I'd known (and feared) her since our time together at Nethermains Primary. Now, I just thought she tried too hard, constantly working so she could remain perfect. For me, perfection was so unattainable that I told myself flawlessness was deeply boring, something for two-dimensional paper-thin people like daft Mr Jackson, still my least favourite teacher at school.

−Hello Arlene, I answered, wondering what she was planning.

−So… I love your new top.

−Thank you, I said, slightly surprised.

−It's *very* Kate Moss. She's on the front page of *The Face*.

—Fantastic, I said, wondering what was happening here.

—Yes, you've got that Kate vibe going on. I love it.

—I'm not doing your homework, I told her firmly. —No way.

—I can do my own homework, she laughed, much to the librarian's irritation. —Or, well... I can get other people to do my own homework.

Arlene stopped and reassessed the situation.

—Does that make sense?

—No, but I get what you're trying to say.

—Actually, I was going to invite you to my party.

I nearly fell out of my seat. I'd never been invited to one of Arlene's iconic parties. Being Arlene, who was part of the closest thing Denny had to a Royal Family, she had a certain cachet, and we all knew it. Though I defined myself as an outsider, sometimes I liked to peek through the window and see how the other half lived. I couldn't help my natural curiosity.

—You're inviting me? Why?

—Honestly? I heard you weren't hanging out with Gregor anymore.

—No, I said quietly. —I'm not.

There was nothing more to say, at least nothing more I wanted to say.

—He was a freak, she explained, leaning over like a conspirator.

—What?

—Haven't you heard the rumours? Gregor's a ladyboy.

I bit my nails, getting too much into the quick, drawing a dot of blood.

—I didn't know that, I said feebly.

—Everybody knows.

She paused, then added:

—He better not try and piss in our toilets.

164

–Your party, I said quickly.

–Oh yes. Are you coming then?

–No, I told her.

–What?

–I can't, I explained. –I'm too busy.

–Too busy! she cried out, causing the librarian to slam her hand down on the desk, making more noise than anyone. –What are you doing? Casting spells or something? Come on! It'll be a fun night. I insist you pop along.

Standing up, I froze for a moment, all the papers I was looking at half-stuffed into my bag. Then I suddenly came up with the perfect excuse.

–I can't go to your party. Honestly, I've got to study for the exam.

Before I made it to the door, Arlene called across at me.

–I've got wine!

I sighed. She knew exactly how to sweeten the offer.

–Okay, I said, adjusting the weight of the bag around my shoulder so I could reach in and take out a notebook and pen. –When's it happening?

–This weekend. My house. Eight o'clock.

Before I could speak, she was away, strolling through the library, waving at everyone, telling them how amazing they looked, how they reminded her of Kate Moss on the front page of *The Face* magazine. As I stood, unsure of what to do next, I touched my hair with the tips of my fingers, feeling the curls, the novelty of the style. Then I looked down at my blouse, jeans and shoes. If I'd known all it would take to make friends was change everything about me, I would have done it years ago, just like Gregor had at Nethermains.

Gregor's name brought her to mind and that made my heart hurt.

165

But slowly, the pain was becoming an echo.
Please, I thought, just let me go.

SMALL SHOES

Everyone remembers their first time. Everyone, that is, except for me. All I know is that it happened at Arlene's party, which started off well enough, until the next morning when I woke up with a hangover and a lad lying next to me.

I turned up at Arlene's door, dressed in clothes I'd borrowed from Lily, who was only too happy to get me out of the house for the night, just so her own friends could visit.

−Take this, she'd said while throwing a pink vinyl jacket at me, −and this, oh and remember to wear the leggings with the jacket. Black sets off the pink. Okay? Take this clutch with you. It's very classy indeed.

I nodded dumbly, not quite prepared for the pressure that style inflicts.

The shoes I slipped on were too tight, for a start. I nearly screamed when I took a step forward in them, but managed to smother it with my clutch.

−You can't be stylish and comfortable, warned Lily, who saw my pain.

In another twenty years, I'd remember her words whenever I caught sight of my bunions. But as a teenager going to a party in 1992, it didn't matter. Nothing really mattered. Life was long, everything was possible and bunions were something old people suffered with, not someone my age.

−Okay, said Lily as I limped downstairs towards the main door. −Don't you dare come back too early.

Hobbling out into Little Denny Road, I walked slowly, taking a rest every few steps. A kid on a scooter whizzed past and whistled at me, but I barely heard anything but my feet screaming at me. The shoes were strapped around my ankles, tiny tools of pure torture, each step making me gasp. Eventually, the pain seemed to lessen as I found a rhythm in my movement. It slowly became a quest to keep my shoes on and taking them off, even for a few seconds, would feel like a surrender of sorts, so I kept walking.

Thirty minutes passed on the ten minute journey to Arlene's home.

THE VIRGINITY INCIDENT

Staggering up the path towards the large white door with the gold knocker (probably real gold if her father's salary was anything to go by), I followed the beats and stepped over some empty cans of beer scattered around the kerb. At last, I'd made it. I pressed the doorbell and waited. The ringing interrupted *Rhythm Is A Dancer*, but thankfully ended before the chorus. When the door swung open, it wasn't Arlene, but someone I assumed was her brother, if only because of their very strong likeness.

−Hey, he said, his words slurry, his eyes red. As I stepped from the street into the party, I caught him looking me up and down like he might a restaurant menu. Somehow, I didn't mind. As I walked past everyone, it occurred to me that Arlene had invited the entire school to her party. Well, nearly the entire school. Gregor wasn't here. According to Arlene, they weren't speaking.

We weren't speaking either. Gregor, I told myself, is gone forever.

While thinking about my friend, a hand reached out and passed me a drink.

Without thinking, I tipped it back, feeling a lovely nip rolling down my throat. It tasted good. Looking around,

I tried to find who had given me the glass, only to see everyone holding similar pint tumblers in their hands. Bugger.

–Hey, said a nearby voice, almost fondly. –Sadie?

I recognised a lad whose voice matched his monobrow.

–Hello Robbie, I smiled, though it was surface level at best. Robbie Ferguson was another refugee of Nethermains Primary, having been there the day Mrs Walker asked her question, the one that nearly ruined my life. I hadn't really seen him much since then, even at Denny High, because I was too square to fit into his circle of friends. Yet something was definitely changing. For years I felt I'd been pushed aside because of my family, Mither in particular. She worked the nightshift and her reputation seemed to be my reputation too. Lily somehow escaped censure, her beauty and pizazzy personality giving her an indestructible aura. I wasn't so lucky. For years I'd cursed my misfortune, but I had slowly started to realise that high school was different. Being the daughter of The Woman Who Worked The Nightshift seemed to earn me a certain cachet every bit as notorious as Arlene's reputation, albeit for a different reason.

At some point, I smelled Robbie's breath. That meant he was too close to me. Weirdly, I didn't mind. We started talking about something we had in common, mostly the past, always better from a safe distance. Then he started going on about Rangers Football Club, his favourite subject. Since I found football completely nonsensical, I just nodded my head, hoping the next song would be one I liked. At this point, I needed something with extreme danceability, even (my goodness) *Sesame's Treet* would work. Thankfully, The Shamen came on with *Move Any Mountain*. At last, I thought, decent music.

–I've been to forty games this year, said Robbie. –I'm aiming for sixty.

That wasn't all he was aiming for.

I got another bottle from Arlene's bar, and there were plenty for everyone. None of us knew that her faither wasn't just a lawyer but an alcoholic, and we were all well into his supply. The more I emptied bottles of whatever down my neck, the more I realised Robbie was actually really exciting and everything he said was completely *fascinating*.

We talked all night long about absolutely nothing.

It was nearly ten o'clock when we went upstairs together.

THE NEXT DAY

I woke up and found myself on a floor with a clean cover thrown on top of me and walls that had not a trace of damp on them. My brain took a few seconds to adapt to my new surroundings – but for a horrible second I recalled being back in Cumbernauld, my grandfaither lurking around, always there, always listening. That was gone. Now I had to figure out this new place. The last thing I remembered was drinking and talking, then... being here on the floor. Pulling myself up from the carpet I'd slept on, something tugged at my brain, a slyly nagging psychic signal. Taking inventory of my body, I knew what had happened before I put it into conscious thought.

I'd lost my virginity.

Worse, I couldn't remember losing it.

Suddenly, I had a weird thought:

After you lose your virginity, can you ever find it again?

Sometimes, even in the most important moment, I had the daftest notions.

–Bugger, I said, crawling around the floor trying to find my clothes.

They were gone too. My jeans, top, underwear and...

oh God, Lily's shoes! That was when I really started to panic. How was I going to get out of this house without my clothes? Nothing could be left behind, and that included my socks. Getting up onto my feet, I took a look around the room. There were three washing machines and dryers, plus washing piled up on a table that sat in the corner. Goodness, a room specifically for drying freshly washed clothes. Even in the grip of a deep existential crisis, I grieved my own lack of wealth.

Then I saw Robbie on the floor, snuffling in his sleep, his mouth wide open. He was slowly starting to wake up, making everything deeply awkward. Feeling slightly self-conscious, I grabbed something from the nearby clothes horse and used it to cover myself. There I stood, trying to be confident while holding a rather threadbare towel no-one would ever hang outside to dry.

It said MALLORCA on it.

−What happened last night?

Although I already knew the answer, I still had to ask, regardless.

Robbie looked at me, blinked once, then lifted up the cover to check himself.

−I think I broke you in, he told me proudly.

For him, it was probably the most romantic thing he'd ever said to a girl.

Sighing, I started looking around for my clothes, eventually finding them in a pile near the radiator, at Robbie's feet. Throwing myself together, I snuck out the house and made my way back to 87 Little Denny Road, not knowing how to feel, what to say or what to do after I closed the door behind me.

LOVE HEARTS AND HAPPY FACES

The summer heat was so intense even the cars broke out in a sweat. The heat I felt at school was a different kind, no less uncomfortable. Someone had started writing on the outside wall facing the car park, meaning it would be seen by everyone, including the teachers. It was the prominent advertising space of the school. Someone had scrawled SADIE IS A HOOR in capital letters using eye-catching red ink. Underneath, someone with better handwriting had scribbled JUST LIKE HER MITHER. When girls picked up pens to attack someone, it always bit harder than boys with pens, because girls liked to add love hearts and happy faces at the end of their insult.

Somehow, a smile made it all feel worse.

For the first time since arriving at Denny High, I found myself walking around with a good view of my feet again. But this was good. This was fine. This stopped me catching a glimpse of the red ink and the insult it communicated. And the red ink bandits had struck everywhere I walked. Their messages were on the walls of houses, communal bin cellar doors outside the rows of flats, even the bus shelter. The insults were usually similar, except some added comments about Lily's beauty and what a monster I was in comparison. It made sense to me. We had a different faither, after all.

At first I suspected Valerie, but she was too good to be so awful.

Really, it could have been anyone at school.

Eventually, I broke. I'd been in my room, windows shut, face on pillow when a gurgling noise in my belly and a weakness in my arms and legs reminded me how long it had been since I'd last put food in my mouth. Nearly two days, actually. When I got out into the hall, I found Lily next to the telephone using a red pen to scribble a number on the back of a cigarette packet.

−Where did you get that? I shouted, glaring at the pen.

−From Mither's handbag, she retorted, clearly shocked at the intensity of my upset. I immediately calmed down. Of course I was being foolish.

−Why? asked Lily, trying to find out the truth. −What's wrong?

−Nothing, I told her, my voice sounding like air sneaking out of a flat tyre.

−Is this something to do with what happened at Arlene's party?

Somehow, she knew all about it.

Then again, it was literally all over town.

I didn't say anything. How could I?

I couldn't remember any of it.

GONE IN THE FUZZ

At some point I decided to stop looking at my feet again and start asking questions. What happened to me? That was the main question. Really, from there I could go in other fearful directions. For a while I was frightened because I didn't know if I might be pregnant or not, but when the old pain came, it brought relief alongside gritted teeth and a hard pressed pillow.

Then, I asked everyone at the party about that night.

Literally, I asked *everyone*.

Arlene took me aside, approaching me in English one day before the lesson started. Looking around furtively, she made her move on the way into the class, as she walked over towards her desk at the far side of the room.

−You took Robbie upstairs, she said quietly, looking straight ahead.

I'd already heard that from other people.

−Seriously, you were all over him.

−I don't remember, I said, hoping not to break down in front of her.

−Do you want to know the worst part of it?

I waited, not believing it could get much worse.

−He can't remember either.

As she walked away, I stood and watched, wondering one thing.

Did I say yes?

EDUCATING SADIE

The only way I knew to keep me living a life I hated was to study myself into a state of silence. Text books became a deliverance from everything happening outside 87 Little Denny Road. Mither was delighted and took to telling everyone who made the slightest bit of noise (mostly the new neighbours upstairs or the barking dogs nearby) to SHUT THE FUCK UP because MY DAUGHTER'S STUDYING FOR HER EXAMS. Sometimes she'd throw things at her victims. The odd ornament, possibly a packet of unopened cigarettes. Whatever she had at hand, she chucked at the offender. Even the postman got it when he buzzed up to deliver a fabulous new coat Mither had ordered from the Littlewoods autumn catalogue. In telling people to stop making noise, she made more noise than anyone. Sometimes, whenever I felt the work was getting too much, I thought about the messages on the wall, the insults in red ink. Then, for no reason other than how it sounded, I uttered some words, hoping they'd sounded better to my ears the more I said them aloud.

−If it is to be, it is up to me.

Oh, I said them over and over again, a half-remembered phrase from somewhere. It could almost have been a spell, even though I didn't believe in that stuff anymore. I repeated the phrase in the morning, at lunch, before dinner and one last time as I closed my eyes at night. Studying became my favourite way of avoiding the world. Social avoidance is easy if you have a book in front of you, easier if you have three or four.

29

GIRL AT UNIVERSITY DISOWNS SELF

I was the first girl from Little Denny Road to be accepted into university. My first choice was Strathclyde (in Glesga) and my results were some of the best at Denny High School. Instead of being proud, most people were surprised. Somehow it didn't occur to them that I could pass my exams. In all fairness, it didn't occur to me either until each time I sat down with the white paper in front of me. Each question had an answer and I knew them all. Unsurprisingly, Mither used my success as an excuse to go on a boozy bender. I didn't join her, not after what happened with Robbie. Instead, I took the praise as humbly as possible. During the exam period, I played around with different ideas about what I'd do with the rest of my life. My first thought was to become a teacher, but I didn't want to see the inside of a school ever again. Eventually, I defaulted to my second choice.

−I'm training to be a vet, I told my mither at a party, the one she claimed was for me. In turn, she told her friends.

−She's training to be a doctor.

−I'm not going to be a doctor, I corrected. −I want to be a vet.

−Doctors get paid a lot of money, explained Mither.

By the end of the night, I was going to be a doctor whether I liked it or not.

FRESHERS

The first week I enrolled at university, literally Freshers Week, I came home to an announcement from my mither.

She sat both Lily and I down, made us wait until she was ready, if only to build the tension, then…

She told us what she was planning.

−Finally, I'm quitting the nightshift, she said with a big smile on her face.

My first thought was that she had a new uncle waiting outside the door, but there was no-one there. The news took a few seconds to process. When it happened, I couldn't believe it. She'd attempted this before, of course, many times in the past. But it always ended the same way − Mither eventually deciding she wasn't cut out for work in a factory. She saw it as drudgery and she hated the hours. Besides, she preferred meeting new people, the people of the night, who drove slowly down her street in a car with their lights down low, engines spluttering, one eye on Mither and the other on everything else.

Crazy, I know.

−You're… going to quit? For real?

−Aye. The polis won't leave us alone.

Lily took this to mean the same thing I did.

−They're trying to arrest you?

−They're trying to take their cut, said Mither darkly.

−Thieving bastards, added Lily ruefully.

Before I could encourage or congratulate Mither on her decision, one I'd wanted her to make for years, it soon became apparent she was about to negatively influence my future. Fearfully, I confronted the situation head on.

−How am I going to pay for university?

She didn't reply, so I tried again.

−I need books, bus fare, food and money for clubbing.

Mither lit up a cigarette before she answered my question.

−Get a grant, she said smugly.

−It's not enough! It barely covers my bus fares.

−Then you'll just have to get a job.

—A job? I laughed. —I can't study and work at the same time.

—You'll have to try, said Mither, a new sharpness in her voice warning me that was the end of the matter.

Later that night, following her lead, I started looking at the back pages of *The Stirling Observer* at the Jobseeker adverts. With the paper open at the kitchen table, two ashtrays full of stubs stinking up the air, I started hunting for a job that would help pay my way through my education. Erratically, I sketched out my first CV, trying to write as neatly as possible. My handwriting always depended on the sort of pen I used to write.

Once I was done, I gave the A4 sheet on the table a quick edit. Sadly, that was the problem. As a girl on the verge of eighteen, my entire life fit neatly onto one sheet of paper. My second attempt at writing a CV was much better because I wrote a load of lies on it. Lying to people was hard, but lying to a piece of paper didn't feel like a compromise of my values. Could I operate a computer? Indeed I could. Did I have experience in handling cash? Of course I did. Could I operate heavy machinery? Duh. Lying, it turned out, was the easiest way to get employers to write back. Once I knew that, I couldn't stop. At last, I'd broken my inconvenient habit of being honest in every situation. The world was there for the taking. The worst lie I told came after one particular question on an application form to work at The Mariner Centre as a lifeguard.

The form asked, *Can you swim to an acceptable standard?*

I wrote YES and sealed the form in an envelope using the spit on my tongue.

Could I swim to an acceptable standard? Could I fuck! Dog shit bobbed along a river better than I did.

Terms and Conditions

Before I could even consider accepting any offers of work, all future employers had to agree to my terms and conditions. The hours had to be part-time. As the first girl in Little Denny Road to go to university, I couldn't work a nine-to-five job. Tea breaks, of course, were essential. At least three a day, fifteen minutes minimum.

The temperature in the workplace couldn't be too hot.

The temperature in the workplace couldn't be too cold.

My uniform couldn't be made from polyester, the frumpiest fabric ever.

That was it. My terms and conditions.

Surprisingly, only one employer got back to me…

Choreography

The Mariner Centre was only a twenty minute journey away on the bus, making it an ideal scenario for me. It was booked and busy during the day, which meant I applied for the later hours. Most families in Falkirk had taught their bairns to swim in its chemical-treated waters. Mither, however, didn't so much teach me as throw me in so she could watch me thrash and splash. The thick discoloured tiles, always rough on the soles of my size eight feet, kept me rooted onto something firm whenever the water wobbled.

Luckily, as a lifeguard, I didn't need to get wet.

The hours were flexible and I got free access to a gym I ignored in favour of the canteen. My dinner was chips, sometimes twice in the same day. I practically lived on chips, counting them as part of an organic diet. When things were quiet, I sat on a stool near the edge of the smallest pool, reading up on my notes from the latest lecture, everything I needed to memorise faithfully underlined in yellow so bright I almost couldn't see it on the white paper. My uniform was shorts, a t-shirt and a lanyard that I positioned so no-one saw my details.

Later, I discovered I got the job because no-one else applied for it.

One night, after a long journey on the Glasgow to Falkirk bus, I managed to arrive at work barely on time. Settling into the chair by the side of the adult pool, using the time to study, I realised someone was splashing water onto my textbooks. I'd bought them from John Smith & Sons and they'd cost most of my wage. Infuriated, I looked up to see a pensioner with her legs in the air.

Choreographed swimming, I thought. How annoying.

It took me a few seconds to realise she was drowning.

−Help, she managed feebly, her voice full of gurgle and gargle.

Something stopped me from reacting. Incredulity, possibly.

She tried again, but this time went under.

A word came out of the water. It sounded like *cramp*.

−Someone, I cried out. −Anyone. Please. We need help!

Eventually someone came out of the changing room and he did the whole Baywatch bit, diving into the water, cutting through until he reached the drowning woman. She was safe, but shaken, with a bad case of What if? Tellingly, no-one asked how I felt, although, considering they now knew I'd lied on my CV, that wasn't a surprise. Later that night, I was asked up to the main office. It was a degrading experience. The manager was barely older than me and had been redeployed from another area in the council. One rumour was that he used to be a gravedigger and now he was in charge of The Mariner Centre. His name was Darren and he had a nose pitted with tiny holes that could be seen from the other side of a room. His hair was greasy and looked like it had been parted by a hatchet.

I stood in front of him, knowing this wouldn't end well.

It didn't.

He screamed in my face, his breath reeking of molten cabbage.

Did the café even have cabbage on the menu? Surely not?

−That old lady nearly died, he raged. −Do you understand how serious this is? She could have drowned while you were just sitting there reading.

−I wasn't reading, I said, hastily correcting him. −I was studying.

This only made him angrier, the residue of hot cabbage cooking slowly on his teeth. But I couldn't say anything. I'd done enough damage.

−You should have told us you couldn't swim.

−But you wouldn't have given me the job if I'd told you the truth.

−Fucking right I wouldn't have!

A few minutes later, I was at the bus stop outside with my backpack, books and a uniform I'd promised to return as soon as possible. Only employees were allowed to wear that uniform − and I wasn't one anymore.

Worse, the bus was an hour late.

PASSING THE TEST

Strathclyde University wasn't what I needed it to be. I'd worked towards being there and when I finally arrived, it felt like another disappointment. Nothing changed how I felt about myself. Every night I stood at different bus stops across the Central Belt, wondering why nothing could shift this feeling in me, heavy and horrible. I turned

180

corners, walked through corridors and sat in great big rooms full of strangers scribbling away in jotters. I had wanted that life, now I didn't know what I wanted. This wasn't meant to be my story. I was meant to break free, not fall into the same traps as my mither and sister. My results were terrible, each test a bigger failure than the last. At this point, Mither was too busy with her new job to care. She had scored herself a position with Avon, representing them in Little Denny Road. She didn't seem to realise how much time I spent in the flat, isolated in my room. On the rare occasions she noticed, I just lied. By that point I was lying more often than not. She believed me. Of course she did. Everyone knew I always told the truth.

It didn't last. A brown envelope grassed me up.

It looked official enough to worry Mither, forever on the lookout for letters with little see-through plastic windows on the front. These were usually notices of unpaid rent or another debt she owed but couldn't settle. Nosiness also played a part in what happened. Even though my name was on the front, Mither steamed it open anyway. That's how she discovered I hadn't been attending lectures. Worse, I'd already failed some modules and was no longer welcome. Academic dismissal, they called it. I braced myself for the shockwave, but it didn't happen. Somehow, Mither's lack of reaction was worse than her anger.

−It's the oldest test in the world, she told me.

−What test? I asked.

−Can you stand on your own two feet?

Just like all my other tests, I failed this one too.

I became the first girl in Little Denny Road to drop out of university.

30

I spent 1995 feeling as ignored as the bad B-side of a single that failed to chart. Without a job or my daily trip into Glasgow to keep me busy, I started to disappear from the outside world. Windows remained closed. Doors stayed shut. The meter in the hall cupboard chewed up power cards by the dozen, if only because the television and kettle never seemed to stop. Feeling guilty at how much money Mither was spending on my behalf, I decided to help around the flat. Every morning, I'd drag our Hoover out of the cupboard, the one Mither bought, back in 1992, thinking she'd get a free flight to Orlando (not even Hoover could clean up *that* mess). I'd spend ten minutes vacuuming the living room and hall, just to give myself something to do.

Mither, especially, appreciated the help, considering she was regularly touring Denny, selling Avon products door-to-door. According to her, being a saleswoman wasn't so different to working the nightshift, except the hours were better and the polis weren't always sticking their batons where they weren't wanted. She was remarkably successful too, always getting orders, forever dispensing wisdom and youth via her little jars of All-In-One crème. Everyone in the area was so terrified of her that they bought what she was selling just to get her away from their front door. From a distance, Mither came across like an amalgam of a mob enforcer and Dolly Parton. Because of her success, I had to divert the Hoover around all the paper bags that quickly piled up on the kitchen lino, jumbled orders waiting to be collected.

Soon enough, Mither mentioned the dreaded 'r' word.

—Rent, she told me while putting together someone's

order. Whoever they were, they really liked their lipstick. Every colour possible was being dropped into a wide open paper bag, the Avon logo prominently placed.

−Rent? I gagged. There was me in the background, thinking I'd get a cuppa without any fuss. −But I'm your daughter. This is my house too.

Without giving me even a side-glance, Mither shot back,

−You're draining me dry, hen. You need to get to the job centre pronto.

The kettle started boiling, like me, and I found myself getting louder, desperation in each octave, my voice peaking at the pitch of a shrill whistle.

−I couldn't possibly be seen at the job centre. What would people think?

−That you're looking for work?

In the pit of my stomach, I felt juices gurgle, giving me the same feeling that came just before I hit the toilet. Suddenly, without a chance to prepare myself, I realised my long-held way of life was coming to an ignoble end. If I didn't get a job soon, I'd be down the street in Denny Town standing in a queue outside the Job Centre, looking at cards on the board, signing my name and explaining to strangers what I was doing to find work.

No fucking way.

So I went out and got a job.

Again.

You're being a little extra

According to a box at the back of the newspaper, there was a company looking for extras for television and film for a new production. It was being partly funded by Scottish Screen, the snazzy new organisation set up to boost Scottish cinema.

−Why the fuck not? I said after reading the advert for the tenth time. It seemed easy enough. All I had to do was fill in a form, take a photograph and send it to a place called Alexa's Extras. The main office was in Glesga, now just another stop on the bus. It didn't take long to receive a call. This was encouraging because it meant I was perfect for the job − or they were totally desperate and had no choice. The next day (after raiding the jar under the sink), I found myself in Maryhill, sitting in Café D'Jaconelli alongside a handful of other extras while two Ewans shared a milkshake. McGregor and Bremner, both hot new talents.

I hadn't been on set for long but already I had realised many of the background extras harboured dreams of becoming serious actors. Me? I couldn't care less. I just wanted Mither to stop bitching about rent money. Also, it got me out the flat for a while. I turned up, sat in a red pleather booth, and pretended to be in a deep, fulfilling conversation with another actor who kept 'talking' over me. At one point, I booted him underneath the table.

−Shut the fuck up, I mouthed, hoping he could lipread and the camera wouldn't catch me. Most of the crew were Scottish, though the director came from Manchester and had had a hit a few years earlier with a film about flatmates who carved up a dead body. I hadn't seen it yet. One of the other extras, a bloke who only talked to me because no-one would talk to him, seemed similarly indifferent.

−This time last year, I was filming *Braveheart*.

−Oh really? I said brightly, hoping for gossip on Mel Gibson. What was he really like behind the scenes? Did he have sparrow legs under his kilt?

−Yes, sniffed my fellow extra in his Edinburgh accent. −Now that was a prestige production. If you press pause during the battle sequence, you can see me in the right-hand corner waving my sword.

I ruined a take by laughing right in his face.

We later moved to the Volcano Club, where I had to dance in the background. My dancing was basically the real-life version of Wile E. Coyote falling off a cartoon cliff, arms flapping, fur flying. The blame rested squarely on the perfectly proportioned shoulders of Jonny Lee Miller. His peroxide white hair yanked my eyes in his direction every few minutes. I couldn't stop looking!

Sadly, it wasn't Jonny but an extra who tried his luck with me.

–We aren't socks but I think we'd make a great pair.

–Ha, I said. –Odd socks don't match.

–Is that a no, then?

–It's a hell to the fuck *no*.

–Fucking hoor, he muttered under his breath.

I was too busy staring at Jonny Lee Miller to care.

THE MADE FOR TELEVISION MOVIE

In the lunch queue on set for another film, some made-for-telly flick filmed in Scotland because the tax breaks were reasonable, I found myself in the queue, chatting to another stranger. Any illusion I had about the glitzy world of showbiz was starting to crumble. Worse, I had to wear a ghastly fake fur bikini and hold a fake spear because I wasn't Sadie Relish anymore, I was a warrior maiden whose name was WARRIOR MAIDEN #8. Lunch breaks became my escape and that's how I ended up meeting my first real boyfriend, another horny extra who'd been stealthily checking me out for five minutes at least. Either that or he had squinty eyes and he was really looking past me at the roast potatoes. He had thick, messy, dirty blond hair, an unkempt beard that was genuinely shabby rather than designer hipster and a nose that seemed to clash with his face. Some of the extras spent hours in the make-up van being transformed into hideous creatures, the large

Orcs that served as the antagonists for the glossy Canadian warriors and their glossier teeth.

–Hello, he said while we waited in the queue.

–Hi, I smiled. –I love your prosthetic makeup. Did it take long to do?

–I'm not wearing any make-up.

I turned away, completely mortified at my mistake. I honestly thought he was one of the extras playing the monstrous Orcs that terrorised the lead cast. He didn't seem to mind though, in fact it bent him over with belly laughter. As we stood together in the queue, I found myself reassessing the man in front of me. He was a bit older. I could tell. His voice was deep, growly, the sort of voice that could get him work as a voiceover artist on a safety prevention film or talking over the 0800-DIAL-A-MAN advert shown late at night on STV.

With all that in mind, I decided to start again.

–Hello, I said, holding out my hand. –I'm Sadie.

–Well, Sadie, I'm Harvey. Pleased to meet you, my ferocious warrior lass.

It was Beauty and the Beast on the lowest of low budgets. As we sat at a table, picking away at the food on our plates, Harvey told me how much he wanted to shift gear into serious roles but couldn't quite get the main spotlight to move towards him. His frustration was visible on his face, even with the beard covering half of it. While taking far too long to chew a piece of chicken (that had been scorched in a deep fat fryer hotter than hell), Harvey explained in that wonderfully drawling voice that he was too freakish to be taken seriously. He knew how it felt to be on the outside.

–I get hired for Halloween parties to dress up as Frankenstein, he moaned.

–Frankenstein's Monster, I corrected helpfully.

Harvey, sadly, didn't read anything other than scripts,

huge wads of paper with plenty of dialogue, none of it underlined for him. The closest he came to reading was the little text that accompanied the pictures of women in the magazines he stashed under his bed in the flat.

I'M SASHA, said one of those little captions. I'M FROM SWEDEN AND I'M GOING TO BE A POLITICIAN BECAUSE I ENJOY SERVING THE PUBLIC. I'M A 32DD AND THE DRAPES MATCH THE CURTAINS.

I found the magazines one night while doing an impromptu spring clean of his bedroom, days after we first slept together. In between gulps of lukewarm tea, I flicked through his magazines, before arranging each edition in order of publication date so they ran in sequence.

Once finished, I slid them tidily underneath the bed.

A few days afterwards, knowing that I enjoyed reading, Harvey bought me a new book. It wasn't my birthday, nonetheless I was excited to see his gift.

–It's *The Kama Sutra*, he said before I even got the paper off.

–I don't believe in karma, I told him, not quite catching his comment.

The next book he bought me was a vintage copy of Leonora Carrington's *The Hearing Trumpet*, and I almost fell in love with him.

THE OFFER

Mither despised Harvey, regarding him as a bone-idle poser with no prospects. Kindness, good banter and manners meant nothing to her if money, steadiness and routine didn't come as part of the package. Though her own life was unconventional, she still enjoyed a sort of stability. In the eyes of my mither, an actor looking for his next big role was worse than useless. Also, and more significantly, she hated the age gap, which was a considerable fifteen years. I didn't know that until our fourth date and by then I was already trying to be in love with him. At one point, Mither even offered Harvey money to break up with me. Harvey, I learned, asked how much he was being offered.

–A lot, said Mither. –Enough to kickstart your acting career.

–Okay, he replied. –Give it here.

He took the money and didn't run.

31

British scientists cloned a sheep and Lily decided this heralded the end of the world. I was twenty-one and she was twenty-six, both of us far too old to be living with each other. The cloned sheep was one thing, but Lily saw signs and portents in the strangest places. Terry Venables quitting the England squad. Mad Cow Disease. The Duke and Duchess of York's divorce. The Spice Girls reaching number one with *Wannabe*. Everywhere Lily turned, she saw nothing but dirt and darkness. At first, I tried to pass her behaviour off as some sort of phase, a lunar eclipse of the brain. But it became increasingly more difficult to understand when Lily locked herself away for a week, only leaving her room to use the toilet and buy bottles of Evian.

Eventually, Mither took me aside and we talked in private.

−I'm worried, she said quietly. How very unlike my mither. She was never worried or quiet. Suddenly everything felt far more serious now.

−You're worried? I asked.

−About Lily. Remember your sister? Look at the state of her. She isn't even brushing her hair, for the love of fuck!

−She's been a bit intense, it's true.

−Intense?

−Well... I tried again. −She isn't quite herself.

−I'm not putting up with this shit. The smells coming from her room. Like shite on a frying pan. Horrible!

I had to tread very carefully. Even though we'd grown slightly closer, I had to remember that Lily would always be Mither's favourite daughter, something I'd learned to

189

accept gracefully. It was a permanent fact of being alive just like the air, the sun, the moon, the stars and Tommy Sheridan's tan.

−We need to find out what's wrong with her, said Mither, looking through entire walls towards Lily's room. Unexpectedly feeling bonded to my mither in a way that rarely happened, I stood up and took charge, hoping to be the favourite for a while. Together we headed out the kitchen into the hall, then we turned left. Lily's door was shut, of course. I stepped forward and rapped on it with my knuckles.

−Lily, I called out. −Can you let us in for a second?

−Fuck off! she yelled.

Mither's eyes were wide as she barged past me.

This time, I pushed back.

−Let me deal with this, I begged.

Folding her arms over her chest, Mither waited, stewing in her own huff.

She wouldn't wait for long though. Already she was tapping her toes.

I tried again, hoping to sort this out before it became untenable.

−Lily, we're worried about you.

The door slowly opened, just an inch, and a single eye, bit of nose and mouth appeared in the crack. I turned and gave Mither a smug look. See, it said, I'm not that useless after all.

−I'm fine, said Lily, not quite understanding why we were worried.

I tried to say something reassuring, but Mither's patience was finally gone.

−Are you on drugs?

Lily seemed slightly unsure as to how this should be answered.

−I'm smoking a bit of weed. Does that count?

−For fuck sake! I cried out.

Her voice came from behind the door again.

−What else am I meant to do? Be an alky like you?

−I'm not an alky, I cried out. −I'm a fan of fine wine and good patter.

−Well don't lecture me! she shouted. −I'm over it all. Just leave me alone.

If I were a stranger and my first introduction to my sister had been her voice behind the door right then, I'd have assumed she was a child, not a grown woman.

−You can't stay locked up in your bedroom forever, I said.

−Piss off! That's exactly what I'll be doing.

−It *must* be depression, said Mither in the background.

Ignoring the unhelpful side voice, I continued trying to reach my sister.

−Is there anything we can do?

…

−Is there anything we can get you?

It turned out, there was something Lily wanted more than anything in the world.

−I want a Pot Noodle, she said, suddenly sounding herself again.

−Okay. What flavour?

She didn't respond and I tried again.

−What flavour?

−Chicken and Mushroom.

Right, I thought. I can do this.

Immediately, I ran to the kitchen. From there, I counted pennies from the jar under the sink and flung my jacket around me, one arm in a sleeve, the other struggling to get itself all the way through. I wanted to see my sister happy again and with luck, gain enough of her confidence that she might open up to me, explain why her behaviour had been so strange over the last few months. Mither,

191

meanwhile, just stood around, not knowing what to do, but understanding that barging in with fists flying wasn't the way forward. The trip to the shop lasted a few minutes. I passed Mr Chadha's garden and ignored the urge to peek in through the gate, take in a little beauty.

The fairies could wait. The munchies could not.

MUNCHIES

Nothing much had changed at Little Denny Mart, other than the owners. The products on the shelves were still the same too. Familiarity allowed me to be a little faster in finding... nothing. At first, I wasn't sure, but a quick look around the shelf proved me right the first time.

There were no Chicken and Mushroom Pot Noodles left on the shelf.

–Fuck, I said, heading back out into the street. Eventually, after wandering around town trying to find what my sister needed, I ended up in the Co-op down in Stirling Street. Forty minutes had passed by the time I returned home.

By then, Mither and Lily were smoking together.

It wasn't a Benson & Hedges.

–I've found out what's bothering your sister, said Mither, sniggering.

–What?

–The Millennium, announced Mither grandly.

–The... what?

Mither suddenly got serious in her cloud of smoke.

THE MILLENNIUM

It was the first time I'd heard that word used, but I'd hear it more often as we all approached the end of the decade. Soon enough, everyone knew about the Millennium. It was a word that buzzed loudly in our consciousness.

'Millennium' looked as good on Scrabble boards as it did on newspaper front pages. Each day there was a new warning in the press about deadly forces waiting to be unleashed on the world the second the long hand passed the little hand. Everything was going to reset, including society. Or maybe it wouldn't. No-one actually knew what would happen and that gap between certainty and uncertainty was the place my sister found herself stuck when she had nothing better to do than smoke, snort and swallow. My sister constantly looked up at the sky, wondering when the madness would begin, not realising it was already happening and we were all caught up in it.

Truth serum

Months passed, stuff happened, but Lily remained locked in her bedroom.

Eventually, even I lost my patience.

−This is stupid, I shouted. −You need to start going out again.

−You just want the house for yourself and your boyfriend, she screamed back, the door between us doing little to blunt her anger.

Well, I thought. This is cool. For once my sister is jealous of me.

−He's auditioning for a role in a panto, I said proudly.

−He won't get it, she told me, much to my irritation.

−You don't know that.

−He's a loser, Sadie. You're too good for him.

No-one had ever told me I was too good for anything.

−He's taking me out tomorrow night, I said quietly.

−When the world ends, there'll no more nights out.

−Do you really believe the world is about to end?

−Aye, she said, lighting up, enjoying what might be her final hours on Planet Earth. −Don't you?

Suddenly I wanted to scream and shake Lily by her shoulders.

−That stuff is frying your brain to bits.

−Nah, it relaxes me. It takes the edge off and slows it all down.

I had no idea what she meant so she attempted to put her feeling into words. −Something really terrible is coming. Can't you feel it?

−That's the dumbest shit I've ever heard, I shouted. −Life is terrible.

Then, in the same breath, I added a caveat.

−Except when it's not.

−But the Millennium…

−It's just a date on a calendar, a line at the top of a page on a newspaper. Anyway, what's the fuss? It's another three years away and…

A door slammed in my face before I could make a case for my sister to give up her weed stash. Alone in the hall, I headed to the kitchen where I found Mither, who was back on the Benson & Hedges. Together, we sat quietly at the table where I nearly started smoking for the first time. I fought the urge, beat the craving and defaulted to food. Suddenly I was happy again.

A CAR CRASH IN ANOTHER COUNTRY

Two days later, Princess Diana died in a car accident somewhere in Paris, her driver too drunk to turn the wheel away from a wall. Suddenly the apocalyptic mood of the nation matched that of my sister, and I couldn't help but think maybe she was right all along and the world was coming to an end.

32

I didn't have a job and university had been disastrous, so what came next? Nothing, at first. I spent my time at Harvey's flat where we watched daytime telly. The schedule was full of game shows and people speaking Gaelic. At night we watched films, including *Trainspotting*, with Jonny Lee Miller being the best part of every scene, none of which included me. Not that I minded being cut. Actually, I could barely stand to see myself in the mirror, never mind on a big (or small) screen.

Curiously, Harvey seemed to take joy in my misfortune. He couldn't help himself. Envy and pettiness had become essential ingredients in our daily routine. We bickered over everything. I started to see for myself how the life of an unemployed actor was as unfulfilling as mine, an unemployable failed student. The glamour was gone. But we made each other laugh and on most days that was enough. When it wasn't enough, I needed more. 'More' meant… something I couldn't put into words… a cloudy, nameless thing that would make my life better if I had it.

Sometimes I thought this might be marriage, that I'd find my direction in life if Harvey got down on one knee and asked the question, but this idea passed quickly, like footage on fast forward. Maybe I needed to start fresh? Leave Harvey and never look back. But where would I go? How would I afford it? Of course, I needed more money. I always needed money. Between us, Harvey and I made a pittance from the dole. Fortunately, he owned his flat. It was a gift from his elderly faither after he passed away. Harvey explained that he had been his faither's registered carer. Each week money appeared in his bank account, cash that kept everything moving smoothly along. Harvey didn't mention his faither much, making him all the more interesting to me. Even his death was mysterious, something that seemed to change every time he told the story.

—I used my grief when I was onstage at The Pavilion, said Harvey, forever trying to appear aloof and enigmatic when I needed him to be honest and human.

His pretentious announcements always made me roll my eyes, giving me a near-constant migraine only the strongest painkillers could shift. Even his post-coital chit-chat felt relentlessly overdramatic, reducing me to an audience of one in a theatre with bolted doors. I often asked myself why we were together. It wasn't the sex, of course. Whenever that happened, I lay frozen beneath the bed covers, wondering when it would be over. Despite that, I liked Harvey's company, the feeling of his warmth in the bed next to me. I decided it was worth enduring one thing in order to enjoy the other.

1998

Somehow, I ended up working in a bar in Falkirk. It was an exclusive establishment, according to the advert at the back of the newspaper, the sort of place where people sipped from cocktail glasses rather than necking booze out a bottle. Without any qualifications, there was no chance of getting a job in retail. Instead, I defaulted to washing and drying dishes. Spending my shift in the kitchen meant being around the chef, who saw himself as a creator of fine cuisine rather than a glorified chip fryer for a bunch of snooty wannabe WAGs. Just like his role model, Gordon Ramsey, his name was Gordon and he wore white overalls. He also swore a lot, thinking that's how great chefs behaved in the kitchen. Maybe he was right? Worse than that, he was never far away from his chef's hat. Whenever he moved, it wobbled unsteadily on his head, which was as shiny as a Dalek's dome. We spent a lot of time together in the kitchen where he cooked, fried and counted the money he was stealing from the bar outside.

No-one knew that, of course. Not at first, anyway.

Nights with Gordon were often surreal and terrifying.

−I lost my virginity to Sharleen Spiteri, he revealed unexpectedly.

−What?

−The lead singer of Texas.

I knew that, of course. Chris Evans played her songs relentlessly.

−Oh, I said, not quite knowing what to say.

−Aye. She wanted more. Can't blame her. I'm a sex magnet.

I almost gagged on testosterone and Lynx. Fighting off the urge to chuck a plate at him, I concentrated on drying the cutlery with a dishtowel that smelled like cat pish. The hotel/bar presented itself as a thoroughly modern establishment from the outside, a gentrified metropolitan place to stay for a few nights in Falkirk.

Behind the scenes things were very different. The owners cared little about their business, only making their presence felt once a year, just in time for the health and safety inspection. As a result, the cupboards were full of jars that had thick layers of stoor on their lids. The freezers badly needed defrosting, even the blood from the plastic packs of meat had frozen into gory icicles, dark red fangs hanging sharply over the rim of the shelf. There was no thought for keeping different meats apart and I must have been the only member of staff who washed my hands after using the toilet.

Eventually, the lack of care dealt a killer blow to the hotel's credibility. One evening, during a themed night celebrating Chinese New Year, I watched Gordon freak out about something so immense that he struggled to physically process it. He couldn't stop pacing around the kitchen while I arranged spring rolls, bought in bulk from a branch of Pharmafoods. Eventually, he came out with it.

−Mark fucking Hateley is here!

−Who?

−He's a famous fucking footballer.

−I've never heard of him.

−He's a fucking Rangers legend.

−Stop swearing, I snapped. No slouch in the department of bad language myself, I'd suddenly decided it was becoming too much. Gordon blinked a few times, seemingly surprised by my outburst. Saying nothing more, I waited for the order so I could start prepping the meal.

−He wants a roll and chips.

−But it's Chinese cuisine night. Thursday is always Chinese cuisine night.

−I don't fucking care. It's Mark Hateley. Give him what he wants!

I began to panic, my fingers tingling with anxiety.

−But he can't get a roll and chips, I argued.

−Why the fuck not?

−Because I've just binned the last roll.

I'd tossed it away only minutes earlier because of the tell-tale patches of blue dotted around its surface. The next delivery of rolls and bread would arrive early the next morning, well before I started my shift. But this wasn't good enough for Gordon, who looked ill at the thought of disappointing a football icon. Quickly, he improvised a hasty decision.

−Take it out the fucking bin and scrape it clean.

−What? You can't be serious. That's vile.

−Do it and put some chips in the fryer.

Something vitally important suddenly occurred to me.

−Does he want chippy chips or fries?

Gordon looked ready to detonate, his terror blotching his skin bright red.

−I... don't know. He didn't say. Oh God, I don't know!

I always favoured fries, they tasted better to me. Something about the way they were cooked, the hot fat that soaked into the potato, made them irresistible. Better still, they were thin cut, while chippy chips were chunky, fat, exactly the way I felt after eating a bag of them. Then again, I never said no to chippy chips wrapped in newspaper. Every now and then I grabbed a pizza supper from The Golden Chip in Denny, always asking for an extra-large can of Diet Irn-Bru to go with it, the best dinner for a boring weekend.

−Look, I said. −Why don't you go out and ask him what chips he wants?

But Gordon was too scared to approach his hero. He held onto the side of the refrigerator to keep from falling to the floor. I craned my neck and peeked outside the kitchen to try and get a glimpse of the football superstar who'd turned the chef into a fool. Seated at a large table was a man with long black hair that reached the nape of his neck. He was dressed in a tracksuit that made him look even more nondescript. Boys have the strangest heroes, I thought. But footballing legend or not, I wasn't going to leave the kitchen.

Gordon suddenly lost his hat and his mind.

−Just give him chippy chips, he almost screamed.

I cut the chips straight from a bag of tatties we had had sitting underneath the sink for over a year and went about frying them for our VIP guest outside.

Two days later, Mark Hateley didn't show up for training.

Food poisoning, alleged the back pages of the Daily Record.

Guess who got blamed for nearly killing a football legend?

It wasn't long before I was looking for another job.

CEEFAX (P400)

By the time I got back from the Job Centre, Harvey was busy skimming through Ceefax on BBC1 to find a cheap holiday. The blocky green and brown palm tree graphic made me realise how much I needed to get away. I hadn't been on holiday in years, not since the disastrous trip to Aviemore. Eagerly, I threw myself onto the couch beside him, hoping to find out where we were going.

The black screen flashed up with bright green letters and though it should have been harsh on the eyes, it actually felt soothing. Each sub-page took time to load up, so we waited patiently for the next screen. Nearly five minutes later, we finally made it to the first page. Since the destinations were listed alphabetically, we were immediately looking at going to America. Horribly, I forgot Aviemore also started with the letter 'A'. Despite my fears, I asked, −Where are we going?

−I'm going to Amsterdam, said Harvey instantly.

−Aren't we going together? You know… like, me and you?

−But Sadie, he told me gently, −I like going away by myself.

I didn't understand, so I fought from my corner of the couch.

−You can't go yourself. What are you going to do? Who will you talk to?

−I don't want to talk to anyone, that's the point.

−Okay, I snapped. −Then you won't mind me not

being here when you get back. (Under my breath, I added:
−Arsehole.)

−I suppose not.

That wasn't the answer I'd expected, but the one I
wanted, only I didn't realise it until he said it aloud. That's
how we broke up. It was nineteen ninety-nine. I had no
job, no prospects and my first real relationship came to a
spluttering end on a couch in front of a television.

There were a few things left to say before I walked out
the door.

−You're a wanker.

−You're the worst shag I've ever had, he shouted back.

For someone whose dick looked like a Clanger, this
was a low blow. My only recourse was to stomp down on
him, really make him feel it.

−Well you're the worst actor I've ever fucked.

This stopped Harvey briefly.

−What other actor did you fuck?

−Jonny Lee Miller, I screamed when I was safely out
the door.

A lie, but it felt so much better than telling the truth.

87 LITTLE DENNY ROAD (AGAIN)

The flat was empty when I got back.

It looked exactly how I felt.

33

Hey Mr DJ

Harvey found himself a new girlfriend and she looked nothing like me. Not that I cared. I was too busy meeting my future husband at a Hogmanay party alongside the Denny locals, everybody partying our way out of one century into another. While Lily braced herself for all the lights to go out as 1999 became 2000, I ran headfirst towards the unknown, hoping to collide with something better.

The party itself had been a last minute decision made on the toss of ten pence. Heads, I go out. Tails, I stay at home on the couch watching Rikki Fulton as the bells chimed. I flipped the coin and got the Queen's side profile in silver. An hour later I made my way down to Sylvester's where I passed a smiling cat and a brand new bouncer at the door. Fraser, who I'd later marry, was also at the club, full of coke, swagger and himself. Not that I noticed him at first. I'd actually spent the night trying to get the very hot DJ to notice me, but his attention was fixed on the vinyl records and turntable in front of him. He filled most of his set playing NME approved artists like The Chemical Brothers, Basement Jaxx, Beck, Missy Elliot and even a bit of Mogwai, who cleared the floor. In a panic, the hot DJ went to the default song that never failed to rescue his sets during the many times he emptied the venue.

It was during a spin of Abba's *Winner Takes It All* that I finally summoned up the courage to talk to him. Actually, I'd already drunk a whole bottle of courage. Casually, I approached the stage, trying my hardest to look confident and attractive with my dyed green hair, the colour of cabbage, an experiment gone wrong.

Finally, after waiting out the chorus, I leaned over and made contact.

—Do you like my sexy dress?

As chat-up lines went it wasn't great, but I had to work within my means. Besides, it *was* a sexy dress. Gold and slick, it shimmered over my shoulders, flowing all the way to my bare knees. Though I wasn't a total fashionista, I had ultimately chosen my New Year outfit for functionality, having endured the pain of a bunion since that time I walked to Arlene's house in Lily's shoes, which squeezed my toes into new shapes. I had managed to score some outfits from the Clearance rack at Red or Dead. So what was the hot DJ's opinion of my sexy dress?

He took a glance at me from behind the booth and smiled.

—No thanks, he said snidely.

Hmph.

SADIE, DON'T BE A DAFTY

This would have been enough to put most women off, but they weren't shameless like me. Undeterred, I watched as the hot DJ raised a fist to the beat, getting into the tune as he spun his records. That's when I noticed he was wearing a Primal Scream t-shirt. He was hip, but not hip enough he couldn't throw a little Abba into the mix. What a quirky dude. My heart ached for something I couldn't have, a strong yearning that came too often those days, the sort of intense emotion that made me feel both sick and strong. Somehow, I had to make him play some love songs for me and me alone. Sadly, there was a problem in my plan, an awkward complication that forced me to be very careful with my next step.

The hot DJ had a girlfriend.

Her name, apparently, was Maria.

How did I solve a problem like Maria?

Not easily.

−Hoor, snarled Maria from nowhere. −He belongs to me and so does this!

The lighting rig lit Sylvester's in spasmodic intervals, making it difficult to see exactly what Maria had in her hand. I had to doublecheck the lights were actually real, rather than a harsh after-effect of the ecstasy I'd popped earlier before my bottle of courage. Lily would never know because I'd never tell her, otherwise how could I be morally superior again? Feeling rather unhappy, I started to think I'd bought a dog worming tablet again instead of ecstasy.

−I don't understand, I said, peering closer. −What belongs to you?

−This!

Maria had reached down and cupped her right hand on the DJ's dick, getting a rather large handful of what was happening between his legs. He didn't pay any attention, his focus completely on the record he was sliding from the sleeve. A few seconds later, Eiffel 65's *Blue (Da Ba Dee)* blasted from the sound system, getting the students up on their feet, bopping alongside each other. Petrified by indecision, I didn't move away from the stage like I should have. I waited dizzily, considering whether or not to fight the crazy girl for the man of my dreams. Eventually, I relented, because Maria looked like a jaundiced She-Hulk and I didn't want to die on a grotty dancefloor.

−You win, I said meekly, backing away before Maria decided to skull-drag me across the dancefloor hair-first. The only time anyone would ever see me wailing and screaming at a party was when I turned forty. As I slunk away from the booth, dejected at my failure to pull, I literally collided into someone doing the funky chicken.

Ironic dad dancing, or so I assumed. That was until I got a chance to size up my assailant. He was too tall, for a start.

−Oafish fuckwit, I snapped.

−Sorry, shouted the idiot, his voice struggling over the beat. Somehow, I felt guilty for being so abrasive. Besides, it was probably my fault we'd hit each other. Even though I was well past twenty, I still found myself looking down at my feet when I walked. In some ways, I was still that girl at Nethermains.

−Don't worry, I said, regretting the way I'd spoke to him.

−I won't, he replied, laughing.

This was the first time I met Fraser, who would go on to make me laugh, smile and cry. Mostly cry. But in that moment, his obnoxiousness seemed more like rebelliousness, charming me even though I was old enough to know better. Maybe being turned down by the DJ wasn't a bad thing? Suddenly another song started in the background.

It was Abba, again.

−Take a chance on me, said the man I would eventually marry.

I did. I threw my future at him.

That's how I ended up married, miserable and in a mess.

34

Because the brainwashing started early, I wanted a fairy tale white wedding, the sort Disney sold to idealistic little girls all over the world. When I walked through the church, I wanted to wear the most beautiful gown, something luxurious with a train that went out the door and around the block. Afterwards, I wanted a huge party with a ridiculously expensive designer cake that would put everyone in debt for a decade. Also, it was essential that everyone on the guest list buy something for the new house that didn't exist. At some point, it would happen. Fraser insisted we find somewhere in Glasgow and I was happy to agree.

Mither, by now practically running Avon for South East and Central Scotland, promised that when my wedding came, my make-up would be flawless. Something of a recent expert in brushes and bronze powders (because no-one in Scotland wanted to be pale), she had ways and means of removing blemishes, spots, and the merest hint of expression from any face she touched. My biggest worry for the wedding was that I didn't have a faither to walk me doon the aisle. Fraser, suspicious of the fact I never talked about him, asked to know why. He was also interested in knowing everything about me, including names and addresses of exes. Not that I had many.

I told him about Harvey, even Robbie. But my faither? He didn't know and he never would. The thought of my secret being told was enough to keep me awake at night, restless on my mattress, head spinning on the pillow. During these bad thoughts, I would imagine Fraser's reaction if he ever discovered the truth about me, found out how I'd been made. But this only happened at night.

Mostly, I didn't think about it at all. Sometimes I even forgot. I had to forget.

Mither had her own bit of wisdom that she passed onto me.

—The past is a haunted hoose. Everyone has skeletons in their cupboards.

Luckily for me, Fraser had a few skeletons of his own stashed away.

THE TOUGH STREETS OF KNIGHTSWOOD

I found myself deep in Glesga, nervously anticipating my first ever meeting with the future in-laws. Knightswood wasn't quite the war zone I'd imagined, the place I'd made inside my head after hearing all about it from Fraser.

—Aye, he told me shortly after meeting him for the first time, —I'm from the streets. Rough as fuck. I wasn't scared of anyone. The gangs? Ha! A bunch of wee bitch boys. Nobody would fuck with me. I learned karate in my garage!

Not only had he sold himself as a tough scrapper who grew up on the mean streets of Knightswood, surviving on his wits, fists and kung-fu kicks, he also made me believe his parents were tough overlords of their local area. The truth, however, turned out to be far stranger. Instead of overseeing a gang, Fraser's faither was the head of the local neighbourhood watch, turning them into a gang of his own. All the faithers in the street, armed with chibs, wandered around Knightswood at night looking for unruly teens to batter. Fraser's faither, it later came out, was on the blue side of The Old Firm, loving Rangers Football Club with an overruling obsessive love. This love was passed like a ball to his son, who wore his strip in bed instead of pyjamas.

The time eventually came for me to meet Fraser's folks.

It didn't go well.

MEETING THE IN-LAWS

I was sitting nervously on an old couch. It was black, the worst colour for furniture because it caught every little bit of dust and dirt. Mither always said never get a black couch unless it's leather and even then, make sure it gets a good wax every week to keep the cushions supple. This wasn't leather. Regardless, I was a good guest and grateful for the seat. I'd walked arm-in-arm with Fraser for nearly twenty minutes because he felt we needed the exercise. By the time we arrived at his parent's house, I could feel dampness spreading underneath my pits, a trickle dripping down my back, between my skin and the shiny blue blouse I'd worn in the hope it made me look classy, not trashy.

Now all I could think about was the possibility of Fraser's family meeting me for the first time and seeing a wet patch under my shoulders. No matter what happened, I'd be the sweaty wife. But if they spotted it, they didn't say anything. They were considerate, at the very least.

−Oh, you're lovely, said his mither, a small woman with short peroxide-white hair and pursed lips. Her name was Loretta and she immediately cupped her hands across my cheeks. Without warning. she started pulling at my face, making noises you'd expect to make any time you patted a particularly cute puppy. While this happened, a large man in a v-neck sweater and a striped shirt sauntered into the hallway. His chest wheezed while he walked.

−Robert, said Loretta, −Come and meet Sadie. Isn't she lovely?

—Aye, said Mr Fotheringham, or Robert as I would start calling him, soon after he introduced himself. —You've done well, son.

Fraser was proud enough to put his arm around my shoulder which felt good until I noticed his faither hadn't taken his eyes off me since I'd arrived at the front door. Suddenly I felt like a cow being looked over by a farmer before a big sale. That sensation of being sized up stayed around for years, impressing itself on me whenever I had to see the Fotheringhams.

After our introduction, I found myself sitting quietly on the couch in the living room, trying hard to make a good impression, other than the one I was putting into the cushion with my arse. Nearly thirty minutes had passed since we'd arrived and the couch felt bonded to me. My legs started to cramp, so I stretched them, drawing unwanted attention to myself.

—Do you want a cup of tea?

—Aye, I replied immediately, grateful to hold a mug, an anchor of familiarity. Loretta headed into the kitchen and I watched from the couch while she boiled the kettle and threw teabags into mugs. She tipped each mug, pouring the hot water like a pint in a pub. As she worked, I waited with Fraser and his faither, who acted like I wasn't there at all. They were talking about the Middle East and weapons of mass destruction. The words 'sexed up' were referenced more than once, the new tabloid-led buzzword that suddenly seemed to be everywhere. Robert favoured a fire of wrath, raining bombs down on the strangers he saw on television or in the tabloids.

—Boom! Boom! Boom! he shouted dramatically, waving his fingers around, pretending they were the fallout from detonated bombs. Thankfully, Fraser didn't agree. No-one cared if I agreed or not. A few minutes of debate continued until Loretta returned with a mug in each hand.

The others were still in the kitchen, because Fraser and Robert always got their tea first. In the years that followed, I'd learn this was typical of the Fotheringhams. Not only did the men get their tea first, they got their dinner before everyone else as well. Life revolved around the men; their views, thoughts and dislikes trumped everything else.

This wasn't just an introduction to their life, it was a taste of things to come.

Eventually, I got my mug and a Wagon Wheel, my idea of a good time.

I lifted the mug to my lips when Mr Fotheringham suddenly began to scream.

−What the hell are you doing to me?

Loretta froze on the spot, knowing what was coming.

−You've used the green milk, snapped her husband irritably.

−No, countered his wife with an eerie composure. −I used the blue milk.

−It's green, he shrieked, acting like his wife had tried to poison him.

−Da, said Fraser, looking over at me, sipping on too-hot-tea.

−But I don't like green milk. She knows I don't like green milk.

Green, meaning semi-skimmed.

Green, meaning *Celtic*.

THE HIDDEN DANGERS OF TRAFFIC LIGHTS

Fraser apologised later that night, explaining that his faither's aversion to anything green made him appear unreasonable at times. For instance, he wouldn't shop in certain supermarkets if they had the colour green in their logo. Tesco was the only shop he used because it had blue in the design.

What I'd observed gave me more questions than answers, one in particular.

—How does your faither cross the road when the lights go green?

Fraser glared ominously at me, believing I was taking the piss.

He wasn't wrong, for sure.

35

We decided to start looking for a house, our first together, only to find we had barely anything in the bank. Life savings? At my age? I had what was in my account and it wasn't much, only what the Job Centre gave me. I'd never held down a job for longer than a few months. Fraser, meanwhile, worked for ScotRail as a train driver, going along the Polmont route, which is how he'd ended up in Denny for New Year. Until we found a house, we lived apart, like teenagers on a holiday romance, instead of adults on the verge of marriage.

Eventually, Fraser found a house he wanted me to look at.

−It's in Glesga, he said excitedly as we sat in my room. The damp patch on the wall had returned and a teddy bear sat on the pillow, a throwback to my days as a wee girl, the same one who believed in magic spells. As a grown-up, magic was still around, except it was called love and I believed in it completely.

−Where? I asked, wanting to do anything to be with Fraser.

−Strathbungo, he said, his arm around me, my head on his beer belly.

−Strathbungo, I repeated, loving the sound of the word when I said it aloud.

Soon enough, Strathbungo, wherever it was, became a promised land.

−But we've got a problem, he said ruefully.

−Money?

−Aye. Money.

It was always about money. We needed lots and we had none.

212

−Look, he continued. −I've asked my folks for a loan.

I knew why he was telling me this, of course. He wanted me to ask my mither for some money too. He was vaguely aware that she had some stashed away, though he had no idea how she'd earned it. The last thing I wanted to do was ponce off my mither, who now spent her life being irritated by everything I did. Nothing was good enough anymore. We were back to hating each other from a distance, the two of us hoping for peace but prepared for war. In the end, I decided to try and keep Fraser happy and I asked my mither for a loan.

It seemed only fair that I make an effort too.

Oh, it was a real effort alright.

THE FAMILY BUSINESS

I found Mither surrounded by paper bags full of product to be delivered to her customers, most of whom appreciated her punctuality. She was sitting by the kitchen table with a thick cloud above her head that looked like the by-product of at least five cigarettes. Sometimes Mither got so preoccupied with her work that she forgot to open a window and breathe some fresh air. She also forgot about lunch, dinner and going to the toilet. Sometimes, she'd stop packing paper bags and realise she needed to pee. Either that or her stomach would gurgle and she'd count the hours on both hands since she'd last eaten something. Regardless, she never ever forgot to light up one of her Benson & Hedges. How customers put up with the stink of nicotine on their face creams, eau de toilettes and whatever else they got in their bags, was beyond me.

Frequently, I found myself in despair at my mither's antics. Though I meant well, along the way I'd turned into the whiny daughter who moaned all the time. I hated it. Keeping that in mind, I recognised a future with Fraser wasn't just something I wanted, but also a desperate new direction I needed. Surely anything had to be better than this life? Stuck in my childhood bedroom at the age of twenty-nine. But even that brought a kind of insecurity. Sometimes I feared that I wasn't really in love with Fraser, that he was a convenient means to an end, a way of escaping everything I'd ever known. If I didn't love him or have his love, who would I be? Would I be anything? Anyone?

−Mither, I said quietly. −I need your help.

−How much do you want?

Stung by her accuracy, I gasped. She had more to say though.

−You're moving out, aren't you?

−Yes, I said, at last admitting it.

−Have you found somewhere yet?

−Yes. It's a wee place in Glesga. Do you know Strathbungo?

−Is it near The Gorbals?

−No.

−Then I don't know Strathbungo.

Neither of us said anything else for a good twenty seconds and I nearly turned my back and walked out the kitchen. Ultimately, Mither decided to help – but it came with a price that was more than purely financial.

−You could always help me with my deliveries, earn the money back.

−No thanks, I told her hastily. Some prices were too high to pay.

−Okay. I'll give you some money and you can pay it back your own way.

I agreed, silently hoping to get the money before she could change her mind.

Later that night, literally a few hours later, Fraser asked why I hadn't accepted a job working for my mither.

−It'd be easy, he said. −You'd just be going around door-to-door.

−Maybe, I said, −But I'm not sure I want to deliver what she's selling.

He seemed unsure, so I let him in on my suspicions.

−I think there's more in those bags than just lipstick, I said quietly.

Ma hoose, ma hame

Flat 2/1, 49 Nithsdale Road was wide and the ceilings ridiculously tall, especially for a girl who had been raised in Little Denny Road her entire life. Directly in front of the main door in the hallway was a large bookshelf and a cupboard door, with all the household junk stashed behind it, the unwieldy objects I couldn't quite place neatly into position around the flat. There were doors on both sides of the hallway, plus a little corridor leading to the bathroom. On the left were two bedroom doors, while the doors to the living room, the Scandinavian-style kitchen for people who'd only been to Scandinavia via IKEA, and a box room could be accessed by doors to the right.

The bookshelf in the hall had a few ugly ornaments on it that I couldn't throw into the junk cupboard. Ceramic cats, weird little fairy houses, little men with frog heads, all unwanted Christmas gifts from my cow of a mother-in-law. Really, I preferred her own ornaments. In every house I'd ever visited, from my granny's flat to my friends' homes, there were always ornaments on display, inherited tat passed down from mothers to daughters, the working-class version of handing down a fine china tea set.

I assumed this is a Scottish thing.

The thin blue line

The test came from the chemist down the road, a small

room with shelves that squeezed all space out. It took me two tries to aim my piss at the test, but eventually I got there. The line quickly went blue and my reaction was to shake the test (flicking flecks of piss into the air). This should have told me nothing about this pregnancy was going to be nice, easy, or clean.

−Fuck, said Fraser over and over again. His first thought after the initial shock was to see if the Rangers Shop did football strips for babies. My first thought? Fear. Simple but powerful fear. Then a lot of questions. Would I be able to do this? Would it be painful? How would motherhood be?

−Fuck, I said.

TRADITION IS HEAVY

At one point we weren't sure we wanted to get married. It seemed so old-fashioned, something for people like the Fotheringhams, with their white plastic doors, fake grass and customised door numbers. We were going to be different, of course. But tradition is too heavy to throw off that easily and Fraser suddenly started to think maybe his folks were right after all. The result of the test, a faint blue line, made him more determined to do everything their way. Me? I had to do everything his way, like his mither with his faither. Even choosing a name presented problems. I'd always wanted to give my kids strange names, the sort you'd see in a fantasy story or a fairy tale. Real life was boring enough without having to go through it with a boring name.

−If it's a girl, let's call her Lilybeth.

−The fuck we will! She'll have a nice name.

I wasn't impressed. Lilybeth, for me, was the height of twee wonder.

−What's your idea of a nice name?

−How about… Julie?

−Julie, I laughed. It wasn't that I disliked that name, but it wasn't Lilybeth.

−I like Julie, he scolded me. −It sounds classy.

−No, I said. −Let's do better.

−Whit will we call our wee boy if we have one?

−How about Caspian?

I'd once borrowed *The Chronicles of Narnia* out of Denny Library as a kid because the cover art had entranced me. Again, Fraser wanted something a bit different. Normal, actually. A nice name to help our child fit in with the world.

−He's going to be called Mark.

−Mark?

−Aye, after Mark Hateley, my favourite footie player. Have you heard of him?

−The name rings a bell, I said mischievously.

Making it official

My dress came from June Bridges, Glesga's oldest boutique shop. Thankfully, it catered to women of all sizes.

−You're getting bigger than a bouncy castle, said Mither in her typically understated manner. She wasn't wrong though. Pregnancy shifted my body around in ways I hadn't expected. Not only did my belly swell up, but so did my chest and ankles, both of which gave me trouble. Standing for too long was a massive effort, while sitting down took a team of people to manoeuvre me into position. Fraser's mither was there to lend a hand, and a kind word. Thank God, because I really needed both.

−We have maternity wedding dresses, said the assistant. −Let's try them.

I'd been trying on dresses all afternoon while Mither

sat in silence, leaving Lily to do the hard work with Loretta, carrying the whole conversation. I knew Mither wasn't keen on Fraser and his family, but Loretta seemed too polite to be anything other than gracious. All of them were dressed in their own versions of elegant, Mither fighting my mither-in-law with fashion rather than fists or words. Loretta, however, was deceptively tough and greeted my mither like a dear friend. Somehow, I found myself liking her more and more, even with my hormones making every feeling both unpredictable and extreme.

−This one doesn't fit me, I said for what was the tenth time that day.

−That's alright, the girl said primly. −We can try the others.

No matter what dress I pulled up my body, none of them were comfortable.

There was a reason, of course. I wasn't just expecting one baby, I was having twins. One boy and one girl. Two names to choose, more arguments to fight. I was tired of being pregnant, completely exhausted with everything, let alone planning a wedding I wasn't sure I actually wanted.

−I look like Biffa Bacon, I sighed, nearly bursting into tears.

−The curtains in that window might fit you, said Mither unhelpfully.

−Don't talk to her like that, snapped Loretta.

Lily closed her eyes and once again waited for the end of the world.

Five minutes later, we were outside the shop and the polis on their way.

−I was just kidding on, said Mither ruefully, but none of us laughed.

Later on that night, when Fraser heard what had happened, he went nuts. Not because of what my own mither had said in the shop, but because of what might have happened to the weans inside me, growing and vulnerable. Whenever he asked how I was feeling, somehow I knew he was really asking if the babies were alright. I'd come to accept this was just the way of things.

−Fuck the lot of them, snarled Fraser. −We're posting the banns and getting to that bloody registry office, just the two of us. Right?

−Let's do it, I said, agreeing because it made sense at the time.

THE BIG DAY

It took just over a month for a slot to become available. Hilariously, it turned out no-one wanted to get married on the thirteenth. We laughed our way to the registry office. After we got dressed, we took a taxi, raised an umbrella, climbed a few stairs, said a few vows, signed a few documents and it was done. The morning went by quickly, thank goodness.

−How does it feel to be Mrs Fotheringham? asked Fraser as we stood outside the office, hiding under his golf umbrella, trying to keep out the rain. The bad weather wasn't an omen, not to me. I still loved rainy days.

−It feels great, I said, but the only thing I felt was pain in my ankles and pressure on my bladder. We waited in the rain, his arm around my shoulder.

The sun eventually peeked through the clouds, but it was a brief shine.

THE PSYCHIC'S PREDICTION

Mrs Menzies at 54 Little Denny Road was a lovely little woman, slight and unpretentious. She was the kind of neighbour who would offer you a mug of tea and listen to you talk about life (and then tell everyone else what you said afterwards). The kids on the street adored her because they knew she wouldn't give them apples or oranges on Halloween, preferring to fill their poly bags with wee Mars Bars. She wore her silvery black hair in a severe bun, so tight it pulled her skin upwards, smoothing the wrinkles of her face, making them appear less recessed. If our street had an unofficial mayor, it was Mrs Menzies, who knew exactly what to say and when to speak.

Somehow, it got out that Mrs Menzies had a gift. She'd descended from a line of Scottish witches in North Berwick and her ancestor had escaped the trial by turning into a mule and running away. Everyone in Little Denny Road knew that Mrs Menzies could see the future, but her visions weren't always clear. She explained they came to her like a face peering out from a muddy puddle, distorted and vague. It was her responsibility to reach out and push away the dirt until her vision became clear, but this came at an unfortunate cost. Even though the kids adored Mrs Menzies for her annual contribution to their rotten teeth and diabetes, a few of the parents were less keen. They didn't want her knowing their business, so only a handful of women courted her wisdom. Mither was one of them, of course. She called me up, excited and talkative. I suspected Lily was off out somewhere, leaving Mither with no choice but to phone me instead. Muting the sound on Scotland Today (eggs and punches being thrown between a protester and John Prescott), I leaned back onto the couch, wincing at the pressure on my bladder.

−I take it you're in a good mood, I gasped.

−Aye, she cried out, her voice high and giddy. −I just went to see Mrs Menzies. She told me my fortune. Bloody hell, she's good.

−Oh no, I said, pressing my hand against my swollen belly.

It turned out Mither hadn't asked about me or the twins. She'd asked something else far more specific and received the answer she needed to hear.

−A tall, dark, handsome stranger is going to knock on the door.

I was not so impressed, feeling less convinced of the magic I once believed in.

−Come on, Mither! That's what all the psychics say to women.

But not all psychics were Mrs Menzies, who could speak to spirits the way she did the children who chapped her door on October 31st every year.

−I believe her, said Mither. −She's never ever wrong.

−With luck he's better than that last arsehole you dated.

Though it came out before I got the chance to think it over, we didn't really talk about Uncle Tam, who'd lasted longer than all my other uncles. Mither kept quiet. She didn't like to think about that time and I didn't want to completely let it go. Our love was push and pull, the knots keeping us together even when the two of us tried to move in parallel directions.

The call ended in a quiet click, but before I put down the receiver, I caught Mither muttering something like,

−A tall, dark, handsome stranger *will* knock on the door.

Three days later, he did just that.

Next time Mither phoned me, it was from a cell. She probably thought I never moved away from the couch and mostly, she would be right. The couch was where Fraser found me when he came into the living room with our new cordless handset, a white curved seashell of a phone.

–Your mither's been arrested, said Fraser in disbelief.

He clearly didn't know her that well.

Hesitantly, I took the handset and pressed it to my ear.

–Where are you?

–Don't panic, she said, immediately making me panic. –I'm alright.

–Where are you? I snapped.

–Denny Polis Station. But honestly… don't panic!

–For fuck sake, I muttered.

–It's a lot nicer than the cells in Govan, she said optimistically.

–Shouldn't you be phoning a lawyer?

–I did. He sorted me out with this extra call.

–I'm… honoured?

–Your daughter's pregnant with my weans and you're stressing her out! shouted Fraser in the background, his arms folded over his chest. He'd taken to walking around the flat in a pair of glossy football shorts and nothing else. I didn't mind. I barely changed out of my pink housecoat, the only thing in the wardrobe that actually fitted me properly. God, I hated being pregnant.

–What's that tit saying? asked Mither from the other side of the line.

–He thinks you're giving me grief, I explained. –What happened?

–So Mrs Menzies was right. A tall, dark, handsome stranger knocked on my door. Actually, he was plain clothed polis and he kicked the door in, but that's close enough, isn't it? The drug squad poured right in behind him.

—Oh my God, I muttered, completely grateful to be out of Denny.

Worse was to come, because life was never easy.

—I'm being done for possession with intent to supply.

I knew it. I fucking *knew* it.

—You were using your business to deal drugs, I said accusingly.

—Hen, dealing drugs *was* the business. The Avon stuff was a front.

—Oh my God, I gasped, suddenly thinking of the newspaper headlines. —Fraser's parents. What will they say? The shame. The mortification!

—Fuck them.

—She's been done for dealing, I mouthed as Fraser paced around in the background, swearing and muttering. While he wore out the carpet, it suddenly occurred to me that I could just end the call and leave my mither to suffer in her cell. I could justify it to anyone, really. My life now was here in Strathbungo, far away from Little Denny Road. Some people forgot their family once they put space between each other. Could I do that? Could I be that girl?

There was only one answer to my question and I already knew it.

—I'll do anything I can to help, I said.

Front page superstar

A few days after the raid, Mither appeared on the front pages of the *Daily Record* and *The Herald* (though thankfully not *The Digger*, which didn't exist in 2001). Somehow, all the papers got their hands on photographs of her looking unbelievably glamorous with her hair done and a lovely faux fur coat draped across her shoulders. The shots had been taken at a party that she'd attended years ago, and the pictures sold to the tabloids for five grand. The press had used these shots strategically, of course. It made Mither look like a rich bitch who peddled drugs and used the proceeds on herself.

This wasn't a completely unfair assessment.

She was, according to *The Record*, the 'new Mags Haney'.

−Better that than the old Mags Haney, I cackled.

Mither, however, didn't laugh, instead reacting badly to the photographs.

−I look fat, she wailed.

−No you don't, I snapped, before adding, −Is that all you can think about?

I needed her to feel the gravity of her situation, because it was likely she'd end up seeing her grandchildren for the first time from the other side of a plexiglass panel at Cornton Vale. I was due to give birth in less than a month. Sometimes I just wanted it over and done with, so I could stop feeling like I desperately needed to pee. The siege on my bladder was constant and half the time I could barely navigate myself onto the toilet pan. Pregnancy was far from the miraculous, wonderful, natural experience I'd expected.

−I'm going on a diet, announced Mither suddenly.

−I'm not, I said glumly.

And there we were, together again, talking about diets while a case was being prepared by the procurator fiscal against Mither for drug dealing. In the background while I listened, I heard Mither lighting up a cigarette.

−It tastes better than Slim Fast, she said.

Mither was being deadly serious about losing weight for her first court appearance. I thought she was being stupid, that she should focus on her defence. At the same time, I couldn't think about it too much. Pregnancy invaded every aspect of my daily life, giving me something to worry about other than my family. Not that it completely stopped. Lily had taken to calling me at all hours, stressing out of her nut.

–I've moved out, she said on the phone. –I couldn't live with her anymore.

–Were you dealing for her? I asked, my voice accusing.

–Of course not, she lied. Years and years later, I'd discover not only was she dealing for Mither, but it had also been her idea in the first place to set up a new business. Lily used her discerning taste to test each product, something she did with great enthusiasm. The only reason she didn't tell me on the phone that day was her fear the polis were tapping the wire.

–It was all Mither. As far as I'm concerned, she's not part of my life anymore.

This also explained why Mither was talking to me all of a sudden, but I said nothing, preferring to try and focus on the positive. I really tried, but it was exhausting. Everything seemed difficult now. Even filling the kettle for a mug of tea felt like a mission. I wanted to shut my eyes and sleep for months, try and get back the energy my babies were leeching from me.

–Pregnancy is the worst thing ever, I declared. –I hate feeling like this.

–It'll all be worth it when you have the bairns.

I sighed. Any time I complained or had a small moan about the changes that pregnancy had inflicted on me, someone always said –It'll be worth it, or –It'll be alright, or −You'll forget when the kids are here. All I could do was grin and hope they were right and everything would get better.

−Where are you staying? I asked, interested despite myself.

−I'm living with Joe now. We're renting a flat in Cumbernauld.

−That's nice, I said.

−It's not, but the rent's cheap and Joe knows the area.

Joe this. Joe that. It was a name I was hearing more and more, usually from Mither, always followed by a tut or a sharp intake of breath. She clearly didn't like him and couldn't hide her distaste, treating his name like the stuff that came out of a burst abscess on her gum.

−So how long before the big day?

Ah. We were back onto my pregnancy again.

−Any time now, I said, suddenly allowing myself to feel optimistic again.

'Any time now' was three days later, when my water broke in the middle of Glasgow city centre, more pish hitting the wrong place. Fraser didn't mind, telling me his friends all pished in Glasgow city centre, so why not his wife too? I was too busy screaming, pishing and pushing to agree with him.

37

The Twins

Mither came to visit the twins when I got out of hospital on the condition we didn't use the word 'granny' once, otherwise she'd walk out the flat. Obviously, this meant Fraser kept saying it over and over again, asking 'granny' if she wanted to hold the babies, telling 'granny' she could babysit them any time she liked. Though she raged quietly, she didn't turn her back and leave. Even if she had, I couldn't catch her. Whatever tiredness I thought I felt in the lead up to giving birth was nothing compared to the exhaustion of becoming the mither of my own two children. A boy and girl. Mark and Lucie. Both names chosen by Fraser, who insisted our wee girl be called Lucie. He loved the name, or so he said. Whatever their names, they were perfect little babies for the most part, except for all the screaming and wailing. I had to whisper, coo and beg them to keep quiet in case the neighbours complained.

Fraser loved his kids but he barely helped with them.

−My job is driving trains safely. Your job is being their mum.

−How much do I get paid an hour? I snapped.

The sound on the telly went up and the conversation was over.

A Stroll through Nithsdale Street

Every morning, regardless of the cold, I took the babies out for fresh air, filling my lungs with crisp winter wind. It felt great. My body, now forever changed, still didn't feel like it completely belonged to me. The babies, one in blue and the other in purple, lay in the pram, both of them throwing punches at each other, a sign of things to come. Every now and then I had to remind them I was here, reaching down and waggling my fingers at their faces. Lucie would thrust out her wee hand while Mark just lay there unimpressed. Another glimpse at the future, though I didn't realise that at the time.

Pushing them, I walked down the street, all concrete and kerb with neatly trimmed hedges, curls of green coming up from cracks on the pavements. A postman walked by and smiled, the same smile he gave me every morning when we passed each other at this time. Small moments like this made me feel like there was more to the world than the four walls of my flat on Nithsdale Street. Halfway through the day, near lunchtime, I realised how much I needed this, how lucky I was to throw my arms around Glesga and be embraced in return. At some point, after having coffee in a wee shop on the high street, I found myself pushing the pram back the way, slowly moving in the direction of home, because it was my home now.

Weight loss (part two)

Mither's diet had been remarkably effective, losing her over four stone, giving her a waist again after years of hiding it with all the tricks at her disposal. But I didn't think she looked good. She was in her fifties and too skinny.

−Stop, I said. −You're doing too much now. It doesn't look right.

−Don't be jealous, she said, not completely inaccurately.

−Lily agrees with me, I shot back.

−How would she know? I haven't seen her in nearly a year.

The trial was fast approaching and Mither seemed

particularly stung by Lily's lack of communication. But if she was worried about the trial, it wasn't obvious. If anything, her entire focus was on her weight.

How short-sighted, I thought.

−Just stop, I said once again.

−You don't need to worry, she assured me. −I'm done with the diet.

She wasn't lying. At last, her diet stopped.

But the weight kept falling off.

That's how I knew something was terribly wrong with my mither.

STIRLING INFIRMARY

Just so she wouldn't be alone when she got her test results back, I headed through to Little Denny Road and accompanied Mither to Stirling Infirmary. I already knew what she was going to hear before the doctor made our worst fears a reality. It was obvious, looking at her, how the diagnosis was going to go. Her faux fur coat, the one that used to sit neatly around her shoulders, now swallowed her entire upper body. But I still wanted to be wrong, hoping there was another explanation.

More often than not, hope got in the way of common sense, but I still prayed things would be good. The hospital, for better or worse, would tell us everything. Stirling Infirmary was close to where I grew up, a short trip in the car, a slightly longer journey on a bus. Mither hired a taxi and spent the journey resisting any attempt at being fussed over, not allowing the slightest trace of sentimentality or fear into her headspace. I sat quietly, thinking about my life in Denny and how different things might be for my own children in Glesga. This was the first time I'd been away from them and even a few hours felt like a holiday in Spain. Mither didn't say much, but when she spoke, it was usually to insult another driver or complain about the potholes, pockmarks along the roads around Falkirk and Stirling.

Things didn't improve once we got to the car park. I almost had to hold Mither back from kicking someone who'd parked in the space *she* wanted, even though the taxi driver didn't seem to care either way. A few minutes later, I realised the other car was a Skoda and somehow it felt like a bad omen. Only when the driver recognised Mither from the papers did he agree to surrender his space to her. We eventually got to the waiting room and sat together. Not knowing what else to do, I reached out to take her hand.

She pulled away.

Finally, her name was called out.

Everyone looked over while pretending to stare at the clock on the wall.

THE DIAGNOSIS

–It's lung cancer, said the doctor, whose name I still can't remember. He was clean shaven yet had a monobrow and that's all I remember of him. Well... that and the death sentence he gave my mither from the safety of his desk. How many other people had he given similar news to? Hundreds, probably.

How many that day though? Was Mither the first? Or just the latest?

–Shit, said Mither calmly, her fingers twitching.

She took a moment to consider her fate before asking the obvious question.

–How long?

–It could be a year, at least. Maybe more. Possibly less.

It was a calm response, delivered by someone who did

this every day, probably before he went out for a sandwich and a coffee.

—Don't you know for sure? I shrieked, not quite believing what I'd just heard. —Can't you do tests or something? Surely you can narrow it down? Maybe more than a year, possibly less… like, what the fuck?

—It's difficult to measure these things, answered the doctor unhelpfully.

—Fuck, I said.

—Calm down, ordered Mither, who got to her feet, sending the chair scraping noisily across the floor. She was ready to go. Not me though. I needed more.

—Is that it? I cried out. —Surely something can be done to help?

The doctor didn't say anything. I filled the void with random statements.

—Chemo? An operation? Something. Anything.

Mither, however, was halfway out the door.

—Come on, Sadie. Let's head.

I staggered behind her, my brain spinning while the world sat still.

—That can't be it.

—That's it, said Mither. —On the bright side, the trial will be postponed.

—Oh, fuck right off, I snapped, in no mood for her silliness. —You're *dying*.

—I am, aren't I? I'm dying. Bloody hell.

Not a single sound escaped my lips. No words. Not a gasp. Only thin breath.

Suddenly, I couldn't get the lungful of air that I desperately needed.

—Oh for God's sake, said Mither, —Why do you need to be a drama queen?

She rubbed my back and seconds later I was calm again.

We waited outside in the cold for a taxi, unsure of what to do next.

Eventually a cab arrived and we headed back to Denny.

−Don't tell your sister, said Mither later that night as I got on the bus.

−Mither! I gasped, completely mortified. −You know I wouldn't say anything.

It was a promise I kept for the hour and a half it took for me to reach the south side of Glesga. Afterwards, I called Lily and told her everything.

38

Mither was with me in the living room at 87 Little Denny Road, her baby with babies of her own. They were noisy, giving us something else to think about other than what we knew was coming. Every time I looked at her, I wanted to cry, but somehow I kept it together. She was on the couch watching me as I changed nappies, the twins on the floor, legs kicking uselessly, little squirming things with fresh pink skin and strong lungs. Mither had a comfy quilt slung over her, a faded floral pattern across it. Her favourite cushion propped her up, a horrible fluffy thing that was constantly shedding everywhere, far worse than any dog. Only her head was exposed and her eyes were closed, opening every now and again, always on me and her grandchildren. At one point, when I thought she was fast asleep, she surprised me by speaking.

−I wish she was named after me, she muttered, half-asleep.

I looked down at Lucie, unmindful to everything other than want and need.

−But she is, I said. −Lucie *Penelope* Fotheringham. I only went with Lucie as her first name because Fraser absolutely insisted. I let him get his way sometimes. It keeps the marriage happy.

Mither gave me a smile. Though it was slight, it was there and I saw it.

−It's funny, she sighed. −I always hated my name.

−I used to hate it too, I said, facing the window, glass rippled by rain.

Mither spent her nights and most of her days sleeping, but when she was awake, she did what she'd done her entire life: she fought hard. Sometimes I got the sense she didn't want to go through with her chemotherapy, having little physical resistance for the cell-killing bombardment. The treatments made her hair thinner. This was almost worse for my mither than any other side-effect.

−I love looking like me, she'd say whenever I told her it didn't matter, that getting better was all that counted.

On short notice, I left the twins with my mither-in-law and went out looking for shops that sold quality hair-pieces. In a cracked mirror version of our shared life, I ended up escorting Mither for her first wig fitting, just like the day she took me for my first bra at Closing Down Sale. This time around I didn't embarrass her or act out in front of the sales assistant.

−I still can't believe you did that, said Mither, yet she found the goodwill to laugh at the memory. It had always been that way for us, of course. Even the worst times made us laugh in the retelling, especially when we had an audience. But now our laughter was tinged with uncertainty. Mither was, in her own words, *riddled* with it. She didn't say the C word. I didn't either. It was always 'this fucking disease', an enemy she couldn't punch, kick or verbally slice to pieces with well-pitched one-liners. That alone frustrated her more than anything else. The fact her favourite daughter was keeping her distance was a bother too. Lily still hadn't reached out to Mither.

I wanted to go to her flat and push my forefinger against the tip of her nose.

But if Mither was bothered, she didn't say. Her attention was fixed on the mirror and all the wigs at her side. She kept trying different pieces, test-driving them on her head. Eventually, she found one that looked similar to her natural hair colour. She put it on, turned around, and asked a question.

−Aye or naw?

−Aye, I said eagerly, hoping she'd buy something. −I'd totally wear it.

Mither immediately removed the wig and handed it to the sales assistant.

−Not for me, she said briskly.

Instead of taking this as a terrible insult to my taste, I took this as a step in the right direction. If she was insulting me, Mither was feeling herself again. I sat on the chair, watching, wondering how long this could last.

UNDERWATER BLUES

Fraser tried his best to keep me happy, though I could tell he felt slightly inconvenienced by the amount of time I was spending away from the flat, especially since he still felt bitter towards my mither for causing his own family embarrassment. He was married to the daughter of that woman on the front page of the newspaper. In reality, he had nothing to be embarrassed about. His photo was never used in any paper. His name was never mentioned. His workmates, however, probably found it funny and Fraser, despite his charm, hated being the joke as much as he loved being the centre of attention. Without trying, he managed to make Mither's situation, her dying days, all about him. But the thing I couldn't do was break down. Not with the kids in the same room, because they knew how I felt about everything. They were attuned to my moods and when I faked happiness, they saw through it.

−I don't know why you're so upset, he said one night while I was in the bath. He was on the pan, taking his

time. –She wasn't there for you. I'm here for you. I just…
I miss you and she's always there, pushing me out.

–She's my mither for fuck sake, I muttered, wondering
if I should submerge and wait until he was finished a)
talking shite and b) taking a shite.

His mood was gloomy, a match for mine, but it came
from a totally different place. He'd grown frustrated with
my lack of reaction to his own problems, all the silly things
he dealt with at work. Maybe I wasn't present enough, but
everything outside of my mither's failing health seemed
so small now.

Now there was only life and death. Everything else in-
between could wait.

–Your sister has the right idea, he said, before standing
up to wipe himself.

I opened my mouth to speak, but I was too deep under
water to form words.

A HELPING HAND

Mither was on her couch surrounded by fluffy offcuts from
her favourite fluffy cushion. She'd bought a set of them.
They must have been in the sale somewhere, possibly at
the Falkirk branch of BHS. Any time I leaned back, it was
with an understanding that my black blouse would end up
covered in fuzzy white bits that I'd have to fight off with
the palm of my hand, static pulling it back. The babies
were with me, by now on their feet, taking faltering steps.
Mark and Lucie wanted to run. Unfortunately for me, they
ran in opposite directions. I had to be alert at all times and
keep them, and myself, together.

–Leave them alone, said Mither as she tried to put
her face on. She'd kept some of her products from Avon
and used them skilfully, always making herself look
glamorous, even during her illness. I'd manoeuvred a

mirror by the side of the couch so she could see herself in the glass. Mither, I learned, got the same enjoyment out of painting her face as the babies got from scribbling over their colouring books. I didn't understand it one little bit.

−I heard from Lily today, said Mither out of nowhere.

−About bloody time, I said sharply. −What did she have to say for herself?

−Nothing. She put the phone down. But it was her.

−Oh.

Mither looked at me and her eyes pleaded for help.

−I can't put my mascara on, she said quietly.

−What?

−My hands.

They were trembling too much. I lifted the mascara brush and applied it gently to her lashes. Afterwards, the lipstick went on and she pursed her lips appreciatively. Ten minutes passed and, in that time, a handful of brushes and glossy-tipped pencils came out of a makeup bag, which looked like a pencil case I'd used at Nethermains Primary School.

Soon enough, I'd finished doing my mither's face.

−There, I beamed proudly. −What do you think?

She smiled in the mirror once, then again from another angle.

Finally, she gave me her assessment.

−Bloody hell, she muttered. −You've made me look like shit.

As compliments went, it was probably the best she could do under the circumstances. I took it anyway, the way I took everything she threw at me.

FINAL RITES AND RIGHTING WRONGS

I did my best to be different versions of me, giving everyone what they needed, saving nothing for myself.

237

Mither was moved into a hospice where she spent her last days, sleeping and complaining about the neighbours, old rivals who she felt had gotten one over on her because they were still alive. I didn't mind because it gave her something to think about other than her painfully thin body. As she lay on her bed, I set about trying to make the room cosy enough for her, even going as far as getting one of the horrible fluffy cushions from her couch back at the flat, plumping it up, sending filaments flying off everywhere. Weirdly, it helped. Mither seemed to relax, giving us both a chance to talk, something we did more now than ever. I couldn't quite reconcile how a terrible disease had brought some good into our relationship. Somehow, it was better to just not think about it.

−I can't believe this is happening, I said quietly. The sound of the rain outside, tiny little taps on the glass, felt comforting in the warmth of the room.

−You can't believe what's happening?

−This. You being here…

She didn't respond and the silence made me talk some more.

−I wish you'd never started smoking.

−It didn't help, but there was every chance it would happen anyway.

For a while I didn't know what to say. I grasped a single word.

−What? I asked.

−This fucking disease runs in the family.

−I never knew that, I said quietly.

−On your grandmither's side. We all get it. I didn't want you or Lily to know.

A curse had suddenly been cast on me and I felt the totality of it.

−The Italian side?

Mither blinked and grimaced

–What Italian side?

–Your mither told me she came from Italy. Oh, years ago she said it.

Mither said nothing and for a moment I thought she'd fallen asleep, or worse. Instead, she laughed slightly. It sounded like her smoker's cough.

–She's a lying cow. Your granny's from Fife. She went to Italy for a school trip back in the 60s, before she married that perv.

Something else had just occurred to me, something horrible.

–I've got a daughter, I cried out, feeling fear in an entirely new way. –What if she gets... what you've got? If it runs in our family, that is?

But Mither wasn't listening. Her attention was caught by something only she could see. Her eyes were locked on the patch of wall over my right shoulder. It was literally a blank wall in a shade of cream, but for her? It was something totally different. Like her, I looked, focussed, but found nothing.

She motioned for me to come closer. I leaned over and caught four words in a whisper, four words I would always remember but keep to myself for years to come. Those same four words became a final breath, noisy and slow. Then her eyes closed and the only sound in the room was the rain outside the window. I stood still, dumbly waiting, not quite knowing what to do next. This had never happened to me before and would never happen to me again. Lifting the cushion, I held it against my chest, not caring if the fluff got all over me. Somehow, it felt like the right thing to do. I pushed my hurt deep into the fabric, pressing hard, letting the fibres float away. In a daze, I watched as bits of fuzz drifted around the room, eventually settling on the furniture and floor, pieces of home to help me to feel a little better as I stood by my mither, a body in a well-made bed.

39

If Fraser lost a parent, he'd know. But he hadn't, so whatever I said failed to translate into something he could understand. Really, he'd been lucky his entire life. There had been fights at home, of course, but his parents were together and alive. Fraser had no way of navigating my grief. And the babies? They didn't care, of course. Their needs were simple. Food, milk, clean nappies and washed bums. But they gave me something to do, keeping my thoughts focussed. Sometimes in a rare quiet minute, I thought how Fraser would only understand this feeling if something awful happened to his mither or faither. Then you'd know, I told myself.

But I'd catch myself and feel remorse, even shame, for being so small.

—What do you need? he kept asking. —Anything, just say it.

From me, it was always the same response.

—I'm fine. Honestly, it's okay. I'm alright.

Even in grief, I didn't want to hurt his feelings, so I lied.

Truth, blunt annoying truth, used to be my thing when I was a wee girl. Now I lied constantly. What happened to me? I missed how I used to be, the silly idiot who went on quests and cast spells. Grief, however, meant nothing happened the way it should. Grief caught up with me when I least expected it. This might happen while I hoovered the house, pushing it around the carpets when I'd think of her, dragging the unwieldy vacuum cleaner around, swearing at it for not picking up the dirt. Every now and again, it happened while I was out in Glesga, shopping to fill the cupboards with tins. I'd be shoving the pram down the street when I'd catch a glimpse of someone with platinum hair whose build was like that of my mither before the disease. It wasn't her, obviously.

Like the girl from Little Denny Road who went looking for blue water in forests, my mither was gone forever. The flat, however, was still there, waiting to be emptied. My hoose and hame would be taken by another family who would fill it with noise and memories. At least, that's what I hoped. Despite my depression, there was still a thin flake of wistfulness in me. Emptying 87 Little Denny Road was my next big undertaking. I gave the twins to Fraser's parents for a few hours so I could take the bus all the way back to Falkirk. There were things to do. Too much for me alone, really.

The funeral was next week. I still hadn't heard from Lily.

A TRIP TO THE GARDEN

I knew the flat was empty before I turned the key.

Not just empty, completely gutted, like me.

Lily had taken everything valuable, including the furniture. My old room was still there, the patch of damp in its rightful place. Memories made me feel like breathing fresh air. There was somewhere else I wanted to see, a place I knew would make me feel happy again, short-lived or not. Peering out the window, I looked across the street at Mr Chadha's garden, with its beautiful little fairy corner dedicated to his daughter. The branches of an old tree blocked my view, twigs weighed down with old Nike trainers, some random junk, even a pair of boxer shorts. Some wishes would never ever be granted.

With a sudden burst of energy, I rushed out the flat, running downstairs like I did years earlier, my feet slapping off each step on the stairwell. Surprisingly, I felt like *me* again, the girl looking for adventure, or a garden full of fairies at least. Not thinking about what was on the other side of the fence, I took the handle of the gate like a handshake, then turned it. Opening the gate just wide enough, I peered into Mr Chadha's garden, hoping to catch sight of the lovely little corner he'd made years earlier.

−Mr Chadha! I called out, hoping he wouldn't be upset with the intrusion.

−Mr Chadha, it's me. Sadie Relish. Helloooo!

But the garden was completely different to what I remembered. The fairy houses in the corner no longer stood. In their place was a shed crammed with wheelless bicycles. The grass was gone, just cracked concrete instead. Dried out whirls of dog shit were scattered around, waiting to be picked up. My jaw dropped so far it nearly fell to the ground. What the hell had happened to Mr Chadha's beautiful garden? It was a dirty dump now.

What I'd failed to consider was the time difference, of course. It was now 2006, and the 80s happened a long time ago. They were now repackaged for easy consumption, they were no longer years in the past but a 'retro' period full of bright colours, silly haircuts and bad politics.

Retro, of course, is never as good as 'vintage'.

Something else I hadn't considered was that dog shit meant there had to be a dog nearby. Suddenly it came at me, barking and howling. I threw myself at the fence, forcing the gate shut as I retreated. The dog, however, was upset that a stranger had crossed into its territory. A large Rottweiler, with a collar that read VERONICA, snapped at me, thick spittle flicking from her maw. Retreating, I yanked the gate back until it was securely in place.

Shaken, I got away from the garden as quickly as possible.

The service was organised quietly and held at Denny Parish Church which had been there for as long as anyone could remember. As a bairn I thought it looked ancient, almost like Denny itself had grown around its masonry. Actually, I was half right. The church, I'd discover, had existed in various forms since 1603. The church had survived centuries of wind, rain, winter, war and Falkirk District Council's rising rent. But Mither's death had given it a frightening new power. No longer was it just a building I passed on my way through Denny Cross – it was now an inevitability. How many of the town's dead had passed through the ornate doorway and out again? Coffins guided by the living, helped along by feet and hands.

I sat through the funeral in the front row, alone with Fraser, who held my hand because he knew everyone (including a journalist from the *Daily Record*) was watching me. Lily, of course, didn't show up. Thankfully, the pews were packed with mourners. Most of them her friends from the nightshift, many putting aside their sleep to make the service. They sat respectfully as strangers in ceremonial robes swung jars of incense, setting off allergies I never knew I had. With eyes streaming (and not just from tears), I managed to trap a sneeze deep inside my nose. One of Mither's old workmates, an older lady with gravity-defying hair and a set of pearls draped around her neck, came over to talk. I'd never seen her before and I'd never see her again. She had some advice to give me, whether or not I actually wanted it. She leaned over to my left ear and I braced myself.

–The older you get, the more funerals you go to.

–Great, I said dryly. –Can't wait.

The service finished, I headed outside to the churchyard.

Everyone followed, keeping a respectful step or two behind me.

That's when I saw her in the crowd.

Someone I never thought I'd see again

Something in her face seemed familiar. She had choppy brown hair, most of it hidden beneath a wide-brimmed floppy hat. Her lips were glossed with a thin sheen of glossy peach, none of it touching her bright teeth. Her smile seemed hopeful. Dressed in black, she might have faded into the audience, but we saw each other and as we looked across the churchyard… something carried itself in a straight line between our eyes. Familiarity. Meaning. Something strong enough to make me stop. I smiled and she gave me a little wave with a gloved hand. She held an umbrella in that hand, tight in a grip the wind wanted to break with each failing gust.

The woman waited as I broke away from the crowd.

−Hi, I said a few seconds later. −Talk about a blast from the past.

−You recognised me?

−Aye. I just don't know what to call you.

−I'm Justine. Pleased to meet you.

Okay, I thought. Justine.

Justine.

Not Gregor.

Not anymore or ever.

Justine.

−You look… so different.

−In a good way?

−God yes! I cried out, then lowered my foghorn voice. −Thanks for coming, by the way. Honestly, I appreciate it. This is exactly what I needed.

−I understand, said Justine. −It's what I needed too.

−Thanks, I said. −I can't believe she's gone.

−It does seem weird, agreed Justine.

We fell into an uneasy silence, but not for long.

−I heard you'd moved to Glesga.

This was a surprise. Not the move, but the fact she knew about it. Had she been keeping me in mind all these years? Somehow this improved my mood.

−Aye, I said. −I love it. Best thing I ever did.

−I find most people in Glesga are lovely until they get behind a wheel.

Despite the distinguished backdrop of tombstones and inscriptions, I snickered. −What about you? I asked. −Are you back in Denny?

−No, she said immediately, shaking her head, letting her hair move. −I can't stay there and be me. My brothers won't call me my name. Fuck that shit.

−I get it. Totally. So does that mean you're just back for me?

Her expression gave me a sense of the uncertainty she felt.

−It felt like the right thing to do, she said quietly.

−You look brilliant, I told her, because she did.

−Oh, she said, −compliments always help. You look well too.

A lie, of course. Grief had taken the weight off my body and put dark circles underneath my eyes. She was trying to make me feel better, something I took to heart. How could I feel this way? Happy on the day of my mither's funeral? Justine's words were a single bright moment in a dreich day.

−So… I started slowly. −What are you doing now?

Justine blinked, her thick black lashes flicking quickly.

−Well, I graduated from uni. I'm a practicing lawyer.

−The more you practice, the better you'll become.

A terrible joke and one that came out cattier than I'd

246

anticipated. How could I not be slightly bitter though? While Justine was transforming herself, doing what Auld Sybil couldn't, she'd also found time to study hard and nab herself a degree. Me? I dropped out of university. Then I got sacked from every job, two of them ending in near death, one for a drowning pensioner, the other for Mark Hateley… *Whatever happened to him anyway?* And if that wasn't bad enough, my scenes got cut from *Trainspotting*, which had been my only claim to fame. Well, that and being the daughter of the only dealer who gave away free lipsticks with lines of coke, all of it wrapped up in a nice paper bag.

−Sadie, called out Fraser. −You're needed over here.

Justine's eyes narrowed and she got to see my husband for the first time.

−Is that who you married?

−Aye, I said. −His name's Fraser.

−I dated a Fraser. He was an arsehole.

−I've got two children as well. Lucie and Mark.

Justine seemed excited. Maybe my adult years hadn't gone to rot.

−Brilliant, she cried out. −I'd love to see them one day… if that's okay?

−Yes, I nearly screamed. −Yes, I said calmly. −Of course.

At this point, Justine seemed to become conscious of everyone looking over at her. Somehow, I knew she wanted to leave as quickly as possible.

−Thanks for coming, I said. −I appreciate it.

−I had to, Sadie. Your mither was such a character. Everybody said so.

−I bet that's not all they said about her!

−No, but would she have cared? They don't make them like her anymore, that's for sure. She was a force. God, I wish I could have what she had.

247

—A criminal record and bad credit?

—No. The power to not give a shit what people said about me.

Another silence came, this time thin and easily broken.

—Is it strange that no-one here recognises you?

—Aye, but the best kind of strange. *Nice* strange.

—Let's do this again at some point, I said.

Justine raised a thin eyebrow, causing me to backtrack.

—Not the funeral. Duh. *This*. A wee catch-up under nicer circumstances.

—I'd like that. Here's my number…

She handed me a card, small and expensive. *Justine Nersesian – Lawyer. Munro & Weir Solicitors.* She was the real deal. Wow, I thought. Just… wow.

—Justine, I called out. —Wait.

She stopped but didn't completely turn around.

—I'm sorry about what I did. You know… laughing at you.

—You weren't the only one, she said matter-of-factly.

—I know, but I'm really honestly sorry.

She smiled before starting on her way again and I watched her leave for a second time. Somehow, it never got any easier. Eventually, I returned to Fraser and his hand immediately wrapped itself around mine, forceful and tight.

He wanted to know all the details, of course.

—Who was that? Was she a friend of your mither?

—She's an old friend from school, I said.

—It's good to have friends, said Fraser, thinking of someone else.

40

Drowning without Swimming

A spectre followed me through the rain from Central Station all the way down to Argyle Street. It was there with me while I looked in windows and browsed shopfronts. Earlier that same morning, I'd decided to get on the train and escape into shopping, a much-needed serotonin booster. But there was something else there, hidden but felt, a weird itch near the back of my brain. Do you know that feeling when you lose your house keys and swear blind you put them in your pocket, but your pockets are empty? That feeling. Calmly, I looked around the shops, wandering and wondering. At some point, two girls passed me, both of them stopping at the entrance to Debenhams.

One of the girls had her hands around the handlebars of a pram.

That pram might as well have been a glass of water in my face.

I hadn't left the flat alone. My kids were with me.

Now they weren't.

—Shit, I screamed. —Fuck!

Have you seen Mark and Lucie?

They were with me when I got on the train. That much I knew for sure. Now they were gone and it was my fault. Frantically, I tore up the street, my heels hitting the pavement so hard I felt the shudder of the concrete on the soles of my feet. Not that my own pain mattered. I had to get to Central Station and report my missing children, and pray they were still on the train.

Thoughts came in fragments, unformed little notions.

My face would end up in all the papers just like my mither's face. What would people say? Hell, what *wouldn't* they say? I'd be forever tarred as the woman who left her babies on a train so she could take a stroll around Glesga, looking in windows without a care. La-dee-da, oh ain't life just wonderful, la-dee-da-dafty?

The other problem was that I had no idea how to go about getting my kids back – if I ever did get them back. Horror movie trailers played out behind my eyes, each one a preview of all the things that could happen to my children because of *me*. I picked up my stride, reaching Central Station in minutes, arriving in a state of heart-pounding panic. For a second I stood at the entrance, getting a dirty look from someone trying to navigate their way past me with a suitcase by their side. Lungs refilled, I staggered on, entering the station, finding myself stumbling over towards Lost Property where I belonged. Really, I should have gone to the police instead, but the inside of my skull was jumbled and untidy. Eventually, I managed to find someone to help me, a man behind a desk, his attention on the latest edition of *Take A Break*. He quickly shuffled it aside when he realised there was a huffing, puffing, sweating mess in front of him. Immediately, he smiled, not too big, but enough to put me at ease. His Paisley accent was thick like Highland toffee.

–Can I help you, hen?

–I've… sob… left my weans… sob… on the… sob sob… train.

–Take a deep breath, he said. –Do you want a glass of water?

–No, I want my bloody kids back!

–Okay. Take a deep breath. Tell me what happened.

Slowly I began to explain, gradually finding confidence in my words. He listened as I told him about my mither's death, how I'd been with her when it happened, how unfamiliar the world felt without her in it. He nodded when I suggested her death as a reason why I'd left my kids on the Queens Park train. It was a shameless attempt at damage control, of course. He understood, because his mither had recently passed away too.

−I'm just back at work this week, he said softly. Without anything in return, the man behind the Lost Luggage desk was on my side, a stranger and a friend for a few minutes only.

But in the midst of all this drama, one thought overturned the others.

Fraser, of course. If he found out…

GOOD NEWS GUY

Things had been tense between us for a while. I was trapped in a cycle of grief from Mither's death, sleepless nights spent trying to read books to kids who refused to sleep. For a while it had been the constant rounds of breastfeeding that added to my misery, but a lack of sleep also made my grief deeper and ongoing. Fraser wanted everything to be perfect, or so he said.

−Just like with my maw and da, he suggested.

It was so ridiculous that I couldn't even laugh. Also (and potentially worse than anything else), Rangers had just been beaten by Dunfermline Athletic, putting Fraser's mood right through the floor. Sometimes I found myself praying for a win just to make him smile again. Other times, more than most, I wanted to see his favourite team fail, just to annoy him. A loss for them, a petty victory for me. His reaction was the reason I had decided to head out in the first place. While he was on the phone crying about the result to his faither, I was standing in Central Station, hoping for good news, while steeling myself for the worst.

At last, good things came my way.

—Your kids are fine, said the man at the desk, who'd spent the last few minutes on the phone, chatting away all of my worries. —The driver brought them in. They're waiting for someone to come and see them.

—Someone?

—You, if you're quick enough.

Before I turned to leave, there was one last thing I had to do.

—Don't tell my husband, I said quietly. —He drives one of your trains.

—Never mind him. You'll be lucky if you don't get social work at your door.

—She didn't do anything last time she chapped, I laughed.

From the sudden frown lines on his face, I knew I'd said too much.

ANY EXCUSE FOR A SKIVE

The twins were having a great time with the ScotRail staff, who were using them as an excuse to skive off work a bit. When they saw the state I was in, all their sympathies immediately turned in my favour.

—I can't believe this happened, I said, trying to make light of a horrible event.

—Don't worry about it, came one of the train operators. —I've thought about leaving my kids behind too.

Everyone in the room laughed except me.

This was a prime example of Glesga banter.

After thanking everyone for looking after the twins (as though they were babysitters rather than people concerned over abandoned babies), I gripped the handlebar of the pram and pushed it towards the door, hoping no-one would try and stop me. Weirdly, I felt like I was about to be busted for kidnapping my own children. No-one stopped me getting onboard the train back home, which arrived late. By the time our stop came, I felt safe again.

–How was your day? asked Fraser when I got back.

–Fine, I replied. –Uneventful.

–That's funny, he said. –I heard you left the weans on the 10.45 train.

I sighed. This was always going to happen. I was kidding myself on if I thought he'd never find out.

–Who told you?

–Never mind who told me. So it's true?

–It was the lost property guy, wasn't it?

–You mean Derek? Aye, he let me know. He was worried about you.

(Under my breath I muttered –Arsehole.)

One of the twins, Lucie, suddenly started bawling, her face brighter than the wee red jumpsuit I'd stuffed her into that morning. Once she started, Mark decided he fancied a good cry as well. His face, angry and snotty, immediately put me in mind of his faither, who wore the same expression as he shouted.

–What the fuck is wrong with you? What kind of mither leaves her weans on a train and fucks off around the shops?

Then he stopped, as though realising he was onto something.

Whatever it was, it took him in the wrong direction.

–Are you shagging someone else? Where were you today? Why the hurry?

Anger, the sort fuelled by indignant hurt, made me lash out with the truth.

–I'm bloody depressed, I screamed. –How can't you see that?

Fraser was suddenly quiet. It took the babies a few minutes to calm down.

–I didn't know, he said. –I'm sorry.

253

−You've got your folks, I said miserably. −I don't have anyone.

Instead of sneering at me for being self-pitying, Fraser surprised me with a flash of thoughtfulness.

−You've got *us*, he said.

I couldn't work out how to tell him it wasn't enough. Before I could say anything, explain how particular the pain of losing a mither felt, he was next to me, arms sliding around my shoulders, belly pressed against my ribs. We stood in middle of the flat holding each other in a stationary waltz, our feet on top of a scabby red carpet that had been a gift from his own mither, still alive to give us things we didn't need. I wanted to cry, knowing it might make a difference. Instead, I took something else from the embrace − the *best* something else. For now, at least I knew my husband still loved me, caring enough about my feelings to try and make me feel better. Maybe things weren't as bad as I felt?

SOMETHING DRY

Later on, I found myself gasping for something to drink, but had to make do with a mug of PG Tips and blue label milk. Standing by the kitchen worktop, my brain ziplined over several thoughts at the same time, all of them competing for attention. Pick me! Pick me! First I thought about Mither, but only for a few seconds. Too painful, the feelings too sharp. Justine swiftly replaced her in my thoughts, taking the edge off. Soon enough, I became caught up in the idea that I'd let myself down somehow.

−Fuck it, I said, raiding the fridge for something nice to drink.

Instead, a half-empty bottle of Buckfast rolled out of the salad drawer. It had been left by Fraser, who enjoyed an after work swally. Quickly, I finished it off, the taste becoming more tolerable with each mouthful.

Depression cured, I headed back into the living room to watch the telly.

41

2010

I wanted to fly somewhere far away, but not on a plane. The only wings I had on me were bingo wings, so I wouldn't be flapping my arms, for sure. But the idea of being strapped to a seat, helpless in the air, squirming like a worm in a bird's belly… it gave me an uneasy feeling. It was a secret, sleekit horror to be avoided at any cost – and the prices of holidays were costly enough.

–Okay, said Fraser, looking up from a list he'd compiled on the toilet pan. –How about Ibiza?

–I'm thirty-five years old, I snapped. –I'm too old to go out clubbing.

The look on Fraser's face was a mixture of disappointment and hopelessness, each competing against the other. He was a little bit older than me, but somehow had more of a problem accepting it. Every weekend he enjoyed going out, having a pint or two in Blackfriars, then heading to Karbon for the night. He also loved being a family. His whole thing was about keeping us all together, doing things with each other until the weekend came, then he was off. He could reconcile those two sides of his life. Me? I understood wanting to go out, but every single weekend? Sometimes I wanted to be there with him, but for some mysterious reason I couldn't get his mither to babysit the twins, both of them six years old. It had been Fraser's idea to get away for a while, enjoy the sun with the family. Sadly, this included his parents as well. They were only too keen to accompany us abroad, because the umbilical cord connected to Fraser might snap if he got too far away.

–Right, continued Fraser, who shouted from the bathroom while I sat on the couch, bathrobe wrapped around me, an adult comfort blanket. —Okay, so how about Benidorm? It's great for kids.

—Is it?

—That's what my maw says.

—Then it must be true, I grumbled, something unbecoming of me, yet it always felt *so* good. He never heard, thankfully. Over the past few years, I'd started openly criticising the Fotheringhams, who weren't just a 'bit much', but absolutely fucking crazy. It wasn't just Fraser's da and his obsession with purging his life of anything slightly green, but how he had an opinion on everything, even matters that had no impact on his own life. The neighbours, a young gay couple in the giddy flush of their first home, made the mistake of holding hands in their own garden. Thus commenced the incident I secretly referred to as World War Gay.

—I complained to the council, said Robert, flecks of foam shooting out of his mouth. —I'm not homophobic, but it isn't right. It isn't. Am I wrong?

—Didn't you say they were in their garden?

It was out before I could stop myself.

—Aye? So what?

—But that's their property. They can do whatever they want.

—Not outside they can't! I'm not just going to shag my wife out there, am I?

—Robert, snapped Loretta, following this with laughter.

—Dad! came Fraser's disgusted response.

But in his faither's mind, a decisive victory had just been won over me, his keenly-held logic and common sense winning out against my over-emotional reaction. He sat there with a smirk, thinking I'd back down.

—They were just holding hands, I snapped, the veneer of politeness completely gone. —Really, you shouldn't be staring at them in their garden.

This debate went on all night and the next morning, Fraser announced we were all going abroad to bring the family back together. The family this, the family that. The way Fraser talked, we were part of a Mafia – but I also understood the bonds that came from a shared history, how much it mattered. Sadly, the Fotheringhams didn't feel like my family.

Actually, even my own family sometimes didn't feel like mine.

–Benidorm! came a voice from around the corner, loud enough to make me jump slightly. –What do you think? Good or not?

–I don't know, I said quietly.

–Come on! We need to find somewhere nice.

–Nice? I asked. –Okay, how about Euro Disney?

Fraser's laughter, followed by the roar of a cistern emptying and refilling, was the answer. Moments later, he sauntered into the living room where he tossed a list of holiday destinations down at me. It was only when I lifted the piece of paper that I realised he probably hadn't washed his hands after taking a shit. Slowly, carefully, I lowered the sheet of paper onto my lap, looking down from a safe distance. God, I truly hated clatty bastards.

–My folks won't go somewhere unless it's sunny, said Fraser. He looked worried at the prospect that we'd disappoint his mither and faither. Eventually (as usual), he won me over and I decided to accept his decision.

Later that night, I booked our family holiday online for the first time, a brave new world for me and much better than dusty old Ceefax.

–We're going to Benidorm, I announced once the money went through.

PLAYPARK IN THE SKY

I spent the flight to Benidorm with my eyes shut, lungs

258

stiff and teeth gritted so tight that my jaw started to throb in rhythm to the pain in my skull. Worse, there were children on board the plane and they refused to shut up. They yelled, shouted, laughed and screamed while kicking passengers' seats, not caring what their parents said to them. It was only when I opened my eyes that I realised the children making all the racket were *mine*.

–Lucie, I snapped. –Mark. The two of you. Shut it! This is a plane, not a playpark.

They sat still, but their energy couldn't be stifled for long. Within a few minutes they were at it again, kicking and fighting each other. Lucie was in the middle of reading a book, something Mark took offence at because he was bored. One of the flight attendants managed to get them to stop, but only by giving them both packets of crisps. They ate obnoxiously loudly, their mouths wide open, a biology lesson of mashed maize, tonsils and awkward uneven teeth. At least they were busy doing something.

Fraser slept through the whole journey, his snoring just as loud as the piston aero engines of the plane, powering the jet from Glesga to the outskirts of the Mediterranean coast. A three-hour-long barrage of noise, sound and misery. Worse than that, everyone on the plane kept muttering and shaking their heads, none of them quite willing to confront us directly. I was ready to punch someone in the face if they so much as looked at me the wrong way.

Eventually the plane came to a soft, smooth landing.

Spain, at last. For real this time.

We entered the airport expecting to see blue sky through the glass partition, feel the heat of 1976 every day for two weeks. Instead, we found ourselves in a ferocious downpour, the sort that soaked all the way down to your underwear. The kids were struck into silence by the sudden monsoon, more ferocious than any they'd seen at home.

It wasn't great, but then again it wasn't Aviemore either. Finally, I was in another country and the rain wasn't doing anything to lower my mood. Strangely, it made me happy. Somehow, I took joy from things that broke other people. Simple things like gushing rain, odd socks or curtains that didn't close the whole way across.

In the rain, we struggled to get ourselves together. Fraser took control, but led us the wrong way. I knew, but said nothing. Contradicting him, especially in front of his kids, would cause a nervous breakdown and right now we were all too stressed to deal with it. In the end we were two hours late to the hotel.

Worse, Fraser wouldn't get off his phone.

It had been an early Christmas present from his parents, a little BlackBerry that fit neatly into the palm of his hand. Everyone seemed to call him at all hours, his phone number given freely to friends and family – but not to me.

We eventually dried off at our hotel room, a bedsit with a balcony. That's when I noticed Fraser's BlackBerry next to a pile of his sodden clothes, always close at hand. The signal suddenly remembered the phone, making it vibrate madly, letting dozens of messages through in one intrusive burst. I raised an eyebrow, but said nothing. His mither or faither, I assumed. They hadn't been able to make it because Robert broke his arm during a punch-up in a pub during a debate about Scottish independence. He was against it and sent out communiqués every few hours, all of them finding us in another country.

−Not again, I moaned. −Turn it off.

I didn't have a mobile yet, but only because Fraser seemed resistant to the idea. Any time I broached the topic, he'd close it down with an excuse. This alone had brought about a sort of bitterness any time the BlackBerry buzzed, giving me the sense that it was providing something to my husband that I simply couldn't, at least that's how I felt. But if I said anything Fraser would just laugh at the idea of his wife being jealous of a phone.

−Let's go get dinner, I said, receiving an immediate chorus of approval.

Fraser was behind us by a few steps, his eyes on the little screen, thumb moving fast to delete the messages. At the same time, a rumbling sound came from nearby, so loud it made the twins grab my hands for safety.

−Is that thunder? asked Mark fearfully. −A bomb?

−No, I said, −it's just my belly. I haven't eaten for hours.

The little hands slipped out of mine as quickly as they'd grabbed hold.

A RELAXING TIME ABROAD

We were at the pool downstairs, enjoying some rare sun and the sight of drag queens teetering around the bar wearing fabulous (but impossibly high) heels, when Fraser's phone buzzed once again. This time I rolled my eyes, but he didn't see because I had a pair of cheap sunglasses hiding them.

−What is it now? I asked wearily.

Before he could explain, the phone stopped buzzing and started ringing.

Again. While we were on holiday. I wanted to scream.

−Hello, said Fraser, cautiously answering, his back suddenly turned to me. I really wanted to take the phone, yell at his parents, tell them to go and get fucked, then end the call by chucking it into the deep end. But I remained on my chair, reclined and relaxed, dressed in a slightly undersized one-piece bathing suit that cut into my underarms. A horrible thing, made from cheap fabric, it was striped like red and white toothpaste. While Fraser

261

spoke quietly, I watched from the chair, my eyes briefly moving to the kids as they did every few minutes. Lucie was reading her book, two boys behind the wheel of a flying car on the front of it, the image having obsessed her since she saw the cover art on the shelf at Ottakars in Buchanan Street. Mark, meanwhile, was in the pool thrashing around, his arms twisting fast, then hitting the water again , a boy-sized turbine. He was enjoying himself while his friends were back in Glesga, sitting in a classroom with their teacher. The only person not enjoying themselves was me.

—Mum, said Lucie, —why can't we get a car that flies like Ron Weasley's car?

—Because there's no such thing as a flying car. It only exists in a story.

My eyes never once moved from Fraser, standing nearby on his phone.

—But… why can't someone just build a flying car?

—Because it's impossible, I said, trying to avoid a debate.

—Why?

—Because it is, I snapped.

—Is it? asked Lucie doubtfully, her eyes briefly looking up to the clouds, now thick and fluffy instead of grey and overcast. At last the weather was starting to feel Spanish, but it was too late to make a difference.

I still carried the cold in me, where it remained even as I boarded the plane back home to Scotland.

REFILLING THE CUPBOARDS

The supermarket wasn't too busy, just the way I liked it. The kids were at school, something else I liked. In the few hours I had between dropping them off and picking them up again, I did the circuit from Fresh to Frozen. Everything but the eggs got chucked into the trolley, which

262

I pushed around like the handlebar was hot to the touch. Eventually, I realised I'd bought too much and wouldn't be able to carry it home. *Taxi for Relish!* It was in the car park outside the Pollockshields branch of Morrisons that I started thinking about my life, something that was slowly starting to obsess me during the recent months. Why now? I wasn't sure. I was older, for sure. Wiser? If only! Cars drove by and I stood there, deep in thought, hoping for someone to call my name. When it happened, I looked up. But it wasn't the driver who'd shouted over at me, someone else who'd shocked me out of the daydream I'd wandered into while I waited for my lift.

−Justine? I cried out, not quite believing my eyes.

From the other end of the car park, I saw her eyes light up. I waved, hoping she'd come over. She did, walking quickly, her hands over her head, as though trying to push the rain off her hair. Quickly, I became very self-conscious of how I looked. The supermarket circuit was part of my routine, just like boiling a kettle, locking the front door or brushing my teeth. I hadn't bothered dressing up for it, preferring comfort over style. When I got ready, I'd thrown on a washed-out pair of jeans and a shapeless black blouse hidden under a satin jacket. Justine was, as usual, put together.

So was the woman standing next to her.

While Justine came over, her friend remained in the background, content to stand a few metres away in the crowd. The heart-slashing surge of jealousy I felt gave me a rush of kerbside seasickness, but it quickly settled.

−Hey, said Justine gaily, −look at that tan you've got!

−I got it in Spain in the sale, I told her, smiling despite the tinge of awkwardness I felt. Did she feel it too? Somehow, I hope she did. Though she reminded me of my best friend, she also had a new face, one that always smiled.

I hoped her smile was for real.

I wanted it for myself.

—Don't you have an umbrella?

—Huh? I asked, suddenly taken aback.

—It's pishing doon and you don't have an umbrella.

Before I could protest, she pushed the handle of her own umbrella into my hand, my palm touching hers, a little brush of skin, just a slight sliver.

—No, I cried out. —It's okay, I don't need it. I'm fine.

—You look like a soggy seagull standing out here.

Laughter came out of my nose instead of my mouth, a snorting sound, but I didn't give the umbrella back, preferring to keep it safe in my grip. We stood there for a few seconds, waiting for the other to speak. That wouldn't last. Somehow, we managed to find something to say.

—I'm filling up Old Mither Hubbard's cupboard, I explained.

—I hope you paid for this, she said.

For a second, I took this badly. Was she saying I was poor?

—It doesn't matter. I know a good lawyer who can get me off.

The look she gave me, the expression on my own face, met in the middle.

—Justine, called out the other woman. —That's our car here!

—We're out for lunch, said Justine apologetically, —well, a few sandwiches.

—Oh.

—For the rest of the staff.

—Lawyers? I asked.

—Aye. They're a bunch of arseholes, but this gets me a bit of fresh air.

—It's fresh alright, I laughed slightly, tilting my head

at a nearby row of cars, their exhaust pipes pumping out bitter fumes strong enough to cover the car park.

−Justine, called out her associate again, this time with more authority.

−Look, I need to go. It was good seeing you. We need to meet again soon.

This sounded familiar, I thought.

−We will.

That too.

As Justine went to leave, I couldn't help myself.

−Is she a lawyer too?

−Stacy?

−Aye.

−No, said Justine. −She's my girlfriend.

Then she was off, the two of them together in one car.

My brain flip-flopped and I found myself lost for thoughts. Slowly, I worked out the logistics of how a woman who was born male was dating a woman. Worse, a woman who wasn't me, the girl who'd loved him, now her.

Jesus, I thought, completely adrift, lost in ideas and concepts that were completely new to me. *How do I process this?*

The cab arrived and gave me something else to focus on, but only for a few seconds. The driver got out and helped me with my bags, making polite small talk, not a bit of it reaching me. Once the bags were nicely packed in the boot, I fell into the back seat, thinking of Justine and everything that could have been. Already it felt like Justine hadn't been there in the first place, our meeting coming and going like a dream, a really good kiss, or a hit and run.

42

My time as Mrs Fotheringham came to an end while stuffing dirty clothes into the washing machine. Laundry, soap powder and fabric softener had all played a large part in my daily routine for as long as I'd been married. I had no idea why, because I'd never enjoyed the drudgery of washing other people's clothes. Who did? Sometimes, while hurling the dirty washing into separate stacks on the floor, I found myself feeling slightly lost, like I'd signed a contract without reading the small print and had to work in a job without the qualifications. Fraser taught me to hate the cleaning aisle in the supermarket.

Marriage with two children meant finding creative ways to navigate dirty underwear, smelly shirts, crusty socks while enduring the turn of the washing machine drum, mesmerising in its frenzied spin. Always, incessantly, I had to empty the washing basket onto the lino in the kitchen, making sure nothing bright got in with the whites, putting it all in order, trying to control chaos. My husband's bright 'quirky' ties, each one a substitute for personality, had to be cleaned separately from the rest of the washing. Then there were his shirts. Sometimes there was a stray coffee stain around one of the buttons, the one that came just above the belt. If not a coffee stain then a food stain – more specifically, usually a greasy smear of coleslaw from the Sainsbury's sandwich he ate in the staff room at Central Station.

But something was different that afternoon.

For the first time since we got married there was a new stain on his shirt, one that didn't belong there. My eyes caught it before my brain could translate. Bringing the shirt close, I examined it with forensic precision. It was undeniable, not that I would ever bother lying to myself. I was many things: highly strung, hyperactive, overly attentive to the order I placed the TEA/COFFEE/SUGAR jars on the kitchen worktop, but never delusional. Not even I could pretend the stain was something else.

Then there was the smell. Cheap perfume worn by someone just as budget. My worries confirmed, I let the shirt fall from my fingers, leaving it to flutter all the way down onto the lino at my feet. For a few seconds I did nothing other than stand there quietly, staring at the microwave on the worktop facing me, but only seeing the stain on the shirt. The lipstick stain. Not just any lipstick. Red lipstick from Avon. Toasted Rose, to be precise, smeared near the bottom button of Fraser's shirt. I tried to imagine the woman it belonged to, but her face just laughed at me.

My anger came out in the form of a compressed little squeak.

Breathing slowly, my chest bursting, I steadied myself on the worktop.

Eventually, I cross-examined myself, starting with an easy question.

−How do you feel about this, Sadie?

−Well, I said to the other voice, *−it's funny you should ask.*

Mentally, I ticked each emotion off as they happened.

First, I felt… surprise.

Okay. That made sense.

Surprise ✓

Then came anger ✓

*−*Dirty bastard! I shouted loudly, my voice drowned out by the furious racket of the washing machine, which wasn't a bad thing because I didn't want the neighbours knowing my business. Then I felt something else. Another emotion on the checklist, this one completely unexpected.

I waited, carefully analysing my feelings, just in case I had it wrong.

No, I was right the first time.

Relief ✓

Finally, the most surprising emotion of the lot:

Happiness ✓

Jesus Christ, I thought, caught slightly off-guard. *Why am I happy?*

Joy ✓ fury ✓ excitement ✓ and misery ✓ also popped by to say hello.

The violent grinding sound of the final spin started in the background, gradually rising until the noise blotted everything else out of existence, including my private existential crisis, the secret little ruminations of a betrayed housewife. Then, without realising, I activated a new cycle. A trance-like state or mother-wife muscle-memory, the kind that only the most boring routine can create, it didn't matter: I'd lost myself over fifteen years of marriage, filling my life with shiny new things bought on the internet, shopping sprees from the comfort of my kitchen. The new washing machine, for instance, had been a spurious purchase, something I'd clicked on during an annual Black Friday event, the same one-day sale that lasted a week. The sales pitch on the website too persuasive to ignore. *Eco-friendly*, said the advert. *Save the planet (and a lot of money) with every spin.*

So there I was, completely alone, wondering what would happen next. What did a wife do when she discovered the truth about her husband? I knew what some women did. They talked it over, stayed the course or they divorced. But this hadn't happened to me before, so I wasn't entirely prepared for my new reality. Yet during the next load of dirty washing, I found myself taking comfort in the knowledge that no matter what happened, at least the towels and socks would be get a good wash.

Bing, bang, Bosch!

After I'd contemplated hanging myself on the same line as the washing, I took a seat at my kitchen table. I'd bought it from IKEA (on credit) during that phase when I wanted my kitchen to look Scandinavian and very slowly managed to turn it into a pristine showroom. I sipped my coffee, bitter like me. Still, I couldn't quite believe what had happened to me. But as I sat drinking, calming myself with a cuppa, the mundane helping to steady me in my shakiest moment, I started coming to terms with a whole new truth.

−He'll have to go, I said aloud, giving myself permission to start the process of breaking up our marriage. Then another thought, slightly unexpected.

−We're still paying for the bed, I said idly.

It was king-sized and there were three more payments left. Being alone is expensive. The prospect of having nothing again was so depressing that I forced myself to think about something else. Revenge, actually. No. Not revenge. Justice. As a woman, a wronged wife, I needed justice. It seemed to be only right that I strike hard and fast, hurt Fraser the way he hurt me with Toasted Rose, whoever she was. Of course, she had to suffer as well. It was necessary for my soul that they felt my hurt, if only to help me recover something they'd stolen behind my back.

Do they laugh at me while they're together? Does she feel pity for the wife at home? Does she know I exist? Does he lie about me? Does he...?

I sipped my coffee, but it was cold.

How long had I been here?

The washing machine had stopped too. Quietly, I rose up from the chair, hearing the creaking noise as I stood. There was a permanent print on the cushion that perfectly matched my bum, heavier on the left side. I walked over to the sink, still full of water and soap residue. The dishes needed to be put away, but that wasn't important anymore. There was something else I needed to do, something vital. But what? I wavered, trying to remember what I'd pushed away.

The shock of the stain on the shirt has made me lose track of time. It's only when I look at the mug I'm about to drop into the sink that I remember my twins are still at school. This would be fine, except the gates shut nearly forty minutes ago. Without giving myself any time for guilt, I run out of the flat, down the flight of stairs, each step bouncing off the walls, taking me to my car and its locked doors. The keys are back in the kitchen where I left them.

Turning around, I bolt back through the communal door, back up the stairs, into the flat where the car keys dangle from the little tree made from wire, with hooks that let all the other sets dangle too, until they are needed. Eventually, I get into my car, bringing it to life, slowly manoeuvring myself out of the driveway. I'm so focussed on the image of my twins waiting at the school gates that I forget all about my husband, his girlfriend and her Avon lips. But like the second between sleeping and waking up, it's brief and I remember again.

43

Marriage is a promise but love is far less dependable. After finding the stained shirt, I started to realise how naïve (or stupid) I'd been over the years. All those nights of extra overtime Fraser kept taking, the times he didn't get into his uniform but still went out for his shift. That sort of thing. But cheating on me meant I didn't have to keep my side of the bargain any more. For the first time in years, I felt free – and more than a little frightened. The monotonous grind that made up my everyday life was finally gone, just like me, the moment I packed my things. Once I walked out, I wouldn't look back. But before I could even think about getting a divorce, I still had a score to settle. After all, I'd taken his name and he'd taken the piss. It was only fair, wasn't it?

With that in mind, I put my foot on the pedal, bringing myself nearer to the gates of Hillpark Secondary, hoping the twins hadn't decided to walk back alone. It was unlikely. They preferred to be chauffeured everywhere. Mark, because he was idle and Lucie, because of her anxiety. While driving, I found my thoughts going off the road and into a fantasy, an alternative history of me where I became the most important woman in the world. In this fantasy, Fraser knows I've discovered his affair. He begs for mercy and I show him none. I'm not a stay-at-home skivvy anymore. I'm now a powerful witch, full of magic and hellfire. My eyes spark and paper-thin beams of hot, killer light flare through the air, cutting the cheating bampot down where he stands. Outside my head (and inside my car), I'm keeping my eye on the road. Mark would be upset, of course. This wasn't the first time I'd been late picking him and his sister up, but I knew from past experience that a Happy Meal could buy their support, silence and love, if only for a while – or at least the time it took for a cheeseburger to digest inside the bellies of two fourteen-year-old kids.

I turned the wheel and the road turned with me, bringing Shawlands Academy into view. They were there at the steps as expected, dressed primly in their standard navy sweaters: a woollen-nylon blend v-neck that could only be washed at 30°C with mild detergent. Mark tried to accommodate a little bit of personality into his uniform, having the shirt untucked, trying his best to look cool, complete with black tie awkwardly hanging insolently to the side, the green and purple shield still in view. Lucie, meanwhile, never had a hair out of place. A wrinkle in her sweater had the power to disrupt her entire day, so she made sure everything was perfect. Mark was a facsimile of my husband, from his complexion to his temperament. As I moved the car close to let the kids into the back seat, I noticed an expression on Mark's face, similar to the one his faither had when he thought I wasn't watching him.

EVERYBODY LOVES ME BUT YOU

Mark was impatient to get home so he could get on his PlayStation 2. He'd plug the controller directly into his brain if the technology existed. *Tekken Tag Tournament*, a two-player game he refused to share with his sister, was the current obsession. I unlocked the door to let the twins climb inside, completely unaware of the storm that was coming.

–You're late, snaps Mark as he rolls across the seat, making space for his schoolbag instead of Lucie. Before I can say anything to defend myself, he slams the door shut. For Mark, an apology was always an excuse, no space in-between for the other side of the story. Looking away from the mirror, I bite my bottom lip, then take the opportunity to defend myself.

–The traffic was bad, I explain. Then, upon seeing his unsympathetic reaction, I tell a lie. –Someone got hit by a bus, I add for no reason.

I didn't feel guilty about lying, not even a little. Lies are like any successful creative endeavour in that the more you do it, the better you become. Lying is easy now, I decide. If Fraser can do it, why not me? I retell the traumatic events that kept me from reaching my children in time, keeping the details as vague as possible. My son, despite being fourteen years old now, is savvy enough to know I'm being dishonest. Most children have a way of sensing the truth, even if they can't quite comprehend the reason behind the lie. It doesn't take Mark long to find a hole in my defence and he tears it at the seam, mercilessly widening the gap until I'm exposed. Childlike logic is the strongest, most inflexible form of intelligence and it tolerates no deviation from cause to effect.

Sometimes it's impossible to defeat.

–Someone got hit by a bus?

–Yes, I reply, trying hard to look traumatised.

I'm an actress now. Danny, put me back in the final cut of *Trainspotting*!

–And that's why you're late?

–Uh huh.

–Then how come everyone else's mums and dads got here on time?

–I'm sorry, I said, my voice as remorseful as I think it'll take to soothe him.

Mark doesn't reply, his attention is focussed on everything happening outside the car window. It's getting dark, late night coming closer. Without saying anything else, I rev the engine and start the journey back home.

Halfway home, I try and make conversation.

273

−Did both of you have a good day?

That's all I can manage in that moment.

−Aye, says Mark, butting in before Lucie can answer, as usual. −But it was better a few minutes ago.

−Why? What happened?

−I saw you.

The words come out of Mark's mouth, but the sentiment belongs to someone else, his faither probably. Thinking of him makes me remember what he'd done behind my back and suddenly my foot is pressing down on the pedal too hard, the dial on the speedometer flying free, peaking too quickly.

Everything outside the car becomes lines.

Houses are grey lines. People are pink lines. The sky is a blue line.

Speed feels good, especially behind a wheel.

−We're flying, squeals Lucie, her voice full of delight.

Just up ahead, a sign warns of speed cameras in the area.

I ignore it and the sign becomes another line.

Scissor time

The day started with scissors. I bought them on Amazon, not because I needed them but because they were gold-plated and cheap, the only reason to buy basics online. I'd only used them a few times, but they never failed to cut whatever I set them to. They were in the drawer, the one next to the sink where I kept a rolling pin, potato peeler and a stash of debt letters I didn't want Fraser to find. They were there, underneath the envelopes. I reached in, pushing my fingers around the hooped grooves in the handle. Lifting the scissors out, I held them up above my head, catching wee bursts of sunlight from between the cracks in the blinds. My face was caught in the coppery burnish – it reflected a grin at me. Two minutes later, I was upstairs in my bedroom, standing directly in front of the wardrobe where Fraser kept everything he wore, everything neatly ironed, perfectly folded and expertly organised. My doing, of course. Before I had scissors, I had too much time.

Now I had a quest.

Fraser's side of the wardrobe was always to the right because it was closer to his side of the bed. No convenience was spared to me, so my clothes sat on the left side, in the far corner of the room. It was a large wardrobe with mirrors on it, too big for the space, squashed against the wall. But Fraser had insisted on it, mostly because his parents had a similar wardrobe in their room and we had to suffer just the same. I sighed.

Out of nowhere... a moment of doubt. Standing at the side of the bed, staring at the bundles of clothes, I started to question whether I could go through with it. A voice stopped me, the inner dialogue I had for company while Fraser was at work and the twins off doing their own thing. Oddly, the scissors felt too heavy for my hand, like they could drop, burying their blades into the carpet. Something else made me hold on tight, giving me quiet courage. Taking this as permission granted, I cleared the right side of the wardrobe, pulling everything out onto the floor. Shirts, trousers, jeans, jumpers, jackets, socks, pants. I piled the lot in a bundle behind me, then got to work. I slashed through the first shirt on the pile, cutting with long continual strokes, the persistent sound of snipping a kind of therapy. It felt great.

I hacked and slashed each piece of clothing as it came to hand, tearing everything into long pieces while imagining it was Fraser's skin. Within minutes, all his shirts were completely shredded. But it wasn't enough. I found myself picking up more of Fraser's clothes. I felt like I was no longer in control of my own body. I'd become an avatar for a powerful, immeasurably primal force, the patron saint of slighted wives. I got into the spirit of revenge. Snip, snip, snip. Oh, it was pure music. I felt like I was in the middle of a strange deconstructive art project: you start with one thing and end up with another – chaos and creation. Again, it wasn't enough. After dealing with the shirts, I attacked the rest. Every piece of clothing Fraser owned fell before the scissors until there was nothing left.

Disappointed it was over, I considered slashing up the bedsheets, but decided against it because I didn't want to be cold tonight. Exhaustion forced me back onto the mattress, my body dropping so hard I bounced up into the air again, before coming to rest. All the excitement gone, I felt feeble and shivery, craving a cuppa with three sugars and none of that decaf shit. I got up from the bed, left the scene of the crime and headed down to the kitchen, whistling a tuneless joyful noise. It was only when I lifted my hand to put sugar in the mug that I realised the scissors were still there, still firmly in my grip. Grudgingly, I dropped them back into the cutlery drawer, knowing full well I could always use them again if I needed to cut off something else.

44

BEING SINGLE IS EXPENSIVE

What next? I asked myself. How do I make a new life with two children in a flat that I can barely afford? Glesga ate money. The rent, council tax and service charges cost nearly everything in the joint account. Apart, we didn't stand a chance. There were parts of the city that were cheaper, but I wanted to be here in Strathbungo, where my children felt safe. They knew the streets, the shops and the buses. The city belonged to them. My housing benefits and family allowance would be stretched to snapping. In that respect, it would have been easier to stay quiet, just keep everything the way it was, bear the burden of unhappiness. And I considered it. Really, I did. But when Fraser came back from work, all kisses and hugs, it was impossible for me to pretend.

As soon as he leaned in towards me, I pulled away.

−What's the matter? he sighed warily, knowing something had happened.

He really had no idea, not in the slightest.

−Who is she?

Taken aback, he tried to laugh it off.

−What?

−Who *is* she?

−I don't know what you're talking about.

Fraser was *many* things. A train driver, a keen fan of clubbing, thwarted DJ, a former reader of *The Broons*, lover of modern tech, a supporter of Rangers FC, a mummy's boy and the faither of my children. But he wasn't too smart. He'd always relied on me as a sounding board. No form could ever be filled in without asking my approval and even his spelling had to be fixed. Somehow, these little moments had made me feel appreciated, like I was needed. I only needed the truth. Unfortunately, I had to lie to get it.

–You've been seen with her, I said confidently.

He faltered immediately and in that moment I had him.

–She was my girlfriend from high school.

–Huh? High school?

–We reconnected on Friends Reunited a few years ago.

Friends... what? I didn't even know he'd been on Friends Reunited.

That was probably the point, wasn't it?

I nearly threw my pricy IKEA table at his head, but a meaningful part of his statement unexpectedly lodged itself in my brain until I thought it over.

This had been going on for years. How long ago? When did it start?

–A few years ago? I shouted. –This has been going on for years?

Another memory. Spain. The phone that hadn't stopped ringing.

–Bastard, I hissed.

–I'm sorry, he said, looking down at his feet, like a wee boy caught stealing. –But look, it's over. It's finished. It didn't mean...

–Why? I shouted. –What did I do wrong?

–Nothing! It's me. I don't know who I want to be anymore.

–That's the dumbest excuse I've ever heard for anything.

–I had history with her, he cried out.

–What's her name? I screamed, no longer caring if the twins heard me. –What's her fucking name? Tell me her name right now, Fraser.

–Her name's Lucy.

I froze in mid-scream. My throat felt hard and tight,

like a blood vessel might burst. Quickly, I swallowed some moisture back into my throat.

–Lucy, I said quietly. –Your ex is called Lucy. The name you gave our daughter?

He shook his head like I was a dafty, full of denial.

–Our Lucie has an 'i' and an 'e'. My ex is Lucy with a 'y'.

He seemed pleased with himself.

–They're two totally different names.

A calm, crawling hatred spread through me like bad pins and needles. He'd pushed a name onto our daughter that I didn't like, a name that I'd come to accept, even love, because I adored my daughter more than anything else in the world, needing her like I needed breath, light and laughter. This wasn't just a violation of my trust, it was a cataclysm of the heart, the most gutting betrayal imaginable. I shook my head, eyes blazing.

There was no way back. Not anymore. How could there be?

–I want you out! I yelled.

–We can work it out. We can…

– You can fuck right off!

Then, once I'd regained some control, I said calmly:

–I'd tell you to pack your bags, but you don't have enough to put in them.

That should have been the end of the fight, but it took a sudden turn in a completely new direction, one that left me feeling staggered.

–No, he told me.

–What?

–I'm not leaving. We're going to work this out. We can't break up.

–Why? Because your parents are still together?

–No! It's nothing to do with them.

But it was everything to do with them. Fraser lived in

two worlds; in one of them, he was a faither with a family, who did everything the right way around. But the other side of him felt trapped, squeezed by the daily grind. He wanted to DJ in Ibiza, go clubbing on the beach, snort coke off tits and not give a shit.

−I don't want to be with you anymore, I cried out, not knowing for sure if that was the case. Maybe I could get over this? Anything was possible. But right now, I wanted Fraser gone. In the past, whenever my mither had fought with any of my uncles, they'd always been the ones to leave. I just assumed that's how it happened in any breakup. She told them to get out (rather, she told them to fuck off) and they got out. But that wasn't happening for me in my own breakup. Instead, Fraser shook his head stubbornly.

−No, he said.

−I'm getting out of here.

−No! he shouted, flipping over my IKEA table, breaking a leg off it.

The noise brought the twins running out of their room.

−Pack your stuff, I ordered. −We're leaving.

−Don't you dare, shouted Fraser, not taking his eyes off my face. −The two of you go back to your room and don't come out until I tell you.

−Bloody hell, said Mark, shaking his head. −What's she done now?

I glared at my son, immediately hating him for taking his faither's side. Of course I couldn't say anything about his swearing, because like my IKEA table, I didn't have a leg to stand on. Swearing was an official part of the Relish lexicon, an essential component of our vernacular.

−I'm getting away from here, I said firmly. −Okay?

−Don't be daft, laughed Fraser. −Where will you go?

−I'd rather live in tramp's troosers than be with you.

−You can't leave! What will I tell my mither and faither?

But I was already dragging my suitcase towards the door. Before I left, I put the boot into the other woman, my replacement who was already off the scene.

−By the way, your girlfriend has a hard face, hard tits and a hard heart.

Fraser didn't know what to say, so he just disintegrated into random insults.

−Right, I said to the twins, −both of you get your things and come with me.

−Why? asked Lucie anxiously.

−Because your faither's a lying arsehole.

The twins looked at each other, then made their choice.

Two of them went off to pack, but only one of them came back.

45

BEDSITTERS

The bedsit reeked of pish and damp, which immediately put me in the worst mood. But no matter what happened, I had to keep going, if only for Lucie. She reacted to my moods, a sensitive little sponge, now split from her twin brother. If she felt deeply about our current living situation, she didn't show it. I was proud and scared and unsure about what to do next. In reality, I'd expected Fraser to go and live with his bit on the side, not stand his ground and cast me out. Now I was stuck in a small single bedroom flat in Regent Park Square, that used to belong to an old lady who'd been disowned by her family for marrying a Catholic, long since dead. The landlord had told me the story for absolutely no reason. His name was Jonathan and he had hair sprouting out of his ears, a distracting bush on both sides. Also, he had a terrible habit of pushing himself into my space. He literally couldn't stay in the same spot, always moving closer to me, each word a footstep forward.

Eventually, he had me backed against the wall of his nasty bedsit.

–The rent is three hundred and fifty a month. I'll need a deposit upfront.

–It's getting sorted, I explained. –I'm entitled to housing benefits.

TELLY TIME

Within days of moving into my new flat, I'd already gutted it clean, throwing the entirety of my frustration into scrubbing the floors, walls and worktops. A 500ml bottle of Zoflora became my new favourite thing in the world, everything it touched gleamed with a surgical sheen. There were two old couches included, a gift from the previous tenant, whose imprint and odour were still in the fabric itself. I had to battle to erase the smell. Every morning, I woke Lucie up from that couch, where she slept with the telly on, watching Top Gear. Mostly, she'd be propped up on some cushions, reading Haynes manuals or books about physics, using the time away from her faither and brother to pondering the mysteries of the vertical take-off and advanced aerodynamics. She soon decided the best way to make a car fly was to find a way to power several autogyros in sync, but keep it environmentally friendly.

–Okay, I nodded dumbly as she tried to explain it to me.

Her grades at school hadn't suffered during the move, but she still seemed a little too withdrawn, her passion for building a flying car, deeply intense. While she had that dream, nothing else could bother her, not even the smell from the couch. Every night we ate dinner on that couch, trays on our laps.

–How's everything at school? I asked one evening, while trying to catch some stray peas that kept rolling across my plate.

–Fine, said Lucie, whose gravy was already starting to congeal over her microwave pie, giving it a slick greasiness that nearly turned my stomach, though it didn't stop me eating.

–Fine? I asked, eyebrow raised, a small smile on my face. I often smiled when Lucie was there. Sometimes my jaw ached from smiling.

–It's *fine*, she sighed, clearly not up for a discussion.

–How's your brother?

That was the real reason I'd brought up the subject of school. Since the split, I hadn't heard from Mark or his faither. Hopefully, Lucie would be able to tell me something about my son, her twin brother. Was he okay? Was he coping? Did he miss me? These were questions I asked myself too often.

−I don't know, said Lucie, trying to avoid my eyes. It was easier in the dark. The only light was the dull gamma blue ray of the television in the corner.

−He doesn't talk to me, she continued. −He pretends I'm not there.

My fork slipped and peas came off my plate.

−He's ignoring you? Your own brother?

−Aye. Him and his friends.

And just for a second, even in the gloom of a late night dinner in the living room with the lamps off, I caught something that might have been sadness on my daughter's face. Her eyes, mostly. When she realised I was looking, she immediately broke into a smile, the same one I forced every day.

It had been passed down through the generations.

−That little shit, I snapped. −Who the fuck does he think he is?

−I don't care, replied Lucie, lying to keep the peace.

But I was already up and at the phone, dialling my old house number.

Someone at the other end answered quickly.

−Sadie, came Fraser's voice. −I'm glad you phoned.

−Put Mark on the line, I snapped. −Right now.

−Wait! I want to talk. I need to see you about something.

−See me?

−Come over. Please.

My initial thought was to stay as far away from my old home as possible, put a wide gap between my old life and this one, the one I was trying to scrape from nothing. Then again, this was an opportunity to make life a little bit easier for my daughter, stuck with her mither in a bedsit.

−Okay, I said. −I'll pop over, but just to talk.

−Aye, he sighed. −Thanks.

The noose had been set up in my old bedroom, made from one of the few bedsheets I hadn't sliced up before I left. Somehow, he'd wrapped the sheet into a makeshift rope. My mouth was agape, because I had no idea this was coming when I had agreed to meet Fraser for a chat. He was standing next to the noose tied to the light fitting, the bulb touching the sheet, patiently waiting for me to speak. He looked dreadful, his eyes narrow with tiredness, his only clothes a manky old t-shirt and a pair of boxers that looked like they'd been worn for weeks.

Motioning at the makeshift rope, I asked, −What the fuck is that?

Of course I already knew, but asking meant talking it through.

−If you don't take me back, I'm going to hang myself.

−With that sheet? It'll pull the fixture off the ceiling, you daft bastard.

He looked up, suddenly realising how little he'd thought this through.

−I can't even do this right, he said.

Somehow, and I don't know why, I found this uproariously funny. At first I tried to stifle my laughter, but soon it came out loud and free. Eventually, even Fraser started to laugh. The two of us were back to how we were when we met, years earlier in Denny, during the bells. But once the laughter died off, we were left in an uncomfortable silence.

−I want you back, said Fraser sadly.

−Would you really have tried this? I asked, looking at the stupid noose.

−Maybe.

−Mark would have seen this. Didn't you think about that? Or do you just think about yourself all the time?

−I'm not thinking about me. I was thinking about you.

Fraser ran a clammy hand through his greasy dark hair, then took a deep breath, suddenly calming down for the first time since he'd let me back into my own house.

It no longer felt like mine. Not anymore. That feeling of belonging, of being somewhere that accepted you, no matter what. The bedsit didn't inspire that feeling in me either. Only one place had felt like home and I hadn't realised it until now. Denny. My hoose, my hame and I could reach it on the bus, an hour's travel up the M80.

For the first time in years, the way forward was clear.

−I can't come back, I said quietly.

−I'm sorry for being an arsehole, said Fraser, his voice breaking.

−Where's Mark? I asked, suddenly wanting to change the subject.

−He's out with his pals.

−Oh? He should be out with his sister.

−I know. I know. I'll get him told to start making an effort.

We went downstairs together and I flung my coat on, getting ready to head out into the rain, make the journey on the bus back to my bedsit. Fraser didn't want me to go. He took my hand and held it until I freed it from his grip.

−Don't do anything daft, I said.

−Just give me another chance, he pleaded, his eyes never meeting mine.

−Maybe, I replied. But I knew that would never happen.

−How are you feeling? he asked, as though realising he should be interested. There was a time he had been interested, so this wasn't a bad sign, just too late.

−I'm not sure, I said honestly. −I'll get there at some point.

Some point was a few more years, but it eventually happened.

I got 'there'.

46

It didn't matter that the Post Office had a small television screen mounted on the far wall. Sunlight from the grimy windows always found a way to reach it, a beam of heat constantly threatening to melt the liquid crystal display whenever the clouds fell back. The TV was an outdated model but had probably seemed like the future at the time. Initially installed as a tool for local businesses to advertise on, the scheme failed after dozens of local businesses were bitchslapped by Brexit. The only business willing to advertise was Hand Job, a luxury nail bar located down the street. Sadly, they were rebuffed. Not the target clientele, apparently.

At some point, in order to justify the expensive TV licence paid for public broadcasting, someone decided that BBC News 24 be shown in place of the outdated business adverts. The channel never changed, even though everything else around it had transformed completely. I was now back in Denny after years of being in Glesga, the urge to realign myself with something familiar proving too irresistible to ignore. A change of location came with a bounce of luck after years of not working. Somehow, I'd managed to nab myself a part-time job at the Post Office, now part of a franchise inside a little convenience store. Everything suddenly seemed to be in place for me again. It turned out that the manager used to buy Avon (and the best ecstasy she'd ever taken) from my mither and wanted to do me a good turn. Somehow, like my move back home, this felt like fate. My only worry was Lucie. For 19 years, she'd only known Glesga and I wasn't sure how she'd cope with new surroundings. Change wasn't something she appreciated. Even her clothes were the same. Every day she dressed in a plain black hoodie and a pair of denim jeans. Not the same hoodie and jeans. Like her grandmither, Lucie was obsessively clean. Her bedroom cupboard was full of identical black hoodies, her uniform in life. What had sold her on the move was the fact our new house came with a garden, a small attic, two bedrooms and a garage.

–A garage, she said, immediately perking up.

I knew that would get her attention.

–Aye, I replied. –A nice wee garage.

Because our budget was smaller than a dot of dirt on a doorknob, I couldn't afford a house in Glesga with a garden or a garage, but things were cheaper out in Falkirk, and the waiting list for council accommodation was shorter too. Within a week of signing the document, we had a new home in Denny. Within a week of moving in, I had my job at the local Post Office.

Somehow, I was finally happy.

At last.

I LOVE BOREDOM

Every day was routine. I didn't mind though. Something about mind-numbing boredom made me happy, putting me in a trance-like state that stopped me feeling anything too strongly. A quiet life was better than all the madness I'd experienced over the years. Somehow, I'd started to value silence. A job at the Post Office suited me. Our customers were mainly pensioners, forever queuing up to collect their pensions, send parcels or postcards to family members who had long since fled Denny for other places.

My journey in reverse, basically.

During a quiet afternoon, while my co-worker, Maria, was off having her lunch, something suddenly felt wrong in the room. A few seconds passed before I realised the television had switched itself off. The sunlight did that sometimes, overloading the circuit board.

—Fuck, I muttered, but it was no big deal.

Standing up, I left the counter and headed around with the remote control in my left hand, a magic wand that always brought the screen back to life. Pointing it up in the general direction of the wall, I pressed the STANDBY button, the rubber having been squashed into a flat dot.

The date flicked up, then vanished, giving me ghostly letters and numbers.

It read Monday 23rd March 2020.

—Time flies, I said to no-one. Then I changed the channel, trying to find BBC News 24, the default station since I'd started my job at the Denny branch. Large green digital numbers slowly appeared, one at a time. *101*, said the display after a slight lag. Immediately, BBC1 popped up, giving me Boris Johnson looking slightly hapless in mid-speech.

—No thanks, I said, raising the control to change the channel again. The Prime Minister was being filmed vigorously shaking hands with people, when in fact he should have been shaking a brush through his hair. *102* came up next as I pressed the buttons in sequence, trying to get the news channel. The hospital was immediately replaced by a garish plastic studio set with a live audience; some sort of quiz show I assumed. Not wanting to see that in the Post Office, I changed the channel once again. *103*, meanwhile, brought adverts. They were all different, yet all very alike at the same time. They all had figures of authority speaking directly to the camera in calm, clear voices. Doctors, nurses, scientists, life insurance salesmen, Esther Rantzen.

—Wash your hands, they said in unison. —Sneeze into a handkerchief and dispose of it immediately in the nearest bin. Stop the spread!

Groaning, I changed the channel, pressing <u>up</u> instead of individual digits.

More adverts, different voices.

–*The impact of Coronavirus on the homeless is something we cannot fight alone. But together we can*...

– *...fight it*...

–*...together we can win*...

–*...ten pounds to help*...

–*...the struggle against*...

–*...Sun Bingo*...

–*...and give a child the gift of*...

–*...Covid-19*...

–*...because Beanz Meanz*...

–*...we are all in this together*...

–Gie's peace, I called out, oblivious to the queue of customers who'd quietly gathered in the background while I fought with the television.

Eventually, after a hot minute, I realised I'd trapped myself in a recurring nightmare of channel surfing, cycling every station on Freeview, running the entire gamut of news stations and afternoon scheduling, until finally I got bored of looking for BBC News 24. Even the shopping networks were selling surgical masks and hazmat suits. In the end, I handed the remote control to the person nearest me, an older man who'd popped in to send a parcel to his mither in Poland. He looked at me hesitantly, not quite knowing what I wanted. How could I tell him all I really wanted was a quiet life?

Oh, and a working television in the Denny branch of the Post Office.

THE NEW LEXICON

New words and terms established themselves into everyday language during the first wave of the pandemic.

Clap For Heroes. Covidiot. Work From Home. Digital meeting. Flatten the curve. The most important word in the new lexicon was, of course, furlough. The Post Office was closed during lockdown and I found myself in my new home, getting to grips with the reality we all shared. Lucie seemed slightly rattled by the changes, but she kept herself busy in the garage, causing a racket with whatever she was doing. I'd hear hammering, which was headache-inducing, but far worse was the drilling, a merciless screech of metal on metal. Every now and then, I headed down the path towards the garage door with lunch, hoping to do my nosy. Instead, I found myself locked out, kept at a safe distance.

In many ways, the pandemic suited Lucie. She could indulge herself in her passion for solitude. Sometimes, out of concern (of course), I'd ask her if she ever wanted a boyfriend or some friends at least. I hated the idea of my little girl being on her own without anyone.

Lucie, however, always had an ideal excuse.

—Coronavirus, she'd say, and close the door, literally and metaphorically.

Our lives continued like this for a while. Eventually, I started to feel wearisome. Even the smallest action required the most considered of thoughts. A trip to the corner shop for a pint of milk meant taking the carton in a sleeved grip. The handles on the bus to keep you steady literally felt threatening to me. Washing your hands without touching the tap handles was a task that needed careful preparation. Basically, the virus was always there, trying to get into you, but I refused to make it too easy. Furlough (another new word) meant I didn't need to worry about money, for once. The Post Office put all their staff on hold, paying us all for the pleasure of staying at home.

I spent the months that followed out in the garden on a towel in the grass.

Eventually, I realised this quiet new life suited me. Peace, I thought. It isn't bad, is it?

47

The swelling under my left breast was hard and tender. Somehow I convinced myself to keep calm.

– I'm still here, I said. While I'm here, I can win.

The semi-solid lump, the size of a marrowfat pea, soon reshaped how I viewed the world, giving me an alternative outlook on life. Not knowing if you have much time left sharpened little details you could easily miss. Time, I soon realised, was vitally important. A fleeting flying thing, time wasn't just something to be looked at on your wrist. It was more valuable than money. Time, like money, had to be spent wisely. I had so much more to do. What? I didn't know. Just *more*. More breathing, more laughing and more living.

Oh, and less drinking.

THE WORLD IS NEW AGAIN

While I waited for my check-up, I decided to fix everything in my life. Unfortunately, there was a lot to sort out. Years after the divorce, the twins still weren't speaking. Timidly, I attempted to get Lucie interested in talking to Mark again, even by phone or text. We were both similarly natured, placid until provoked.

I'd been inside all day, stewing in silence, bored and a little frightened. Finally, frustrated at the lack of progress, I spoke up.

–I was thinking about Mark, I said.

Lucie cut me off before I could say any more.

–You're always thinking about Mark, she said flatly.

–He's my son. Don't you miss him?

–Not particularly.

−You know… this would be a good time to call him up. He's probably stuck in the house too. I bet he'd love to hear from his sister.

−Ha, said Lucie, who was on the other couch, her fingers tippity tapping on the keyboard. Swallowed in her extra-large black hoodie (because she liked loose fitting clothes), she looked like a wee face and hands. Physics was her thing and before the pandemic struck, her degree in Geophysics had landed her a job… at The Cathouse in Glesga, setting up their sound equipment for live gigs. It paid a pittance, sadly. Luckily, the council didn't know Lucie was living with me, so I claimed everything that was going, just to keep the rent low. Mither's tips and tricks had proved useful through the years.

Once again, I tried to get my daughter to do what I wanted, while making her think it was all her idea.

−When did you last hear from him?

−Two years ago, she said blandly.

They'd met accidentally in Glesga, at Renfield Street's branch of KFC. According to Lucie, it had been pleasant and promising. Then nothing.

−You should reach out to him. Find out how he's doing.

−No.

−Why not?

−Because I don't feel like it.

I'd already tried to reach out, but couldn't quite do it. Any email I typed always made its way into Drafts instead of Sent. I'd even set up a Fakebook account just so I could see what my son looked like now, but his profile picture was the Rangers Football Club logo and everything else was private.

−Look, I snapped at Lucie, suddenly turning her into the target of my frustration. −You can't just ignore your brother.

−Why not? she replied calmly. −You've ignored your sister for years.

From the look of triumph on Lucie's face, she'd been waiting to use that one and I'd walked right into it. My first instinct was to tell her to fuck off. Thankfully, reason prevailed, because really... she was right.

−Your Aunt Lily didn't come to your grandmither's funeral.

−Och, that was years ago, she said, eyes and fingers stuck to the laptop. −You can't just ignore your sister forever.

My own words lobbed back at me.

−It's tough, I explained. −I walked out on your brother. I left him with his faither. In his head, it looks like I chose you over him.

−That's a load of shite, snapped Lucie. −He chose to stay. I chose to leave. He wasn't abandoned. If I felt you did something wrong, I'd tell you.

−But that's how I *feel*, Lucie.

−Well don't. Honestly, he'll come to you at some point. It'll be fine.

−It was never easy with him. I could never get anything right.

−He was seeing faither and copying him. It wasn't personal.

I hadn't thought of that, actually. Maybe there was something in that?

−Look, if you speak to your brother, I'll phone my sister. That's the deal.

Lucie seemed to consider my offer.

−Okay, she said. −I'll try.

−Good! That's all I want.

That was one problem solved, at least.

Now for the next.

Lily's old number started ringing the first time I dialled it into the keypad, the digits being recorded for posterity in an old notebook. But I couldn't finish the call, ending it before the ringing gave way to a voice.

Eventually, I stayed on the line, refusing to disconnect the call.

—Hello, came my sister's voice, years since I'd last heard it.

—Hey Lily, I said quietly. —It's me.

—Bloody hell, cracked my sister. —I never thought I'd hear from you again.

—You nearly didn't!

—Well…

She paused, as though considering her words carefully.

—I'm glad you did.

To my surprise, I was glad too. Like Mark and Lucie, I'd never been close to Lily. But my perspective had recently been shaken by what I found on my breast, so I was willing to be flexible in my attitude, even after she abandoned me at Mither's funeral. This was something I wanted to talk about.

Lily, meanwhile, seemed excited to hear my voice. Times had changed.

—I've missed you, she claimed. —Why did we let this happen?

—Because you didn't come to Mither's funeral?

Immediately, I regretted my honesty. It wasn't worth knocking down my sister, not now we were taking cautious steps to renewing our relationship.

Until I knew my test results, I wanted to be careful.

—I nearly got arrested because of her, said Lily quietly, her voice still slightly bitter. Maybe it was anger or guilt, but it suddenly seemed so trivial now.

−So how are you coping with the lockdown?

−Oh great, said Lily. −I've prepared for the end of the world. Remember?

I laughed and she joined in, the two of us ha-ha-harmonising.

−What was that all about? I asked.

−A lot of pills and powder, came her blunt response.

We were quiet for a second or two, suddenly remembering our lives. I knew who she was thinking about. The same person was in my head too.

−Do you still think about her? I asked.

−Recently, aye.

−It's funny this happened, said Lily, all of a sudden.

−What?

−The number of weird calls I've had this week…

−Scammers?

−No, family. Just out the blue like you.

−Who?

−Believe it or not, Grandfaither. He was asking about you.

I ended the call immediately without saying another word.

The dirty old beast was still alive.

Worse, he'd contacted Lily, my sister. He was fishing for information.

I felt sick. My hands wouldn't stop shaking and I thought maybe there was a heart attack on the way. Calm down, I told myself.

Nearly an hour passed with me holding the phone in my hand. It was something physical to hold onto, a talisman of power that could finally put an end to an evil old man. If I could just press three digits on the keypad! Did I really want to do this though? Not particularly. But I had to do it.

For me. For her.

Without giving myself a chance to change my own mind, I called the polis.

—You're through to Police Scotland, said a woman. —How can I help?

—I don't know how to start, I said nervously.

—At the beginning, said the voice. Whoever she was, she sounded nice.

—The beginning? That's easy. A bus going to Denny in 1976.

Wait. That wasn't right. Now I sounded like a dafty.

I had to go back nine months earlier.

—Sorry. I'll start again.

—That's alright. Take your time.

My thoughts suddenly aligned and I was ready to try again.

—I'm calling you because…

How the fuck did I put this into words?

—Because…

Finally, I said it out loud for the first time in my life.

—I think my grandfaither abused my mither.

—Abused?

—Physically. Sexually.

—Do you have proof? asked the voice.

—Aye, I replied. —Me.

48

The polis might have taken my grandfaither away, but they couldn't keep the cell door locked long enough. He was out again in days, pending the results of the DNA test. All I seemed to do these days was wait for test results to come through. With theatrical eagerness, I had sauntered into the Denny polis station where someone escorted me into a small office area. He was young, clearly insignificant in the polis pecking order.

−I need to swab you, he said. Not that I cared. Covid had given me a blasé attitude about having my tonsils tickled with cotton-tipped brushes. Anything that helped get that pervy bastard locked away was worth it, not for justice but for revenge. Oh yes, revenge. It filled my thoughts, my dreams, all of my ambitions.

Revenge was the first step on my road to recovery.

It would be a long walk. Some arsehole at the testing lab had leaked the results to the media and made me front-page famous again. Suddenly, I found myself being bombarded by reporters. Oh, I was ready. They emailed for exclusives I couldn't legally give. I was bombarded with messages, each offering to tell my story. Readers were fascinated by true crime, apparently. I kept quiet. The story would be the same, regardless. As a result, the way people regarded my mither fell into two categories, not an inch of space in-between. Some were disdainful, remembering her previous stint as Denny's number one drug dealer and prostitute (never 'sex worker'). But more were supportive, seeing a woman who took control of her life, successfully keeping her independence.

Then there was me, a problem in plain sight.

I was the result of incest, a daughter and granddaughter to the same man.

Hiding my secret was now completely impossible. Any time I went out, people pointed, whispering while I walked by. If Mither had been around, she'd have told them to fuck off. Sometimes, I felt like doing the same, but I suddenly became aware of something important, a small, incredibly vital lesson I'd learned during that mess of a week. I didn't care what people thought of me. Not anymore. Call it confidence, age or lived experience. Maybe it was just the healing power of not giving a shit? I didn't know. But whatever it was, it helped. I no longer walked with my eyes on the ground, a good view of my feet. That was an amazing thing. Useful too, because it meant I could stare right into my grandfaither's eyes when I saw him again.

14ᵀᴴ MARCH 2022

As the pair of decapitated horse heads became more prominent in the windscreen, my heart kept up with the car, thumping fast. There was no point in getting worried. The Kelpies at The Helix in Falkirk, inspired by the myth of a shapeshifting creature that lived by the lake, were an iconic addition to the countryside. Named after a creature from Scottish lore, the kelpie was a mystic predator, a powerful shapeshifter.

According to the stories, it would assume a pleasing form, drawing you close, lulling you into a sense of safety… only to pull you underneath the water, drowning you in the murky depths. The Kelpies of The Helix still had the power to bring people towards them. Tourists mainly. I didn't think about them too much, my thoughts far away on vacation. But I couldn't completely avoid them either. No-one could. Thirty metre tall horse heads with steel skin weighing six hundred tonnes combined; you saw them no matter where you looked. They were the skyline and everybody knew it, especially Falkirk Council. Luckily for me, the park wasn't too far away from home. Eighteen minutes in a car, in this instance a Bruce's Cab. The park was perfect for what I had in mind. It was open, busy and there were plenty of places to sit. It was, for me, the perfect place to set a trap. I watched from the back seat of the taxi, sitting without a seatbelt, something the driver hadn't bothered to correct. Then again, he wasn't wearing a face mask, so I took my victories where I found them.

This, I hoped, would be another victory.

If I failed, it was over.

−Doing anything exciting, said the driver and not for the first time.

−Naw, I said. −I'm meeting my faither.

A SPECIAL DELIVERY

Instead of chapping my grandfaither's front door, I'd personally slipped a note through it giving him the time, date, location… and a threat. *Meet me or I'll tell the neighbours everything.* The time and date were added in different ink, the sort found in a bingo pen, big blocky red lines, an obvious addition to a note that had already been written. I had delivered my note three days earlier, not wanting to leave the Royal Mail to do my work. The old Greek columns had developed a thick moss-grown skin since the last time I'd seen them, years earlier when I jumped on a bus to Cumbernauld, hopping off with my backpack and a hangover. Once I slipped the note through the letterbox, I ran up the street, using muscles that hadn't been exercised in years. Huffing and puffing, I slowed down when I reached a safe distance.

It's time to stop running, I decided.

The taxi driver kept talking during the journey, but I couldn't hear anything he said, not one word of it. One thing I couldn't ignore was the fare.

−That'll be twenty-five quid, hen, said the driver. In no mood to argue, I handed over three tenners, accepting a pile of hot coins in return, smash from the driver's bum pocket.

−Thank you, I said, my tone slightly sour.

As I got out the cab, my purse mortally wounded, I watched the car pull out of the car park, which wasn't as full as I'd expected from The Helix during a weekday afternoon.

The car was a red Ford Ka, a teapot on wheels.

But it wasn't a Skoda, at least.

Suddenly aware I was standing next to an unused bus stop (it felt nice), I turned and head in the direction of the main park. Juices in my belly bubbled.

Could I do this?

Like I had a choice!

Several things instantly came into view, including The Kelpies themselves, who were always there in my line of sight. First, the gardeners. They were working hard, grafting over huge lawnmowers that seemed to splutter soon after being powered up. One of the gardeners, a woman with blondie hair, deftly fixed the mower, making it snarl again. I smiled and passed by. Another gardener mowed the opposite patch of grass, not keeping in the lines quite as neatly as his colleague. He smiled, giving the brightest smile I'd ever seen, literally, because his veneers gleamed like glass. Nodding, I kept walking ahead, cutting closer to the horse's heids and my appointment.

Near the canal, two park attendants were sitting, both eating sausage rolls out of bags. They didn't notice me nor anyone else, just each other. Dogs ran loose too, but they weren't aggressive. Their owners were always nearby, throwing a ball, or chucking a stick.

At last, I found a metal bench near the water.

There, I waited.

WHAT TO DO WHEN THINGS GO THE WEIRD WAY

Somehow, I zoned out. Soon enough I realised someone was blocking the view, momentarily taking The Kelpies out of sight. Two tiny eyes, watery and weak, blinked down at me. My breath caught and words failed. He was older, of course. His face withered, body supported by a stick – but he was there in front of me, my grandfaither, my faither too. I felt sick, but kept calm.

−What do you want? he asked, his tone sharp.

−I want you, I told him.

−Well I'm here. Do you know how much the taxi cost me?

−Sit, I said, offering space on the bench.

−I said…

−I know what you said. Make this easier for both of us… and sit.

It was a command and one he obeyed. Falteringly, he got himself into position and I smelled pish, crisp and vinegary, it almost made me gag. He had no-one looking after him, clearly, and it was obvious he couldn't look after himself. Normally, I'd feel something like pity. But not now. Not for him.

−Where's grandmither? I asked, knowing full well she was gone and had been a long time. A guess, more than anything. Mither hadn't said anything.

−She died years ago, he said, his voice a clattering weak thing. His breath came out in small irregular bursts. My skin crawled, being near him felt corrupting, as though his evil was transferable through exposure.

−How did she die? I asked.

Old age, I thought. Please let it be old age.

−Cancer, just like your mither.

Lily must have told him during the phone call. Either that or he was checking up on her, something I wouldn't put past him. Mither had always hinted that he was deeply controlling, always needing to know everything.

He was still talking.

−It'll probably happen to you at some point, maybe it's already happening.

The last bit of fear left me and suddenly I wanted to shout at him.

−You better hope it isn't, because I'd have nothing left to lose.

−Oh, there's always more to lose, little girl.

What an arsehole, I thought.

To his face, I smiled. −You'll be dead before me. Probably in a cell too.

−I don't want to be here, he said, ignoring my put-down.

−I don't want you to be here either, but this has to be sorted out. Right?

He couldn't look me in the eye. Why hadn't I noticed that? Every time I looked right at him, trying to seize his eyes with mine, he dropped his head.

−The trial is coming up. I wanted to see you before it.

He snorted and made the sound of horrible laughter.

−What the fuck are you laughing at?

−You've probably buggered up your trial by asking me here, he answered.

Was that true? In my anger, I hadn't considered the ramifications of my plan. What plan? All I wanted to do was see him, confront him outright. Somehow avenge my mither. But I started to feel slightly unsure again.

−I know what you did, I said, hoping to recover some power again.

−Please, he begged, now looking at me with his grey watery eyes. −I didn't do anything. Your mither's lying. She made it all up because I wouldn't let her be a wee hoor with her boyfriend. I swear on your grandmither's life.

−Don't you dare, I hissed in outrage. −You can't lie to me. I've done a DNA test at the polis station. You know that, don't you?

At last, I got to say what I'd travelled from Denny to tell him.

−Everyone is going to know what you are and I cannae wait.

His eyes, bleary and tired, widened as my voice climbed higher and louder. −I'm sorry, he said, trying hard to make me believe him. Even though his walking stick kept him balanced, his head sagged, giving him the appearance of a condemned man. −I'm so sorry, he said. −Please, I'm sorry about everything.

−For what? I said snidely. −If you didn't do anything, why are you sorry?

He didn't know what to say. That was clear. His mouth opened slightly, then closed, before opening again. A fish in a tank without water.

Or, I considered, a man in a cell without freedom.

He looked away again, but wasn't quite ready to leave.

−I've been so lonely, he said. −You're the first person to speak to me in weeks. Not even the postman wants to stick around anymore. Your sister only speaks on the phone, but it's not the same, is it? I never thought I'd miss that daft cow as much as I do − and I really do.

Wait. Daft cow? Huh?

−Who's a daft cow?

−Your grandmither.

Before I could say anything else, he started mooing.

Literal, actual mooing like a cow.

306

People started to look at us, the park attendants stopping in mid-bite.

Oh my God, I thought. He's going for an insanity plea.

−Do you know what cows eat? he asked as I stood up from the bench.

−How the fuck should I know? Do I look like a farmer to you?

−Cows eat grass, and that's what you are. A grass. Moooooo!

This was a mistake, I realised. Why did I think meeting him face on could give me what I needed? What the hell had I been thinking? How dumb.

−You're going to Barlinnie, I said as calmly as possible. The slight tremor in my voice, however, was impossible to ignore. If anything, it only made my grandfaither more aggressive in his loudness. Now he was screaming, a horrible howling shriek that made me turn my back on him. I'd arranged this meeting to face him one last time, look him in the eye, break him with my truth. Maybe, on some level, I had wanted to know why he did what he did to my mither, but there was no rational explanation other than a bad man doing bad things. As human beings, we often overcomplicated our lives looking for reasons and explanations, trying to find order in random cruelty when there was none. Really, why did I even need to hear what he had to say?

Quickly, I started walking in the opposite direction.

In hindsight, it was stupid of me to turn my back.

Something hard and heavy smashed onto the top of my skull.

The park tumbled and I followed through.

−Fucking hoor! came a voice buried in the buzzing, a horrible tinnitus that faded slowly as I came to. −I told you I always get the ones who got away.

Two horse heids were looking down at me when I opened my eyes.

He'd hit me with his walking stick.

I'd been clobbered the second I turned away.

Furious, I got up onto my feet, swaying slightly.

That's when I punched him.

An eighty-year-old man.

My fist smashed into his face.

He hit the ground a split second later.

—Oh shit, I cried out. —I'm sorry.

Then, upon realising I'd just apologised to a pervert, I snatched it back.

—Actually, I'm only sorry my mither isn't here to see you now.

—Did you see what she just did to that wee auld man? came an indignant voice from nearby. The park attendants, still eating, were pointing in my direction.

—Get a fucking job, I screamed at them, my hand pressed hard on the back of my skull. It was matted, moist and possibly even fractured.

—Help, shouted someone else in the park. —Call the polis!

—Please, begged my grandfaither from the ground, —she's trying to kill me.

The stick came at me again, landing on my knee, forcing me down again.

—Bitch, he hissed, though only I heard it. Though diminished by age, I got an echo of how this man must have seemed to a little girl growing up under the same roof. Terrifying, most likely. In that second, I suddenly morphed into my mither, crawling on the ground to get away from my faither.

—Keep that stick away from me, I yelled, but it didn't stop him. Obviously it wouldn't. Giving little thought to the end result, I kicked the walking stick out of his hand, sending it flying through the air. While he was distracted, I booted him in the shin. Something broke under my heel.

−That's for my mither! I shouted as he rolled on the grass, a pathetic squeal coming my way.

Staggering onto my feet again, I made it safely out of The Helix. On the way, I passed the gardeners, who were still busy working hard.

It started to rain, a light summer drizzle, warm and nice.

Somehow it felt soothing, a nice shower of sorts.

I stood there with my eyes closed.

In my ears a roar.

Then sirens.

But not for him.

49

Students passed the window on their way to Europa Records, laughing and pushing against each other. Best friends, I think. They didn't notice me watching, hoping to spot a familiar face in the crowd.

I'd spent the last ten minutes trying to make my glass of orange juice last just as long. Friars, I decided, was a nice place to meet an old friend. Eventually, I caught sight of someone walking down the street, dressed in a tailored black collarless blazer and matching flared trousers. At last, Justine had arrived. Ten minutes later than we'd arranged, but it really didn't matter. I was just thankful to see her again. Everyone in Friars stopped to look when she entered the bar, a shooting star, blink and you'll miss the dazzle.

–Hello beautiful, she said boisterously.

–Hello yourself. Did you get here okay?

–Did I hell, she said, snorting with laughter. –I made a wrong turn and nearly ended up at St Andrews. Cobbled streets and these heels? No thanks.

–Everyone would think Kate Middleton was back for a photo-op, I joked. –Anyway, never mind all that. We've got loads to talk about. Not just my stuff.

–I think your stuff's more important.

–My ego's on a diet, I declared. –Honestly, I feel like all I've done is talk about me. 'I did this'. 'He said that'. I'm over it now.

–Polis interviews are tough, said Justine sympathetically. After settling down, Justine ordered a drink, soft like mine.

–I'm driving, she said apologetically.

A minute later, she was sipping some Irn-Bru from a

paper straw, her peach lipstick staining the tip. Glancing over, I caught a glimpse of headphones in her bag, a discovery which immediately brightened my mood. She still loved her music, it appeared.

When we started chatting, our conversation flowed nicely, like it had when we were teenagers. She knew everything, of course. Everyone did. Trials, mistrials, accusations and counter accusations. The phrase 'Scottish Joseph Fritzl' came up in more than one newspaper. Caught in a barrage of legal fuckery, I felt like Alice when she first discovered Wonderland, except in my version of the story, there were lawyers, journalists and grifters instead of talking cats, murderous queens and mad hatters. Caught in a tight position, I had called in the only person I knew who understood the weird world of Scottish law. After giving a few vague details, Justine had offered to meet me in Stirling.

−Neutral ground, she told me. −Also, I need to get away from the office.

Jesus Christ, I thought. She has her own office. Whenever I tried to imagine something, part of me became what I was imagining. But even I struggled to see myself sitting behind a desk in a room with my name on the door.

−Well, started Justine, −how are you feeling?

−Like someone shat me out and stood on me, I said.

Justine, to her credit, burst out laughing.

−Is it true? You know…?

−What the newspapers are saying? Aye, it's all true.

The test results had proved everything my mither said was true.

−The auld bastard's eighty. Do you think I waited too long?

−No, said Justine firmly. −He still needs to pay for what he did.

We sat quietly, but it wasn't the worst kind of quiet.

311

It promised something exciting might happen soon, a statement or comment big enough to break the silence. Somehow, I didn't mind those moments of peace. They'd provided the soundtrack to some of my favourite daydreams.

−I'm thinking of quitting my job, said Justine abruptly.

Ah, I thought. Something exciting at last. Not about me, for once.

Until I made it about me.

−You can't quit right now, I cried out. −The evil auld bastard is doing me for assault and battery. I need you to be my lawyer and crush him in court.

She seemed unconvinced.

−Remember I used to share my Slush Puppies with you, I said slyly.

−Look, she said, cutting me off. −I'd love to represent you, but I don't work in criminal law. Everyone just assumes I spend the day sending criminals to Barlinnie. My job is really boring. I help shitty landlords sue their tenants for not paying their rent. I've sold out, Sadie. I have. And I hate it, because I worked hard to get here. The things I've done to get my foot in the door!

−Does it matter? You're there now.

−Not for long, said Justine, before adding: −I'm taking early retirement.

−And what the hell will you do all day?

It seemed like a sensible question. Actually, Justine could do nothing if she wanted. I got the impression she'd be happy making playlists and watching cult cinema. Her bank account was probably stacked, so financially she was in a good position to set herself free. But it wasn't enough.

−I'd like to open a wee café somewhere, she said wistfully.

−That's a good idea. You could have a stage for local bands to play.

−Yes, she said, suddenly enthused. −But where?

−How about Denny?

Justine looked away and her expression made me regret my suggestion.

−Come back, I said quietly. −Just one time so you can see it again. We could go together, like old times. Nethermains is still there too. Not Denny High though. That moved. Oh come on! Let's do it.

She raised the straw to her lips again, but there was only a loud slurp, large ice-cubes rattling away as the straw circled the glass.

−I can't. I just can't. My brothers are still there too. Fuck that. I couldn't. Honestly, I don't know how you can live there again.

−It's home, I said simply. −Why don't you try Glesga for your café instead?

−Or Cumbernauld? It's near here and you could work for me.

−I'd really like that.

The conversation trailed off. Justine wanted me to tell her more about my stuff, specifically what happened after I got away from my faither. And I would, in time. But I still had a problem saying a certain word aloud. It even sounded strange when I said it in my head. Faither. My faither. Him. Our last meeting had ended with me being escorted away from The Kelpies in a polis car. Assault and battery, they said. Afterwards, I spent hours at the station, explaining why I'd arranged to meet him in the first place, especially when a court case was being prepared. Now there were two trials in my immediate future. Me Vs Him. Him Vs Me. In recent weeks, I'd considered running off somewhere far away, a place no-one would find me until I was ready.

Aviemore, maybe?

—How's that lump? asked Justine abruptly.

Catching me off-guard, I nearly gave her my test results. But I froze, catching myself in time. She was referring to the lump on the back of my skull, the one dealt to me by my faither's walking stick. Actually, that was healing nicely.

—It's fine, I said.

The other lump, however…

OLD HABITS

We were out on the street, walking in the direction of Stirling Bus Station, both of us fighting the weather, bursts of chilly air that came between brief moments of sunshine. We'd spent hours drinking, chatting and laughing. I was thankful for her in more ways than she could ever understand, but more than that, I was thankful I could be a cameo in other people's lives.

Justine was the first to lean in for a hug, though she stopped halfway, her back arched uncertainly. She seemed to realise it might not be a good idea. Years after the pandemic first started, many of us were still lost in two thousand and twenty.

—Sorry, she said, mindful of Covid. —Old habits.

She stopped, as though suddenly remembering something.

—Do you know why old habits are like Bruce Willis?

—Because they Die Hard, I said, snorting out a half-laugh.

—We've still got it, said Justine with a snap of her fingers.

As we spoke, I turned to the right and Justine moved the other way.

We were nearing the end of our day out.

−I'll message later, I promised.

Before I could leave, Justine stopped me.

−Wait. Sadie!

I stopped and looked back.

−If there's anything you need, just ask. I mean it. Anything.

−Represent me in court, I said.

−Ha, fuck that.

Her expression suddenly turned serious.

−Take care of yourself, Sadie.

Maybe she knew after all?

She was gone before I could ask, off to live her own life on her own terms.

OPTIMISM IS HARD WORK

For the first time in the longest week of my life, I felt a bit lighter, even (whisper it) optimistic for the future. People spun off in different directions around me while I walked to my stance, speeding up so I'd get there in time.

From the corner of my eye, a woman overtook me, clearly in a hurry to get a seat onboard a bus before anyone else. If she hadn't been running in heels, I wouldn't have looked over. Her hair was brassy blonde and she wore a black fur coat around her shoulders, similar to one I wished I'd rescued from my sister before she cleared out the flat. Thinking of my mither again (it happened far less these days), I wondered whether she'd be proud, or even slightly impressed with me. After all, I'd taken charge of my feelings and fears, finding certainty in my situation. Even though things were starting to feel overwhelming, somehow I sensed everything would settle. I still had my daughter and maybe one day I'd have my son too. Covid. Chemo. Court. They'd take their turn and I'd do my best, facing each problem one by one, quests as important as any I'd taken on as a wee girl. Only now there were no magical blue pools or wishing trees in my immediate future – just a bus waiting to take me home and a hope that everything would go well in the end.

For now, that was enough.

ACKNOWLEDGEMENTS

Thank you:

Clare at Fledgling Press for saying no to the flying car.
Andrew Forteath for giving me my dream book covers.
The booksellers, librarians, readers and reviewers who
supported *Happiness Is Wasted On Me*. The nice person at
the Inland Revenue for waiving my tax penalties. Thank
you for making this experience feel a little less stressful.